I0700889

Praise for
Topping the Willow

Debut author Lori Closter taps into the drama and emotion of young adulthood in *Topping the Willow*. Like most teenagers, Brittany Warner manages to drive her high-power attorney mother, batty. Until she doesn't. Her mother ends up in a coma and Brittany ends up with guilt. Closter walks us through guilt, finding out detrimental past secrets, and into forgiveness in this well-told story that introduces us to the greater power of love and to the one who really gives it.

> —Cindy K. Sproles, Christian Market Novel of the Year, author of *What Momma Left Behind*; best-selling, award-winning author, mentor, speaker, conference teacher

What *The Cross and the Switchblade* did for the previous generation, Lori Closter's sensational *Topping the Willow* does now for ours. Through searingly real descriptions, gorgeous imagery, and brilliantly realized characters, Lori immerses young adult readers in her protagonist's harrowing journey from doubt to despair to joy, showing them that, through Christ, her heroine's salvation can also be theirs, no matter how dire their straits. Lori is the most gifted writer I know, and her gift to us, this astonishing book, will uplift, entertain, and transform all who read it.

> —David King, screenwriter

A beautifully crafted story with insight and compassion packed into every page. Unforgettable!

> —Susan D, writer

Topping the Willow is a deeply moving story about broken people and their buried secrets, revealing how the ripple effects of one person's guilt and shame can damage the innocent. But forgiveness, grace, and hope also have ripple effects, which Lori Closter authentically weaves throughout this raw and multi-layered debut novel.
　　—Karen Sargent, author of *Waiting for Butterflies*, the 2017 IAN Book of the Year

At its best, storytelling will reach into your chest with both hands and grab your heart. It says, "I want you to listen to my pain, my sorrow, and my hope." *Topping the Willow* does that. Lori Closter pulls no punches to tell you a story that is raw, real, and hard to put down.
　　—Bethany Clemons, screenwriter

Topping the Willow had my heart aching for Brittany from page one. This story explores the visceral feelings of an emotionally wounded teen wrestling with a tragic situation of her own making. Lori Closter beautifully brings her protagonist through a journey of finding hope when all seems lost, and love where there was none.
　　—Elizabeth Soule, writer

I got so into Brittany, I had a hard time putting this down to go to work.
　　—Catherine A

A sincere story about relationships, particularly parent-child pain; what kept me reading was that it tapped into my deep need for hope.
　　—Bob J

Wow, what a wild and beautiful ride, just tremendous. Loved it, very riveting, it really kept me coming back. So many wonderful stories woven in, loved the dreams and the way she spoke to herself as she experienced it all. Loved the characters, and the way Brittany lived on the edge of dark and light. It was a tremendous description of how God really works in people's lives. Great work, just monumental in my opinion.
    —Steven J

It's great! It's really great! I cried three times.
    —Greta B

Lori Closter opens a world to us in which anyone familiar with the follies and frailties of humanity will be able to relate and also feel understood. Through the realistic turmoil of an angry, jaded teen, we are reminded of ourselves and relearn the way from anger and jealousy, to how to grow from our haunted hearts into hopeful and faith-filled lives.
    —Katy J

I'm on page 29 and am swept away.
    —Pam F

Lori Closter's characters are so true to themselves, there is never any doubt how they react in any given situation. The tension moves beautifully between low and high. A satisfying read with a satisfying ending that will leave YA readers yearning for her next novel.
    —Douglas C. Atkins, author of *Diminishing Horizons*
        and *The Watchers.*

TOPPING THE WILLOW

Lori Closter

Narrowgate Media | Hubert, NC

Narrowgate Media | Hubert, NC

For those who need hope

TOPPING THE WILLOW

1

Ten years ago

Midnight. In a large colonial outside Manhattan, five-year-old Brittany Warner lay awake thinking about death. Just like last night, and the night before. The room was dim, made even darker by the lace canopy over her four-poster bed. It was as if she lay in a narrow box … maybe one that was about to go into the earth forever, like a grave.

She peered at the bookshelves filled with her stuffed bunnies and teddies, a few picture books, the justice scales hanging by thin brass chains, the unused tea set with its painted blue flowers … but none of it helped. The clock on her bureau, with its two bells on top like ears, lit up the room with its green numbers. Telling time was still a mystery, but she knew, because her mommy and daddy had told her, that both hands pointing straight up meant either it was lunchtime—which it wasn't—or very, *very* late. Which made her tummy feel sick.

Tick-tock, tick-tock. The minutes of her life were ticking away. Somewhere downstairs, the tall, pale-blue grandfather clock began to chime in as well. *One, two, three … ten, eleven, twelve.* And the air conditioner hummed through it all, as if it didn't care. Would she know if she were going to die today, or next week? She was perfectly healthy, but …

She squeezed her eyes shut and rubbed away a tear. Her mommy didn't like her to cry, but she needed … something. Clutching the soft, silky edge of her blankie, she slid from her bed and landed on her bunny slippers. They couldn't help either, so she kicked them aside. Barefoot, the tattered blanket dragging behind her, she crept out of her bedroom and down the thick carpet of the hall toward her parents' bedroom. She passed the same lighted paintings, polished tables, and tall vases with dried flowers she saw every day, but was careful to look straight ahead. Who knew what scary things might wait to pounce on her?

Ahead of her, Mommy and Daddy's bedroom door seemed to call to her, its creamy paint shining in the dim light. She raised a shaking hand and tapped. Waited.

No answer. They must be asleep. But she couldn't go back to her dark room and awful thoughts without her daddy. Her heart thumping wildly, she knocked louder and waited again. Still nothing. If she tried again, Mommy might be angry. She jammed her thumb into her mouth and turned away. Took one tiny step, then another. Halfway to her own room, she stopped.

"Brittany?" Daddy's voice, muffled with sleep.

She whirled and raced toward the shiny door. Turning the knob, she pushed the door open, edged a foot into the room, and stopped. This room was even darker than hers. Holding her blankie across her chest, she inched forward.

"It's me," she whispered.

A few feet away, Daddy yawned and switched on his bedside lamp. "What is it, punkin'?" Next to him, on the far side of the bed, her mommy adjusted her blue eye mask and flipped onto her side, facing the wall.

Brittany burst into tears. "I can't stop thinking!"

Her mother gave an impatient grunt and tugged the comforter around her shoulders. Daddy raised himself onto his elbows and glanced, his eyes blurry, at the nightstand clock. His eyebrows came together.

He sighed. "Again?"

Brittany gulped, trying to calm down like Mommy had taught her. "Always, Daddy. It's like a big black monster swoops down and all I think about is—dying. How after you die, you never *ever* wake up again. And the whole world goes on forever without you." She swallowed a sob and peeked at the still form at the far side of the bed. "I wish you and Mommy didn't tell me," she wailed.

Silence. Her daddy blinked, his eye sockets big and black above his pale, bony cheeks. "Brittie, is this about that dead possum—"

"No. Why do *people* have to die?"

A pause. He shot a look at her mommy, the elastic of her eye mask tight against her smooth blonde hair. Brittany clutched her blankie. Her own gingery braids were a wild mess, as usual. Brushing out tangles was a job both she and Mommy hated.

"Punkin', we've talked about this, haven't we?" Daddy said. "You'll live a long, long time, and so will Mommy and Daddy." His fingers twisted the edge of the comforter.

She stared back. "And then—"

The blanket twitched in his hand. "Well, when people are very, very old, they become … tired. They've lived so very long, and done so many wonderful things, they're ready for a rest. So they lie down, real peaceful, and it's just like going to sleep." He eyed her. "Doesn't that sound nice? It won't happen for ages, of course."

"But are you *sure* I'll live 'til I'm old, Daddy?" Her small thumb found her mouth.

From the far side of the bed came a long sigh. "It's late," her mommy said through gritted teeth and the muffle of blankets.

"Well, I can't be positive," her dad said in a rush. "But most people—"

Her mommy threw off the duvet and swung her legs to the floor. They were bare below her silky pajama shorts, and the flowery scent of her body lotion filled the room. *Gardenia.* Brittany had tried it once, smoothing it onto her skin the way her mother did, but it made her sneeze. Even now, her nose felt tickly.

"I have court tomorrow, remember? We can't do this now." Mommy shrugged into her fluffy white spa robe, yanked the belt tight like she was mad, and lifted her glossy hair from the collar. "Brittie, you're too old for this. So take that thumb out of your mouth, how often do I—never mind, let's get you back to your room." Rounding the end of the bed, she bent to remove the thumb from Brittany's mouth. But the child resisted. The mother tugged harder. The thumb popped out with a *blip*, and she folded Brittany's spitty hand in her large, dry one. She gave Brittany's dad an odd look. "Don't wait up," she said.

She led Brittany into the hall, leaving the door open. But when they'd gone just a few steps, the blanket rustled from inside the bedroom and they heard the gentle thud of feet hitting the carpet. Then Daddy was standing in the doorway, his hair rumpled.

"Agatha?"

Mommy's nose pinched white. "What." It wasn't a question.

"I just—" He stopped.

She blew out a breath. "Stay here," she ordered Brittany. She pushed past Daddy into the bedroom, turning to pull the door half-shut behind them.

The little girl listened from the hall, her ears bunny-sharp. "Should we tell her something about heaven?" her father whispered. "She could decide for herself later."

Her mother snorted. "You want to give back her pacifier too? It's ridiculous, Steven. I won't lie to a child."

"But we already are." His voice dropped even lower. "We have no guarantee how long any of us will live, or what happens afterward." A pause. "She's upset almost every night now."

Mommy stomped out of the bedroom, her tall form ghostly and her beautiful face stormy. She gripped Brittany's wrist and towed her down the shadowy hall. "Trust me," she threw to Daddy over her shoulder. "She'll live."

Back in her room, alone again, the child lay rigid on her back. Holding her tummy, she stared upward. The white canopy looked blacker than before. As if she were inside a grave.

Mommy doesn't understand.

2

"Brittany!" my mother screams from downstairs. I stop dancing and yank off my floppy straw hat, the bikini top I'm wearing over my T-shirt, and the sarong from my waist. I toss them onto my bed, now piled with sunbathing gear: sunglasses, flip-flops, a Frisbee, a beach towel. And three bikinis, including my new chartreuse. I'm packing for Hawaii! Or was, before this rude interruption.

Reluctantly, I lower the music. "What?" I yell.

"We leave in five!"

Five *minutes?* I stuff clothes into my rolling duffel, then the beach stuff and my bathroom items. I had to buy travel sizes, now that airline rules are so strict. The duffel zipper sticks, but at last it's closed. I take a last look around to be sure I'm not forgetting anything. Beneath my music posters and a couple of friend pics tacked to the walls, my bookshelves are pretty bare: a few paperbacks, knickknacks, and the justice scales hanging by thin brass chains that my mother bought me right before she threw away my stuffed animals. A baggie of gummy bears in each pan means one is almost always higher than the other, though I try to keep them even, to be fair. On my desk sits a medium-sized fishbowl with my Siamese fighting fish, Orangina. I pick up the cylinder of fish food next to her. A quick shake tells me there's just a whisper of food left. *Shoot. Benny will have to buy more.*

Tucking the fish food under my chin, I pick up the fishbowl with one hand and drag the duffel downstairs with the other, bouncing it against each step. I nudge open the study door with my knee and drop the duffel. Fishy water sloshes onto the parquet floor, which hasn't a speck of dust but will be cleaned twice while we're gone.

"I've got to—"

My mother frowns and waves me to silence. She stands straight-backed and stunning by her mahogany desk, recording a new message on her cell phone. "Agatha Warner speaking. I'll be away from my office for the foreseeable future. If you want a comment on the Hartwell case, just say justice was served."

She smiles, catlike, until she spies the wet floor. Grimacing, she taps the tissue box on her desk with a perfect, manicured fingernail. Once, twice.

I cradle the fishbowl against my side, pluck out a tissue and drop it, and dab the puddle with my toe. "I need a ride to Benny's!"

Instead of answering, she slides a piece of paper into my free hand. I scowl, then read aloud: "Ninth grade: Track Team. Tenth: Student Council, Class Officer. Eleventh: Peer Mediation. Peer *what?*"

"It's unfortunate that all you did this year was track." She folds her arms across her chest, creasing the sleeves of her favorite raspberry linen blazer that she wears in court for closing arguments. "We didn't make the most of your ninth grade; my cases this year took way too much—anyway, it's done. But you've got two years left to build your high-school resume for college. By senior year, it's too late."

I toss the paper onto the desk. "So we talk after vacation. School ended just three days ago, remember? And there hasn't been a drop of sun to enjoy summer." The fishbowl is pressing against my ribs, and I'm dying to get out of here.

But she thrusts the paper into my hands again. "I realize that, but the timing's right for me to take a break. And this will be more of a working vacation, to get your fanny in gear. I hope you aced your exams, because each aspect of your application—grades, test scores, what kind of *citizen* you've shown yourself to be—is vitally important if we're going to get you into an Ivy. It's no exaggeration, Brittany, to say these next two years will determine the course of your entire life."

Sweeping generalizations clothed in parentspeak make me sick. I growl a protest, but she steamrolls on.

"Admissions officers will pore with a magnifying glass over everything you've done. In the next week or so we'll map out your high school career, including after-school activities, and find something productive for you to do the rest of this summer. Maybe volunteer on a political campaign, or at a nature center." She bites her lower lip. "I didn't even register you for camp. And naturally your sainted father wouldn't dream—" The wall clock chimes twice, and she slants a look at the Roman numerals. "Never mind."

"But—"

"Don't worry, you'll have breaks. Pack a swimsuit if you want a tan."

I scowl. Much as I love going to the beach and gathering shells, I can't swim. Ever since a wave knocked me flat and almost drowned me at Hilton Head Island, the summer before kindergarten, I haven't gone in the water past my knees. Not even for lessons in a quiet pool. It still infuriates her, along with a million other things about me, from how I do my hair—a single, long auburn braid—to my distaste for wearing socks. She'll go ballistic when she sees the B I got in Social Studies this quarter. I bet she grounds me for a week—once our "working vacation" is over.

Every so often on the news, some tearful woman laments about her tattooed, pierced, teal-haired daughter who's been kidnapped or murdered or died in some drunken car crash or overdose, "We were so close!" Right away, whatever sympathy I might have had vanishes and I think, *You're lying*. My parents won't even let me wear a nose ring, and when I'm finally old enough to get a tattoo without their permission, it'll be on my hip, below my bikini line, where my mother won't see it. I'm a model teen, or try to be, flying below her fish-eye radar whenever possible. I learned that lesson when I dyed my hair purple on an overnight to my friend Chelsea's. It was only a rinse, not even permanent color, but when my mother saw me she flushed and chased me right out of the kitchen with her palm raised to slap me. Luckily our maid Harriet appeared in the doorway, her mouth an "O," and my mother pretended she'd stumbled. That time.

Lesson learned: crossing the line isn't worth the hassle. I'm biding my time for the day I can make my own decisions. But meanwhile, she never says she loves me, and the last time she hugged me was—well, some-where in the misty past. And I'm supposed to believe that this sobbing woman on TV laughed and joked with an inked-up kid with aqua hair?

Don't think so.

But now my mother's words sink in. "So, you expect me to work in Hawaii."

She lifts her chin. "We're not going to Hawaii."

"What?"

Smoothing her hair, she checks her reflection in the mirror propped on her desk, right where people often keep family photos. "Didn't I text you from court? I meant to." She ignores my expression. "Anyway, we're driving to Vermont to spend two weeks in a gorgeous cottage on an island in Lake Champlain. You'll love it. The water will be frigid, of course, it's only June, but it's not as if—"

"*T-two* weeks?" Our Hawaii trip was to be one week. She always does this, shoots stuff at me rat-a-tat-tat so I have no clue where to fight back first. It's an arcade game, and I'm the rubber ducky facing her rifle barrel. But I've got to try. "W-what about celebrating the Fourth at Waikiki?"

"Last time I checked, Vermont was part of America. I'm sure they've got fireworks."

But I can't afford two weeks. Some people train for cross-country the whole summer, I try to explain, keeping an eye on my fish. Orangina's racing around her bowl, bumping her nose against the glass. She's upset too, and I'm pierced by fear she'll do something stupid, like leap out of the bowl and hurt herself flopping on the floor. This is my battle, not hers.

"You're done with track." My mother cuts off my train of thought. "I called Coach—"

"You *w-what?*" My voice shrills, despite myself.

"You heard me," she replies coolly. "Running's too … individual. Colleges today value teamwork, and Peer Mediation will prepare you for law school."

I set the fishbowl down hard, sloshing water on the mahogany desk. Orangina swishes her beautiful filmy fins, struggling to right herself. Her round jet eye reproaches me. I grab the end of my braid and twist it furiously. "But I don't want to be a lawyer! I can't even talk without s-stuttering."

Her mouth quirks in amusement. "Only when you're angry with me, correct? Not to worry, there's plenty of time to fix all that. Now bring your bags to the car."

Something in me sags. This battle's clearly over. But it's not true I stutter just with my mother. I stutter when I'm upset. That's almost always with her, though, so in a way she's right. I'll miss Coach Mullen, who always found something positive to say about my cross-country times. And a good run always leaves me, if not exactly peaceful, too tired to care much about anything.

I point to the fishbowl. "Benny's taking care of Orangina. I just hope he can do that second week. So are you going to drive me there or not?"

"I said I'd be home by one. You should have gone earlier."

I actually feel the blood drain from my face.

It was a rhetorical question. Her specialty in the courtroom, which she uses to stump the opposition's toughest witnesses.

"So w-what, I let her d-die?"

My mother jerks her chin toward the powder room. The door's open, the toilet in plain view below the embossed, plum-colored wallpaper on the upper walls.

"*She* swims, doesn't she?" my mother purrs. "You can get anoth—"

My jaw falls open. *She means it.* My cheeks burn. My whole *body's* on fire. I rip her stupid paper down the middle and again crosswise and throw the pieces onto the desk. Then I walk out, my knees shaking.

I blast out of the house. The screen door to our kitchen slams behind me, making the hydrangeas on either side tremble. In the driveway, my father's half-hidden behind our silver Lexus SUV, surrounded by luggage, laptops, and the twelve-packs of Evian we always bring on a family car trip.

He knew about Hawaii. And didn't tell me.

I break into a run, to get as far from here as I can. But as I pass him, he steps into my path and we collide. Leaping away, he adjusts his faded-to-pink cotton baseball cap. Once upon a time, it was red and said Yankees. Beneath the visor, the Gucci sunglasses my mother bought him last Christmas reflect my own discomfort.

"Hey, where're you going?" he says, but I scoot past him. In the best of all worlds, I'd ask him to drive me to Benny's. But I've just been betrayed twice and don't dare overrule my mother. Sure enough, he glances toward the house, chewing his lip. "Don't tell me you've upset your mom."

Okay, I won't. I jog down the driveway and onto the street.

"We leave in ten!" he calls after me, half-heartedly because I'm tuning him out. Giving instructions isn't part of his job description at home. We all know who's top dog, and it sure isn't Steven Warner.

I run. My feet pound past fancy white fences, emerald lawns, shrubs mulched to their necks like smocked ladies in a beauty salon. High above me, a lacy canopy of oak, elm, and sycamore has already darkened to summer green. But the soft garnet leaves of a Japanese maple brush the top of my hair, and without slowing I snap off a twig and draw its feathery edges over my lips. I've had a soft spot for trees ever since I did a school project on our town's upscale, quasi-rural habitat. They freshen the air and are kind to everyone, unlike the uptight people around here. Seriously, clotheslines and even For Sale signs aren't allowed. People have to call a real estate agent or go online if they want to buy a house.

From nowhere, a muffin-sized kid barrels toward me on a red trike and topples at my feet. Before I can even move, he's bawling at the top of his lungs. His mother rushes out of the house. My palms shoot up—*don't blame me, I didn't do it*—but the whole time she's helping him up, soothing him, and setting the trike upright, she's giving me dirty looks. *Fine, lady, think what you want.* I lope away and overtake a woman pushing a stroller the size of a sub-compact. She's all gussied up, with sunglasses, lacy blouse, spiky heels, and bright red lipstick. To walk an infant. An au pair, probably, hoping some CEO will cruise by in a Mercedes, and all I can think is *good luck, lady, the big fish all work in the city. Unless they're home sick in bed, tapping at cell phones and iPads.* A tiny face peeks out from a blanket plastered with ducklings, and I shudder. Babies creep me out. I have no idea why. They're so helpless, and their clueless mommies think the world revolves around them.

My parent never thought that. It's sort of a dull, constant ache.

A gray-muzzled spaniel limps, yapping and wheezing, to a fence I'm passing. Him, I pity. One day soon he'll fertilize a shrub in his yard with his decaying body instead of the contents of his bladder. Or maybe his owners will plant a tree over him, marked by a little tombstone. I'd want my ashes scattered at my own happy place, wherever that is. Hawaii, maybe, if I ever get there. But it won't matter. Death ends everything, my parents have always said, and I've no reason to doubt them. Though when I was little, the idea sure did a number on me.

But I grew up.

As I pass Elm Street, I turn my face away from the second house in, the hulking Tudor where Jeff Cox lives. He's my school's star quarterback and we flirted for weeks, last fall. I don't think he knew I was just a freshman. Then after the last game of the season, after his victory ride on his teammates' shoulders and the locker-room cleanup, he practically attacked me. Right under the bleachers, where I'd been waiting in the striped shadows of those huge overhead lights. His breath hot and soda-sweet, the smell of fresh deodorant filling my nostrils. My icy sockless feet, his cold hands tugging at my jeans zipper until I reared back—luckily, we were still standing—breaking the gluey seal of our mouths and in sheer reflex, punched his face. His shock, disbelief, and curses as I stumbled away are still vivid in my memory.

I should have been ready, I guess. Fifteen is plenty old for sex these days; in some cultures, I'd be married. But I wasn't. Ready, I mean. Not even close.

I duck beneath the commuter train underpass and enter a different neighborhood, literally the wrong side of the tracks. Here the houses crowd together amidst tiny lawns littered with ride-on toys and plastic baseball bats, and driveways crammed with trailers, aluminum boats, and rusty cars on blocks. Pizza boxes and boxing gear—mats, a punching bag, a glove—protrude from the half-open lid of an overflowing dumpster. A kid wearing actual holey jeans, not the fashionable kind, bounces a rubber ball against a garage door. But it keeps hitting the ridges, so he's mostly just chasing it around.

Does it matter? No. Here I sense no expectations, which is why I'd rather hang out at Benny's dingy split-level with its rust-streaked, faded shutters than my own home. And sheesh, what dark thoughts I've been having. It's not who I want to be. I resolve to be more cheerful at Benny's as I trot along his driveway, through the scrag-gly side yard, and down the stairwell of the concrete bulkhead. Music blares from inside, so I pound the steel door with my fist. To my surprise, the door swings open. Picking a paint flake off the side of my pinky, I step into my buddy's basement lair and a massive wall of amplified sound.

3

I'm on sensory overload. Besides the screech of heavy metal music, there's trash everywhere, plus a brownish couch with torn cushions, a combo TV/DVD player on a metal cart, a kiddie dart board with chunks of foam gouged out, and a knotty pine coffee table strewn with loose change and linty peanut M&Ms. A plastic yellow bowl holds greasy popcorn kernels drowned in salt. *Blech.* Benny thinks popcorn's a food group.

The place also smells. Of dirty laundry, rancid popcorn oil, a tang of mildew from the air conditioner that thrums in a window, a pungent aroma I recognize … and unwashed teenage boy, who now emerges from his bedroom at the far end of the room. He's skinny, oily-haired, and carrying a purple bong.

"Hey," he says loudly. "Wassup." He crosses to the stereo and kills the music.

My ears ring in the silence. I shrug, take a can of ginger ale from his mini-fridge, and pop the top. The icy fizz shocks my brain.

"Where's the fish?" my buddy says. "I wanted a snack."

So much for being upbeat. While I'm running, I forget my problems; but once I stop, reality hits. "Ha ha," I say, and am about to explain about Orangina when he cuts me off.

"We all got problems. You live in a mansion, my heart bleeds." He drops onto the couch, lights the bong, and stubs out the match on the coffee table. A thin spiral of smoke blends with the aroma of pot.

"To me it's a prison," I say. "With parole in three years to some fancy college."

"So you say. From where I sit, you got a sweet life and a condo in Ha-wa-ii."

Yeah. I snort. "That was just a timeshare, and anyway it's canceled. What's with you?"

Benny holds out the bong, his expression hard. I ignore it.

"Come on, gonzo, speak," I say.

He takes an endless drag of cannabis. Finally, he mumbles, "We might lose the house." His mouth twists.

Whoa. I sink onto the couch, weak-kneed. He casts the bong aside, pulls out a flask, and makes as if to spike my soda. I shake my head. Even if I didn't prefer to keep my wits about me, my family's driving to Vermont today. Climbing into our SUV reeking of booze and pot would be an unwise choice, to use one of my mother's courtroom buzzwords.

"You need a plan," I say. "What's your mom do, again?" I only met her once—her name's Carolyn—but when I said hello, she just dragged on her cigarette and warned us not to burn the place down. Benign neglect, it's called, except in Benny's case it wasn't: his dad died of lung cancer three months ago. He ran a liquor store, until his wheezing fits scared away the customers.

Now his kid takes another hit off the bong and coughs. "Home … health aide. She washes old dudes' butts, makes nothin'. But hey, check this out." He pulls out the fanciest digital Nikon I've ever seen and hands it to me.

"*Benny.* Where'd you—"

"Chill, I didn't steal it. My dad took it in trade for a booze bill. Before he got sick. And this dude I met? He pays cash for, um, artistic poses. You know."

I power the camera on. "Aka porn. Forget it. You'll be caught, and in even more trouble."

"Not porn," says my pal. "I always liked art class in school and wasn't too bad, if I don't mind my saying so. And this chick Rita said she'd model for me. But she never showed, so Ma and I are screwed. Unless …"

"What?" Only half-listening, I pop off the lens cap and zoom in, then hastily pull out. Benny's beaky nose and lip rimmed by tiny bristles are not the stuff of close-ups.

"Listen, Britt," he says. "I wouldn't show your face. No one would know it was you—"

Huh? "Oh, no, you don't." I thunk the camera onto the coffee table. "No way in Hades am I modeling in the buff." Even my mother doesn't consider the Greek word for hell a curse. Not that Benny would care. But sometimes I blurt things without thinking, so it's safer to be consistent.

His eyebrows arch in fake surprise. "Buff? Did anyone say such a thing? I got stuff for you to wear."

I bet. I eye him. "No. And no."

"But …" He cocks his head and leers at me. "Hey, you're all grown up. That reddish hair's sort of pretty, and you got peachy skin and a cute lil' bod. You're your own woman, right? And what's that thing you always say? It's so cool, how does it go?"

I snort. He's flattering me. If I got caught doing his stupid idea? My mother would boil the flesh off my bones, spray-paint them a classic ivory, and suspend them on a mahogany frame. Then she'd donate my skeleton to some impoverished medical school in Central America, if there is such a thing. But it can't hurt to answer him.

"It's simple," I say, and quote myself in a singsong. "In a thousand years, whatever's bothering me today won't matter one bit. So if it's not important in a millennium, why should it be in five hundred? Or even one hundred? And if it won't matter a century from now, why should it in fifty? Or five, or one?"

"So-o-o …" He smirks in anticipation.

"Nothing matters now," we say in unison, and despite my annoyance, I grin at him. It's my own philosophy, which helps me not get upset about things. Of course, when I explained it to my mother, she sneered.

"Your theory and a stick of chewing gum won't buy a cup of coffee," she said, studying her still-wet toenail polish. It was a year or so ago, and we were sitting on our back patio. The mani-pedi lady at her salon had called in sick, and my mother was doing the job herself because she had some party to go to. Her words deflated me a bit, though I'd bet she hasn't enjoyed a sunset in a decade, except maybe on a screensaver. But I shouldn't have told her my idea. Sometimes I'm stupid like that.

Now I scowl at him. "There's no future at that gas station, you know. You've got to get your butt in gear and find a real job—"

"So you believe that thing you always say," Benny says.

He's not even listening. I sit back and sip my soda. "Yep."

"In the end, nothing matters."

"*Yes.*" I guess he's stupid, too.

His natural squint widens, making him look earnest and innocent. Which he definitely isn't. "So what harm could a few pics do?" he says.

Um. My palms break a sweat.

"You'd help us out, y'know," he presses. "Keep me and poor Mom off the streets. She works so hard, she doesn't deserve—and I wouldn't show anything *private*, just ..." His hands carelessly trace the shape of a female torso.

What nerve. I jump up, banging my shin on the stupid coffee table. I try to shove it away, but it won't budge. But Benny's been there for me these past few months, when other friends ... weren't. And to have *no* place to live, not even this dump? He and his mom really might become homeless, living in a shelter, or even a tent upstate. Those things happen, even if they're usually not in Westchester County.

I glare at him. "If I did this ... insanity, and please note, I said *if*—it'd be once. *Once.* Got that, Benny? Then you'll be on your own—"

"Sure, babe. Awesome!" He twists to rummage behind the couch, his skinny white belly bare above his sagging jeans.

"What are you doing?" I say, suspicious. My banged shin is still sending distress signals, and I rub the bruise.

Moving toward me, he dangles a fistful of risqué lingerie so close to my nose that I practically go cross-eyed. The sales tags are still on. *They're stolen* flashes through my mind. But the knot in my gut tells me that's not the issue here.

I straighten and bat away the underwear. "*Now?* You sleaze, you set me up—"

"We got another letter from the bank, Britt. Certified." His expression is as solemn as a judge's who just confiscated a case of whiskey. "They're closing in on us."

He's closing in. On me. I edge myself out from behind the coffee table and take a deep breath. "Would these photos be black-and-white?"

"You're joking, right? Who'd buy that?"

"Right. Well, listen up, Benny. Here's the deal. Forget turning away my face. If one *millimeter* of skin or hair shows above my neck, so anyone could even *suspect* it's me—this mop of mine is a dead giveaway, that's why I asked about color—you'll be sorrier than you can imagine. I'll cut off your extremities, pour gas on your privates—"

"*Eek!*" He mimes terror, laughing. "No worries, peach."

Seriously? My mouth is dry as paper in a dust storm. "I mean it. You'd be famous for what I'd do to you."

Now he's mock-serious, with a wounded-puppy pout. And I cave. Against my better judgment, I reach out.

Benny's bedroom reeks of mildew and is as trashed as the living room. My running shorts and T-shirt lie rumpled on the unmade bed. I eye my reflection in the cheap mirror above the dresser and flush, embarrassed in front of my own self. Who knew such a thing was even possible? It's not that I look *awful,* though fuchsia is not my color. My hazel irises, identical to my dad's, shine greenish in the dim light. A teacher once said they resembled a doe's, meaning their shape and my eyelashes, which I guess are unusually long. And I'm slim, even a tad underweight. Our total snack supply at home consists of carrots and apples, and who likes those except horses? But this outfit screams … hooker. All that's missing are false eyelashes, a platinum wig, and a fake beauty mark like Marilyn's.

It's for my pal, I tell myself. *So his mom won't smoke herself to death worrying about being homeless.*

From the living room come knocks and thuds, then a muffled curse.

"What are you doing!" I yell.

Benny huffs something about how the tripod got away from him. He's a mechanical klutz, even when he's sober.

Then it happens. "What's taking so long?" he calls and flings open the bedroom door. I shriek and cover myself before I even take in what I'm seeing: over Benny's shoulder looms a pair of dark, bottomless eye sockets like the ones in those Scream paintings by Edvard someone-or-other. *My father.* He's clearly horror-struck, and so am I as he points toward the outer door. From his shaking fingers dangles a pencil with a tissue rubber-banded to the eraser end, and I recognize a pathetic, jokey attempt at a peace flag. Obviously, the family boss sent him to find me. But he hates conflict, so he always turns things into a laugh.

I slam the bedroom door, pull on my shorts and T-shirt, stuff my feet into my running shoes, and dash into the living room where my buddy's collapsed on the couch. Giggling hysterically. He's higher than I thought.

The outer doorway's empty, just a bright, sunlit rectangle framing the bulkhead stairs.

"Did you see his mug?" Benny hoots. "Hey, leave the duds!" he says as I rip past him, and even though it's ridiculous to obey, I unhook the tiny fuchsia brassiere with trembling fingers, pull it through the armhole of my T-shirt, and fling it at him. It lands on his forehead with the cups over his eyes like goggles, which I'd find hilarious if I weren't so panicked.

At the bulkhead door, I pause and peer back at him. "If my m–mother finds out about this … I'm toast," I half-choke and stumble up the concrete stairs. Some ridiculous loyalty has kept me from spilling the beans to my drop-out pal about my parent's rages. How her nostrils pinch white and she screams like she's demented. She's even thrown plates a few times, and more than once, fishing under a piece of furniture for some mislaid item, I've come across broken bits of china that the vacuum missed. Benny knows nothing of this, and would deny that life in our huge, elegant colonial could be anything but perfect.

But, I don't know him either, I discover when I reach the scraggly yard. The basement door's still open, and his voice booms up the stairwell, piercing my eardrums: loud, smarmy, and, well, stoned.

"Sheena? It's me. Hey, doll, wassup?"

We drive home in silence, my father gripping the steering wheel in a perfect Driver Ed ten-and-two. Behind him, I gnaw a hangnail and focus on the wispy curls that poke from beneath the baseball cap he wears to hide his thinning hair on top. It's a compromise: my mother would rather he wear a toupee or even undergo a hair transplant, but he hasn't done either, and I don't blame him. He's decent-looking, tall and lanky with preppy clothes, a nice GQ escort for a lady, except for his teeth.

Unfortunately, they're rather crowded and even a bit yellow, and today it's huge, white Chiclet teeth, not clothes or money, that make the man. Or woman. Or whatever. But until he smiles, you'd think he went to Andover or Dalton, or some other fancy prep school. His crooked incisors bothered no one, I'd bet, until he met Agatha Olsen. But now he's self-conscious and keeps his lips pressed together in public. It makes him appear stern, the furthest thing from the truth. The man's an invertebrate, with no spine at all.

These thoughts distract me nicely from what just happened, but now my hangnail is bloody. I spit out the tiny comma of flesh and suck the side of my thumb, willing the stinging to stop and the dread twisting my stomach to go away. My father turns onto our street. Our house looms on the left, the grounds manicured to within an inch of their life. Azaleas, rhododendrons, and yews in front, hydrangeas along the sides. A dogwood placed just so in the loop of our perfect lawn, and I'm just pondering how nicely my family treats its plants when I remember Orangina.

It's a gut-punch. Is she still alive, or did my mother do the nasty deed herself? I'm not even sure which I prefer. I sort of wanted to say goodbye, but that means I'd be the instrument of her death myself. Murdering my pet! Can I really do it?

Before I can figure it out, my father eyes me in the rearview mirror. "Your mom's been working hard," he says. "She deserves a break. For now, let's keep this between us."

What? My initial relief evaporates as the implications sink in. Where my father found Benny's address, I have no clue. But it's obvious there'll be no punching out my false friend, no trips to the police station to teach me a lesson, no lecture about my indecent photos maybe going viral or me possibly being blackmailed. Nada. It's nothing new, and most kids would envy me a parent who so thoroughly shirks his dad duties. But along with relief, a thin worm of betrayal slithers through me.

"Whatever," I say tonelessly.

We pull into the driveway. He opens his door, sticks out one long leg, and pauses. "Five minutes 'til we leave." Then he's out of the car and striding away, obviously clueless about Orangina.

Suddenly I'm boiling. It's my third parent warning of the afternoon, not to mention everything else that's happened. "Dad," I call. He half-turns. "If I were lying on a railroad track and a train was about to run me over … would you yell, 'Hey Britt. Get out of the way'?"

He scowls. "What kind of question is that?"

"Or would you just whisper? In case Mom heard you?"

"Don't be ridiculous." He whirls around and stalks into the house.

My sweet Orangina swims in her bowl on the mahogany desk, right where I left her. She's the only pet I've ever had, my mother claiming allergies to everything from puppy saliva to frogs to tiny turtles. Okay, the turtles carried salmonella and were banned. You can still buy them in Chinatown, but she's not about to risk her professional reputation by buying an inch-long illegal reptile for anyone, much less her flighty daughter. So, no dice, which is sad because they're so cute. You just have to wash your hands after holding them.

Now, a fish—especially a Siamese fighting fish—isn't exactly cuddly. But whenever my shadow falls on her, Orangina understands she's about to be fed and swims to the surface. This has always made me feel warm inside. Until now. She trusts me, and I'm about to betray her in the worst way possible. I shake out a few "vitamin-and-mineral-enriched, color-enhancing" pellets and she digs in, her mouth opening and closing as if she's singing an aria or burping spaghetti sauce. "Even prisoners get a last meal," I tell myself, and slam down the thought like the bars on a jail cell. What I'm about to do stinks. But if I don't, my mother will. Plus, I'll have to deal with her rage. The way I see it, I owe Orangina.

My pet snarfs the last pellet. I lift the fishbowl and carry it into the powder room next to the study. Straddling the toilet, I lift the seat ... and pour in the contents of the fishbowl. Orangina plummets to the bottom in an avalanche of bubbles. But my mother was right: little O swims. She rises to the surface and noses the ceramic perimeter of the toilet bowl, checking out what she has every reason to think is her new home. All agreeable and adaptable, putting up no fuss whatsoever. *She's wonderful.* Suddenly I can't bear it, and grab the toilet handle. "B-bombs away," I mutter. My fish disappears, on the ride of her life.

And death.

There's a one in a bazillion chance some sewer worker will open a pipe right when my fleshy bit of orange streaks by—but no, this isn't a Disney movie. Orangina's doomed, and I can only hope that however she dies, it'll be quick.

"You're going to a better place," I fib, iron banding my throat, and am halfway across the parquet floor when I realize, astonished, that my lower lashes are damp. I *never* cry. On my sixth birthday, my balloon blew away by the gorilla habitat at the Bronx Zoo, and I sobbed as it shrank to a pinpoint in the sky. But I haven't since, and if my mother saw me now, I'd be mortified. My whole life, she's referred to crying as being "reduced to tears." I mean, whenever some witness falls apart in the courtroom, especially if it's a guy, she talks about it later at home in a tone so scornful that I itch to smack her.

Her message got through loud and clear, though: only the weak cry. So this must be allergies. Anyway, I yank a tissue from the box on her desk and blow my nose, gazing at the wall behind her chair.

Before me hang three framed posters of fake newspaper pages, the kind old people are given on important birthdays. Facsimiles, they're called, though they're probably going as extinct as printed news. "Learn what happened the day you were born," the ads say in upscale magazines devoted to history and culture. It's sort of interesting, I guess, if someone in a nursing home has nothing better to do. But these posters in my mother's study aren't real. They're fantasies she commissioned from some copy shop to portray her goals for the three of us. Success means nothing if you're still surrounded by losers; the whole *family* has to be top dog.

The middle poster's headline trumpets her ambition: "Agatha Warner Named to Supreme Court!" Her toothpaste smile gleams from within the frame ... 'nuff said. Just looking at her makes me queasy. To the right, the second poster announces, "Steven Warner Designs Skyscraper"—plausible enough, unless you've caught him puttering for days on end with an architectural model of some fantasy village green, dreaming of the country life. I mean, the man practically lives in an imaginary world.

He'll love Vermont. On the other side of my mother's poster, subtle as a bomb blast, my nine-year-old self grins like a fool: "Warner Girl Wows Princeton!"

As if. I'd rather do almost anything than read, even pick trash along a highway with prisoners to help our environment. I only manage decent grades and occasionally sound quasi-intelligent because I retain whatever I hear. Which most people don't, I guess. As for Princeton, a lifetime ago my mother read some novel that mentioned the scent of magnolias in the spring there, and somehow it stuck in her brain. An unlikely soft side, but there it is.

"Let's move!" Now she's yelling from the kitchen. My insides twist again and I raise the empty fishbowl, gripped by an overpowering urge to hurl it at her smug image and Photoshopped justice robes and shatter *her* dream. But for once, I force myself to resist. I lower the fishbowl and stand over the metal wastebasket by her desk, the way I did the toilet. She can't blame me for this; she loves to quote natural consequences, both at home and work. And renouncing fish as pets makes perfect sense since she's making me kill this one. Any idiot would agree: ditching the bowl is the logical next step.

I let the fishbowl fall. It smashes into smithereens.

The impact of glass on metal is unbelievably satisfying. I savor the moment.

But. Turning away, I imagine our cleaning lady Harriet reaching blindly into the basket while we're gone, and … *ugh.* That can't happen. I tweak a blank sheet of computer paper from my mother's printer, scrawl CAUTION— BROKEN GLASS in large letters, and fold it across the open top of the wastebasket. Then I scotch-tape it on, so it can't fall off or blow away.

It's not Harriet's fault she works for such a dysfunctional family. And there's been enough collateral damage already.

4

My father cracks his gum while he drives. In the passenger seat, my mother orders her iPhone to cough up driving directions to Vermont. Behind them, I've mentally put up the kind of plexiglass wall you see in taxicabs and retreated into my iPad. Although I don't abuse substances or cut myself, and tattoos and piercings aren't worth the hullabaloo they'd cause, I admit to one teeny addiction that keeps me sane: YouTube videos. In my humble opinion, the internet as a parent substitute would make a great subject for some grad thesis. You can learn anything in cyberspace, even if some of it—like how to build a bomb—could land you in jail.

Right now, I feel so rotten about Orangina that my goal is to focus on anything but my little O-fish. So I'm glued to a video of my favorite online guru, a twenty-something Aussie named Angora Flatline—her real name, she claims, and why not believe her? In this one, she shows how to get rid of ants. She often shares valuable practical stuff—how to tune a guitar, clean a coffeepot, or make a wasp trap from a soda bottle. She even helps you figure out the right amount to tip in a restaurant, and suggests ways to cheer yourself up: French-braid your hair, thank the sun for keeping us warm, or sample makeup at Sephora. If you're feeling energetic, you can run fast for fifty yards and time your pulse, or if you prefer self-indulgence, you can make fudge, the one dessert that doesn't come in a mix. Some of it's cheesy, but I stay tuned because, drum roll, Angora obviously enjoys her life. Which I can't exactly relate to. At the end of each video, she lifts a wineglass full of smoothie in an Aussie toast her grandpa always made: "Here's fluff in your watchspring!" I guess it means to slow down time, and not race through your days, which makes sense. No matter how bad things get, you only live once.

"Five hours." My mother peers at her cell phone. "Not counting traffic, which will be terrible. It's the first real summer weekend, so we should have left by two. Brittany!" She raises her voice.

Now what? I pause my video, freezing Angora with her mouth wide open. Where her gleaming white teeth would normally be are huge, pink tonsils. One looks slightly larger and whitish, and for a moment I worry whether she's prone to sore throats.

"Get out the plaid tote behind you," my mother commands.

Sheesh. The bag's heavy, awkward, and jammed in with the luggage. I tug it forward, onto my lap. But when I adjust my grip to heave it to the front seat, she raises a hand to stop me.

"It's for you."

I roll my eyes and peer inside. The tote is crammed with huge, glossy paperbacks, all with "SAT" or "COLLEGE" blazoned along the spines. Stuffed in beside them are highlighters, snack bars, index cards … I pull out a Mozart CD and give her an *are-you-nuts?* glare. Aside from the fact that I do everything online and download my music these days, my tastes are anything but classical—which is why my mother made me fork up my allowance when I lost the expensive ear buds I got for Christmas.

"Mozart is scientifically proven to help concentration and memory," she purrs.

"My SATs are two years away. But what's this?" I pull out a brown leather notebook, obviously not new, that I've never seen.

"I'll take that!" she says quickly. I hand it over and heave the bag behind me again. She tucks the notebook out of sight with a side glance at my father, but he keeps his gaze straight ahead. Then, to my shock, she just shrugs, pulls out the travel pillow from Nordstrom she "can't live without," and nestles it against the car door. Her eyelids droop, though she didn't act tired a moment ago. If I had fairy dust, I'd make her sleep the whole way to Vermont.

My cell phone beeps. I pull it from my purse with an odd pang of hope. Who could it be? No one has texted me in weeks, maybe even months, about anything other than a track meet. Benny just calls. His phone's so outdated it's got a numeric keyboard, which is almost impossible to text on.

The thing is, that day under the bleachers when I slugged Jeff Cox, I didn't do much damage. The guy's twice my size. But he minded, big-time, and floated some horrible rumors about me. The fallout: in addition to my boyfriend, I lost my two best friends. Chelsea and Marissa and I had been like Siamese triplets since third grade, sharing Breyer horses, American Girl dolls, mascara … and track team. But Chelse in particular acted like a real turd, saying I was crazy to send Jeff packing. We got into a huge fight, shouting at each other in the Junior section of Nordstrom, and now haven't talked in months, even though we took math together. I'm still in shock she took Jeff's side, even if I didn't explain how creepy it was when his huge, meaty football hands—anyway. He got nasty when I hit him.

All those years as besties, my friend should have known I had a reason. I never would have frozen her out like that.

I didn't tell my mother about Jeff, either. ME TOO isn't part of her vocabulary, and she'd accuse me of leading him on. But I was kind of alone after that, and this spring I bumped into Benny in the convenience store of the gas station where he works. He seemed familiar, and as the clerk rang up my gummy bears and Dr Pepper, he reminded me we took French 1 together his junior year. But then he'd quit school, he said, and invited me to hang out. So I did. And that's when Marissa got all critical and dropped off the scene, calling Benny a lowlife. What a snob. I bet she'd rather go to an Ivy League university than meet John Lennon. *FYI Marissa, colleges don't care who your friends are.*

Well, my mother got what she wanted. Benny's history. I check the text, and sure enough it's from him: "im a cad." Six whole letters and no apostrophe. No wonder he dropped out.

"You said it," I text, and block his number from my contacts. It feels kind of weird, even a little sad. But I'm well rid of him; whoever I hang with next, it won't be a loser, soft-porn pimp.

We get on the Taconic Parkway, winding through the hills between the Hudson River and western Connecticut.

I set aside my iPad and watch green ribbons of scenery unspool outside my window, as if I'm in an Impressionist painting. It's funny how intense colors are on a gray day. The road curves and bends, my body swaying with the car's motion. I close my eyes and let my mind roam. I'm riding a glittering wave off Maui beneath a cloudless sky, ogled by a crew of tanned beach dudes. And I'm a different person, with doting parents who are proud of their only child, and have plenty of friends to gossip and swap clothes with.

Delicate snores drift backward from the passenger seat, and I force my attention back to the ribbons of scenery. Daydreams have no place in my nothing-matters philosophy.

Rain pummels the car. Lightning flashes and thunder cracks. It's hours later, and we're creeping along a two-lane highway. Red brake lights and yellow headlights of a hundred cars blur against the dripping darkness, like those time-lapse posters of Times Square where car lights form long neon trails that look like fireworks. My mother yawns, stretches, and frowns at the traffic.

"What a mess. Where are we?" She checks her cell phone GPS and peers at the speedometer, then at the city to our left. "That must be Burlington. But it's five more miles to the cottage—and we're only doing five, so we're still an hour away. Great. I have to say, *this* is why I wanted to leave early."

She had to say it.

A diner looms above us, on a bluff by the roadside.

"Hey." She snaps her fingers and points. "Let's stop, Steven, unless you brought food. It may be our last chance."

My father starts visibly. "You were right near the deli, didn't you—"

"All those reporters, when could I shop? But *you* were home all day, doing whatever you do in that study of yours …"

He swerves into the right lane without signaling and winds up an incline into the diner parking lot. It's jammed, and he cruises maddeningly slowly past a row of cars.

"There." My mother points again, but he gestures to a white-haired couple coming toward us in a Taurus. They swing into the space, beaming and waving their thanks. She snorts. "I'm driving after this. So we arrive in the foreseeable future."

My father doesn't answer. Why bother? He won this one. Sometimes I suspect he does things just to annoy my mother. They're the only victories he gets.

But I'm glad we're taking a break, because my back aches from all that driving. On a plane, you can get up and walk around.

The diner is crowded, noisy, and humid with cooking smells and the exhaled breath of too many yakking people. I pull off my damp hoodie and run my palms over my wild, wiry hair, but it's hopeless. There was no time to re-braid it following the disaster at Benny's, and on a car trip nobody sees you anyway. I still can hardly believe my misbehavior brought no major consequences—though I should cross my fingers; that could change in a snap.

My mother surveys the room like a general. At a booth by the kitchen door, a lone waitress with her hair in a messy bun serves a Coke to a light-haired guy in his late teens. He's wearing a white dress shirt, of all things.

She says something, he nods, they trade grins. She lifts her tray and bumps open the swinging kitchen door with her hip.

Then she notices us. "Be right there. Sit wherever you like," she calls.

"Maybe this is a mistake," my mother says.

"We're here, Ag, can't you just deal?" My father ambles past a glass dessert case loaded with nine-inch-tall cakes and sticky, oozing pies and slides into a booth. She shrugs and follows.

So do I, but after just a few steps I trip over … a boot. Stuck right in my path. I spin, fists knotted, and face the most intense pair of eyes I've ever seen: light amber, deep-set, thick-lashed. They're gorgeous … but below them, a long, misshapen nose skews to one side. His skin is rough, medium-toned, with no five o'clock shadow but not pale, either. He's maybe in his early twenties, glossy dark hair slicked back, and long-legged enough to trip me without leaving his stool.

The guy radiates magnetism, a sizzle that zaps me to my toes. He's either devastatingly attractive or horrendously ugly; I can't decide which. But when he murmurs, "Name your price, princess" in a gravelly voice, the insult jolts me. I stiffen and lift my perfectly straight nose.

"Beyond your wallet," I say.

A hefty guy on the next stool giggles, and a beanpole on the other side tugs his scrawny mustache. The dark dude skewers them both with a look that makes them freeze. He takes my hand and smiles broadly. Unexpectedly fine teeth and a twist to his lips somehow balance the crooked nose. And his gaze is so compelling that despite myself, I don't resist when he leans over my palm.

"With such beauty come superior charm and wisdom," he pronounces.

My enchantment dims. *That's the best he can do?*

"You will endure … surprising events," he adds. "But a special treasure awaits you in the end." He presses warm lips to my damp palm.

Only half-annoyed—he *is* attractive, if pathetically unoriginal—I yank my hand away and move on to the booth where my parents sit. The guy in the booth by the kitchen door is obviously watching. Between the dress shirt and his light hair, he's downright anemic compared to that … sorcerer. I stick out my tongue. White Shirt is taken aback, but a dimple flashes in his cheek as the waitress serves him a large, juicy burger. His plate's over-flowing with fries, and I'd bet my chartreuse bikini she gave him twice the usual portion. She obviously dotes on him, but even though she's old enough to be his mother—if she got pregnant in her teens—I doubt she is. They'd never be so cozy.

I slide onto the cracked vinyl bench next to my father and peek at the dark dude. And, *whoa.* He and the blondish guy are in a stare-down. Not just locked gazes, either, but with crackling animosity. Something's obviously gone down between them, which isn't surprising as they seem polar opposites. Without breaking visual contact, the kid in white snaps open his napkin like he's dining on some cruise ship, spreads it on his lap, and picks up his burger. Finally, he chomps in.

The dark dude smirks. In my view, he lost the stand-off—the other guy's pretty self-possessed—but the goons obviously think their man won. They grin idiotically, their pupils glowing like live coals in a firepit.

Ugh. So far, I'm not too impressed with Vermont.

5

The waitress appears and hands us plastic menus so sticky that a whole daycare might have used them first. She and my mother do a push-me-pull-you, 'til at last the woman takes the menu back with an indrawn breath that tells me she's practicing patience.

"We're ready," my mother announces.

Surprised, the waitress glances at my father. When he doesn't protest, she sticks the menu under her arm and pulls a pencil and order pad from her apron. A mousy lock falls against her cheek, and she tucks it behind her ear. "Great idea, your food will come quicker. We're slammed today, what with the weekend coming."

"I see that," my mother says. "Do you have San Pellegrino? Or Perrier?" They won't, of course. It's just a greasy diner, but giving people a hard time is part of her shtick.

Our waitress isn't fazed, though. "We got seltzer. I could—"

"Never mind. I'll have iced tea, unsweetened, three lemon wedges on the side." My parent frowns. "Make sure the lemons are washed. I will not drink pesticides."

"Yes, ma'am," comes the prompt reply.

My mother shoots the waitress a look, suspicious she's being mocked. But the woman just says to my father, "Sir?"

"Uh … I'll have a Diet Coke, please." He glances at me. "Make it two."

"And three chicken Caesars," my mother says. "On mine, hold the croutons, the *parmigiana*"—spoken with correct Italian pronunciation—"and the anchovies. Slimy, disgusting creatures. Serve the dressing on the side."

The waitress's pencil stops. She pinches back a smile, tiny lines deepening the edges of her mouth. "So … that's two chick-Caesars, one lettuce-and-chick?"

Uh-oh. My mother gives the waitress her dagger-look, and the humor lines bracketing the corners of the woman's mouth smooth out and reappear between her brows. But she just says mildly, "This place is famous for wings and fries." Obviously, high-maintenance people don't faze her. Then, her pencil poised, she asks me, "Honey? Sure you don't want something else, maybe a root beer float?"

I shake my head and pass her my unopened menu. My glaring parent is our family's food sheriff, and I save my strength for major battles, limiting my dietary rebellion to the odd, smuggled Cow Tales candy or packet of peanut butter crackers.

But my father peers at the waitress's brown plastic name tag, the letters etched in white.

"Actually … uh … Cassie. Cancel my salad, would you?" he says. "I'll have the roast beef and mashed potatoes."

I stare at him. My mother grunts and toys with her knife, scowling.

"It's vacation, sweetie," he tells her. "And you said yourself, there's no food at the cottage."

The waitress's eyes meet mine, but I betray no further reaction. No matter what this woman thinks, she's not part of our family.

"Not for your triglycerides," my mother says. "Remember what Dr. Vaughan said …"

He winks at the waitress. "I bet I can convince this young lady to bring me a slice of that scrumptious apple pie I spotted when we came in."

So, the woman's maybe in her mid-thirties. And my father's forty-three, so calling her young is ridiculous. Not to mention, he's nuts to goad my mother.

The waitress grins, revealing a snaggletooth high on her gum. Otherwise she's pleasantly attractive, but in a washed-out, tired way. Her features would come alive with some lipstick and eye pencil. YouTube must have makeup videos for women like her, whose skin is already aging.

"Sure thing," she says. "That comes a la mode, with vanilla ice cream and"—her expression holds a hint of mischief—"the tiniest sliver of cheddar. Both locally made. Pure protein."

My mother's nostrils pinch white as she raps her knife on the table. "Would it be asking too much for you to just bring what we ordered? Also"—she thrusts out her fork, tines-first—"you can bring me a dinner fork, not this Lilliputian … *implement*. And we don't expect to be here all night."

The woman's eyes pop open as if she's swallowed a bumblebee. She nods, takes the fork and the last menu without meeting any of our gazes, and leaves.

"Mom. That was rude!" I tell her.

"Indeed it was," she says. "*Cassie* needed to be put

in her place. Unless you'd allow her to endanger your father's life?"

She exaggerates like, well, a courtroom attorney arguing a case. And it works. My father slaps his palms on the table, rattling the silverware and making me jump.

"You win, Aggie-Poo. But if I die first, embalm me in … Chocolate Overload ice cream. Deal?" He leaps to his feet and strides over to Cassie, who's setting another Coke in front of the white-shirted kid. Startled, she scribbles the change on her order pad and jabs the pencil into her messy bun.

My mother lifts her chin, triumphant. I can't stand to look at her, fiddling instead with the maroon container that holds packets of sugar, artificial sweeteners, and raw brown sugar. Mostly what's left are pure chemicals. She won this round, but the penalty was being called Aggie-Poo, a detested name which must have stemmed from childhood. My father wouldn't dare make it up, unless he did it while they were dating. Even that's hard to imagine. They must have fallen in love at some point, of course—I mean, here we are, a family—but she's hardly a gooey romantic. To call her Aggie-Poo is to risk her wrath.

Maybe he's steamed he can't tell her what happened at Benny's. Until he does, the responsibility for dealing with me is his. And that's something he avoids like a pro.

We step outside the diner into pouring rain. My mother ducks her head and hurries toward the parking lot. I slop through puddles in my flip-flops, concentrating on avoiding worms. Behind me, my father mutters something and dashes back inside. I stop and watch through the large diner window as he taps our waitress's shoulder and slips her an extra bill. It must be a fiver at least, because she grins in pleased surprise. He comes outside again and stops at the sight of me waiting on the walkway, dripping wet and scowling.

"Mom's rude to a total stranger and you pay her off," I spit at him. "But when it's me, you throw me under the bus."

For a split second, he appears uncomfortable. Then he retorts, "What do you call not telling her about Benny's?" He heads for the car, forcing me to scurry to keep up.

I break into a trot and give him a withering look as I pass. "That's for her too. And you."

Our footfalls are perfectly out of step. At the car, he slides into the empty passenger seat. We slam our doors in a quick *one-two* staccato.

And we're all supposed to survive two weeks in a cottage without killing each other … how?

It's thundering again, with lightning flashing around us. Gusts of wind buffet our SUV from side to side. Maple leaves splat against the windshield and fold in two, their spines and undersides the exact color of inchworms. We pass a farm, where a windblown couple leads two panicky horses toward a barn. Thunder rolls, and the woman's horse breaks away and bolts through the muddy barnyard. It skids, almost falling, and its muscled hindquarters bunch as it disappears into the barn. The woman lifts her arms, helpless.

My father fiddles with the radio. There's static, and a male voice announces: "Winds 20 to 40, possible gusts to 70. A Travel Advisory is in effect until midnight. It may be summer, but this is a real nor'easter, folks …."

He switches off the radio. "Think that's near here?" His tone is casual, but that he even asked shows he's worried.

My mother shrugs. "An advisory's just advice. Which we don't have to take." Her eyes skewer mine in the rear-view mirror. "Speaking of which … Brittany. I've already said this, but it bears repeating. These next years will affect your whole life. Thousands of kids will compete for ridiculously few spots at the most distinguished universities in the nation. You've got to find something unique, something spectacular, to make you stand out. Like an exceptional personal statement. And then you'll have to wow them in an interview."

No pressure here. "It doesn't matter," I mutter. "In a hundred years we'll be dust."

Her pupils glitter like a bobcat's at night, waiting to ambush some unsuspecting prey. "You can drop that two-cent philosophy right now, young lady. It's both false and disrespectful. Your great-grandparents came here with nothing, to give you a better life."

I yawn. "Really? They did it for me?" An attorney's kid, I can seize an opening too—especially one an armored truck could drive through.

"You little *miss*. Check this out!" She thrusts her four-thousand-dollar Prada bag at me. It's heavy, black, and smooth, the metal hinges cold to my fingertips. "Feel those stitches," she snaps. "Do you have any idea the vinyl crap I carried at your age? Of course not. You're spoiled rotten, everything you've ever owned is top-of-the-line …"

Her voice saws across my nerves. I push the bag onto the console beside her and shift in my seat to face outside. My window's fogged over, so I draw a line with my fingertip and above it, a stick figure. "ME," I write. *Top-of-the-line* … lame, I know.

"… and you lend your belongings to Chelsea as if it's nothing," my mother natters on. "She doesn't need them. Her grandfather's on the board of one of the biggest banks in the country."

"Which is why you forced us to be friends."

"Don't give me that, you chose each other. All I did was set up a playdate. And don't think I'm not aware something's wrong between you. You'd better patch it up. She hasn't been to our house in weeks."

A pang goes through me. It's actually months. "She's a jerk," I say. "And I have other friends." *None like Chelse, though. I miss her loony laugh, and how she always shared her homemade cupcakes with me at lunch, and wish—*

My mother swerves to pass a subcompact and stays in the fast lane. Beside her, my father shifts his weight uneasily. "Agatha. Please, pay attention."

She ignores him. "Sure … what's-his-name, Benny. A dropout who pumps gas and can barely zip his own pants."

She knows where he works? Adrenaline sizzles through my veins. "Talk about unzipped pants," I shoot back. "What about the dirtbag you just set free? Didn't he rape a cashier?" I hate that the sole lawyer in our family earned her reputation—some would say notoriety—by defending the scum of the earth. Rapists and child molesters are her specialty.

"His own mom swore he was home playing video games the whole night," she says.

"So she's loyal, lucky him. But the jury must've ignored his arrest record." I don't often follow cases, but you'd have had to be dead in Madagascar to miss the publicity on this one. And of course I have to keep up, in case some kid at school says something and I have no clue what he's talking about. Or she. Girls are the worst.

"He had no convictions. The verdict was innocent, just read the papers." My mother's conscience seems as clean as a baby's bottom after a bath.

"And another perp is free to walk," I say.

"I wouldn't put it that way, but obviously it bothers you."

"It doesn't *b-bother* me. I just think it's hysterical, my mother defending rapists."

"This is America. Everyone deserves a fair trial." She's a quarter-inch from smugness as she tucks a strand of blonde hair behind her ear.

"But the victim's in a w—wheelchair!"

"So? A whole jury said he didn't do it."

In the passenger seat, my father rubs his neck. The speedometer needle tips eighty. My mother honks at a slow-moving sedan with rusty fenders and passes it on the right. The teen girl clutching the wheel looks over, wide-eyed and guilty. I peer backward. Sure enough, her blinker pops on and she drifts into the right lane.

We regain the fast lane, and my mother narrows her eyes at me in the rearview. "By the way—your pal Benny is over."

She did not say that. "Over—how?"

"Over, as in out of your life. So you're not caught in some drug raid, ruining your chances for a decent future."

"You can't do that!" I shriek. Sure, I've already deleted Benny from my cell phone, but it's the principle of the thing. "And you're g—gone every day. You have no clue what I do."

Her eyes flash at me in the mirror. "Don't underestimate me, dear. I have ways."

And that is when I make my worst mistake ever. Something so purely evil I didn't know I had it in me.

I grab her Prada bag off the console and lower my window.

"What are you doing!" Her voice is hoarse with rage and shock.

"This bag's your favorite, right? You bought it after the Harrington case—yikes, it was more bounty, wasn't it. Well, looky here, Ma!"

Clutching the strap, I stuff the bag out the window. I'd never drop it, of course, but man, it feels good to turn the tables on her. She's driving, so no way can she win this one. For a split second, I gloat.

But her arm snakes backward, groping, her pale oval nails flashing in the gloom. "Give me that. Steven, get that bag," she hisses.

"Watch where you're going, Agatha!" My father's voice pitches high with alarm.

"My bag!" She lunges backward, gripping the wheel with one hand, and clamps my knee with the other. The car swerves right, then left. Her nails dig into my muscles. I struggle to peel them off. My father peers forward and suddenly punches my mother's upper arm. Once, twice … I look up. A giant silver cylinder is rounding the bend ahead of us.

A semi. Barreling toward us. In our lane.

"Look out!" I pry her fingers off my knee and fling her hand away. She peers through the windshield, and the car swerves again.

"Agatha!" My father finds his voice and grabs the wheel. The truck's headlights sweep over us as my parents fight for control in slow, strobe-like motion. A horn blares loud and long, its overtones seemingly disconnected from the tons of metal and whatever else that's hurtling toward us. We swerve again. The semi's brakes squeal and hiss, piercing my eardrums. When it's almost on top of us, practically filling the whole windshield, the whole rig skids sideways. For one frozen moment, I dare to hope it will miss us.

My mother screams, an honest-to-goodness, terrified Fay-Wray-in-King-Kong's-fist ear-splitter.

The silver cylinder slams into us with a roar of shattering glass and twisting metal. Light flashes and sparks fly in electric reds, blues, yellows. Something is burning. My head spins—

The world goes black.

6

A rustling. I open my eyes and instantly squint against glaring sunlight. Cool fingers grasp my wrist and wrap something around my upper arm. I yank it away and struggle to sit up, shading my eyes with my palm. Despite the glare, a darkness hovers at the back of my mind … *something bad happened.* An Irish-looking woman with bushy white brows—*a nurse?*—sets some sort of monitor on the nightstand and lowers the shade over a picture window. During the split second between the glare being blocked and the shade descending, I catch a glimpse of hazy green mountains. *Vermont.*

"What happened?" I croak. My head's stuffed like a vintage Raggedy Ann, but I'm not grinning. *Something's wrong. I shouldn't be here.*

"You're awake!" the nurse says. "This is a hospital in Burlington." She takes my arm again, wraps the monitor cuff above my elbow, and pumps a bulb. Blessed silence while the needle drops on a gauge, but the ripping of Velcro when she whips off the cuff is so loud that I wince. Her fingers tap rapidly at a laptop on a cart and pause.

"Do you remember the accident?" she says and pops a thermometer in my mouth.

Suddenly, memories flood my mind. *Damp air glass everywhere ceiling's a collapsed tent rain hisses. I moan, unable to move. Something digs into my left side. A uniformed male arm reaches through the shattered car window and rubs my forearm. Outside, lights flash. I crane my neck and peer forward. The front seats are empty.*

"We'll get you out of there, chiquita. Don't be afraid."

Some sort of machinery roars. A chainsaw? The car shudders, and I steel myself against the vibrations. Twin ambulances wait nearby. A wiry EMT in a jumpsuit slams the double doors on the nearer one and calls to the driver. With its lights flashing and siren wailing, the vehicle rolls forward and gains speed.

"Mom? Dad? Don't leave!" I shriek, louder and louder until the arm patting mine withdraws. A moment later, with no warning, I feel the sting of a needle.

Now the nurse removes the thermometer from my mouth. "Looking good," she says. A baby-faced doctor with a receding hairline appears at her side, and I look from one to the other, unable to form a thought but trying to stifle my growing panic.

"Hello there." He pulls a penlight from his breast pocket. "I'm Dr. Robbins. You're a lucky girl, escaping with a few scratches. We only kept you here to rule out concussion. And—well, if I may ..." He flicks on the light and leans close, his white jacket filling my vision.

A white jacket. An orderly pushes me along a hallway on a rolling trolley. We pass a doorway. Inside, two surgeons wearing seafoam green scrubs rinse their bare arms in a wide sink. One half-turns and gives me a piercing stare before I roll past and out of his life. Someone needs surgery? I'm afraid, but sedated so my fear is not all-consuming, just a small, fanged mouse chewing the end of my arm. Still, I wish I held a hammer to smash its skull.

It doesn't strike me that this is abnormal.

Dr. Robbins tucks the penlight into his pocket and beams. "Your pupils are the right size. It's safe to say you don't have a concussion."

"My parents?" I whisper.

He frowns at the nurse. "Maggie. Hasn't anyone—"

She holds up the thermometer. "I'm just doing vitals—"

"Tell me!" My voice is stronger, my head clearer.

A pause. "You'll see them soon," the doctor says.

A deep plunge, relief. *But ... those ambulances.*

"I'm sorry to tell you, though—I regret to say, your mother has sustained a rather serious ... what we call a Traumatic Brain Injury."

A shudder jolts me. "Traumatic—how?"

He hesitates and glances at the nurse. "Again, I'm sorry. She's in a coma."

I grab his sleeve. Pain shoots through my shoulder, and I wince. "When will she wake up? And what about my father?"

The doctor plucks a rubber hammer from his jacket pocket and taps his palm, seemingly unaware of my hand on his jacket. "I'm told he has no major injuries. Maggie, let's test this young lady's reflexes." He turns to face me, breaking my grip. "Then we can discharge you and get you over to the ICU."

"Maggie" swings my legs over the bed and helps me sit up. The doctor raps my knee with the hammer, and my foot jerks, as if I'm kicking him. I'd *like* to kick him. If I watched crime shows, I'd know: *what's an ICU?*

But the sight of blood, even fake theatrical blood, makes me sick. So, I don't. Watch *or* understand.

I brace myself against the armrests of the wheelchair and stand. In front of me loom massive double doors with a black-lettered sign impossible to miss: INTENSIVE CARE UNIT. *I-C-U*, my mind makes the connection. *No.* My Irish-looking nurse—Maggie—hands a sheaf of papers to an exotic-looking woman, maybe from some Caribbean island, who could be a model. Tall, slender, coral lipstick … *she* doesn't need makeup tips.

"For her dad," Maggie says. She leans across me, squirts foam from a wall dispenser, and slathers it on my hands like I'm a kid. I view my sudsy palms as if they belong to someone else.

"Bloody," I say.

She gives me a quick, worried look while she wipes me dry. "What?"

"I'm Lady Macbeth. Out, out, damn—" Now I'm giggling hysterically. But losing it is better than crying.

The good-looking nurse presses a blue wall plate depicting a wheelchair icon. Double doors swing open to reveal a hushed diorama that instantly sobers me. I force myself to put one foot in front of the other.

Behind me Maggie says, "It sounds like an awful accident. I wonder what happened."

I walk faster, so I miss her reply.

I tiptoe past a row of curtained cubicles. Each partly encircles a patient in a hospital bed. One after another I peer in at an aged lady, a battered teen who must have fought someone meaner than himself, and a sixtyish woman with an anxious younger one seated beside her, patting her forearm. At the next cubicle, a skinny oldster quavers, "Have you seen my Sarah?" With a quick head shake I hurry on, to another geezer hunched over by a patient so surrounded by equipment that only the sheeted legs are visible. I stop short. This visitor's light curls appear gray in the fluorescent light, but I recognize my father, his head buried in his hands.

"Dad?" My voice sounds eerie, disembodied among the beeping machines.

He pushes himself out of the chair and faces me. My whole body jolts at the sight of his red, swollen eyelids, his skin ashen with exhaustion, the bandage visible inside the neckline of his polo shirt.

His bony arms reach out and, to my shock, pull me close. "Thank heaven you're okay," he mumbles. "I got lucky too, just a mild concussion and a cut. Got a few stitches." He touches the bandage. "But your mom—"

I wait for his reassurance that everything's fine.

Instead, he sets me away from him and stares at the floor. "What'll I do, Britt," he says in a monotone, "she always knew ... *knows* ... what's best." His jaw muscles work, and for one horrible moment, I'm afraid he'll cry.

"You'll just have to deal with it," I say, hoping to snap him out of this. But he doesn't seem to hear.

"I've got to stay with her," he mumbles.

"With Mom? Here?" A chill slices through me. "What about me?"

He regards me as if I'm a stranger. "I … I don't … know."

Whoa. *Whoa.* I push past him to the bed. My breath whooshes out as if someone hit me, and my knees go so weak I have to grab the metal bed rail to keep from falling.

She's so still. To either side, banks of machinery blink and beep. Details leap out at me like B-roll shots in a horror movie montage. A purple cheek, swollen but oddly flattened where it shouldn't be. Dry lips taped around a tube that rasps like Darth Vader. IV poles standing guard, their bags dripping clear fluid. Neon electronic lines on the monitors that trace the damaged mysteries of my mother's body. Bandages encircling her head, hiding her hair except for a stiff blonde lock that sticks straight out above her forehead. Agatha Warner would not be caught dead with a hair out of place, and this tiny spike, more than anything, shows her utter incapacitation.

My mother has been felled like some giant tree.

"It's m—my fault, I've k—killed her." The words jerk out of me, through sheer terror.

I stumble backwards. Whirl. Flee.

"Brittany!" my father calls hoarsely. But I'm gone, past the curtained cubicles and through the double doors.

Never have I run so fast, as if a pack of ravening wolves is chasing me in some medieval fantasy. At the end of the hall my stomach heaves, and I vomit into an empty laundry bin. I wipe my mouth and pound along another hall, my toes clenching my flip-flops so they don't fall off. A nurse sitting at a desk glances up, startled. At a bank of elevators, I smack the Down button with the heel of my hand. When a door opens I dart in, hit B for Basement, and dig my fingernails into my palms until the doors glide shut. *I've got to get out of here.*

The elevator opens opposite a door labeled Morgue. Shuddering, I dash through the bowels of the hospital toward a neon red EXIT sign at the end of a corridor. Someone enters the hall behind me, but I keep going and shove open the emergency door. An alarm blares.

"Miss!" a male voice calls behind me, but I ignore him and step outside.

I crash down the wooded slope behind the hospital. A branch lashes my cheek. My toes cramp and one flip-flop drops off, so I kick off the other. Dry pine needles and leaves snap beneath my bare soles. Something stabs my arch, and I yelp. Finally, I reach a busy road and halt so fast that I become dizzy and almost lose my balance. To the right, a sign points to a cemetery. *Handy to the morgue.* But right now I couldn't bear to see headstones honoring beloved mommies and daddies gone to heaven. Bad enough to plow each year through racks of syrupy Father's and Mother's Day cards, trying to find one that doesn't rave about perfect parents who are "always there." Does everyone lie twice a year? Why can't someone design a card that says, "We both know you failed me in every way possible, but …"?

I slam down thoughts of how badly my family does love and turn left.

Normally, a mile's an easy run for me. But the pavement's hard and I'm barefoot—and limping, by the time I reach downtown. Storefronts blur as I pass, I have no idea where I'm going, and my side hurts. At last I stop and bend over, panting. Spring track ended just two weeks ago, and already I'm in lousy physical shape—but part of this must be panic. Crazy thoughts snake through my head. *Don't let yourself dwell on her, don't, don't …*

I straighten up in front of a wide, windowed store-front with elegant bottle-green trim. BENNETT'S APOTHECARY arcs across the top third in fancy gold letters. Sunlight bounces off the glass, mirroring my disheveled self. I inch forward to peer at my reflection and jerk back, shocked. *Is that blood trickling down my cheek?* Suddenly a face looms just inches away, on the other side of the glass. Shrieking, I leap backward and crash hard on my bottom onto the sidewalk.

A bell jangles, and a door opens beside me. "Hey, sorry I scared you—are you okay?" It's the kid from the diner, the pale-shirted dweeb I stuck out my tongue at. He leans down and helps me to my feet. Upright, he's taller than I'd have expected, the whites of his eyes a striking contrast to his dark irises and tan. He reaches toward my cheek, and I knock his hand away.

"Don't!"

"But you're bleeding. Come inside and I'll fix you up." He gestures at the open door.

I wipe my cheek and check out my palm. He's right. I slit my eyes at him sideways.

"It's a pharmacy," he says patiently. "We've got per-oxide, bandages, tape—"

"I'll take a Band-Aid." I duck past him and limp inside.

＃ omitted

7

The place is vintage. Black-and-white checkered floor, tall glass-front cabinets crammed with first-aid stuff, and along one wall, an old-fashioned soda fountain with a gray laminate counter and red vinyl stools. I perch on the nearest. Opposite me is a wall of old-timey poster ads for liniments, salves and miracle cures, plus a few Norman Rockwell prints I vaguely recognize from eighth-grade art history. On a shelf below them, a plastic radio with round knobs plays Oldies, so low it's more of a suggestion.

"Be right back." The guy disappears through a doorway behind the soda fountain. I plant my elbows on the counter and bury my face in my hands. There's mumbling in the back room, then he's with me again, pocketing his cell phone. I watch through slitted fingers as he grabs a tall glass and fills it from the soda fountain, his motions smooth and natural. But now his brows knit together in a frown.

"What are you doing? I said a Band-Aid," I snap.

"Coming up," he says. "But first—I make a wicked chocolate malted, aka a Bennett Supreme. This one's on the house. I'm guessing you don't have a wallet on you."

I exhale. "So, your dad owns the place and you give freebies to all the girls."

He pauses. "Did I say that?"

"Whatever. I … could use some water."

"To wash with?"

Is his brain impaired? "To drink!"

He brings me a glass of water and finishes making the malted. Fine gold hairs glint on his arms. He does have a nice tan. Not a city dweller.

I drain the glass, still edgy. "What's with this place? It's, like, a time warp. Has your pharmacist even heard of penicillin?"

A dimple on his right cheek deepens as he sets the milkshake in front of me with a straw *and* spoon. He gets a point for that, even if he loses one for the environmentally-toxic plastic straw. I slurp some froth. *Delicious.* Another point. I try to use the straw, but the concoction's so thick I finally just spoon the cold, creamy malt into my mouth. I shut my eyes, concentrating on the separate flavors of chocolate, cream, and malt. It may be the best thing I've ever tasted.

"We do have penicillin," says my amused host, "but today they mostly use modern derivatives. And this décor's from, like, the fifties. I think. Anyway, hang on a sec." He moves along the store shelves and picks out an armful of first-aid supplies. Then he fills a metal basin with warm water, settles on the stool beside me, and dabbles a washcloth in the water. Squeezing it out with one hand, he gently tugs me toward him with the other.

A thrill of nerves shoots through me. Then our eyes meet, and I sense he's feeling awkward too. If we were in a commercial, this would be his cue to check if his deodorant's working. But he's neat and clean, wearing another tailored shirt, khakis with a braided belt, and squeaky-clean athletic shoes. He gives a slight impression of a nerdy prepster, but the leather cord around his neck and stud glinting high on his ear say otherwise—and he did stare down the dark guy in the diner.

The boy leans in to dab my scratched cheek. Close up, his irises aren't brown or even hazel as I'd thought, but an enameled mosaic of mocha, green, gray, slate, and gold, shiny and lapped together like the pebbled bottom of a stream or the side of a fish that's just been caught. Not that I've ever seen one in real life, but again, YouTube is handy for learning all kinds of skills. His eyes reflect the light amazingly. When I was younger, I thought various-colored eyes felt different to look out of: brown would feel thoughtful and serene, maybe like a cow or lamb, but blue would be fiery or frosty and passionate, like Julie Christie's in *Dr. Zhivago*. I know better now, but how cool it would be if irises changed color according to their owners' feelings, like a mood stone. Though revealing so much might cause problems, say if my mother—

My whole body stiffens. *How could I forget, even for a moment?* Guilt gnaws me, like those hair shirts religious fanatics wore ages ago to punish themselves. Warm water trickles down my cheek, and I focus on that. At first it stings, but soon soothes me. I could almost imagine I'm at a spa. The chattering and clattering of people eating off coarse beige china fades, and now the boy and I seem to be encased in a private bubble. My irritation drains away, and my eyelids lower. Finally, he pats my cheek dry and gingerly dabs on ointment.

"It's really just a scratch," my rescuer says. "You don't need a bandage."

I duck my head in a half-nod and swivel away. But the boy stops my stool with his foot and points to the floor I've just crossed. Hashtags of red appear at regular intervals. More blood.

"Ugh." Mortified, I lift my heel, revealing a gash in my arch. Mystery solved on the stabbing pain on that slope behind the hospital. The boy lifts my foot onto his knee and bends over it with the washcloth. His hair is the color of wheat, with golden streaks that appear natural. It's shiny and heavy and straight, reminding me of a small boy with a bowl cut. Now I smell his shampoo, sort of woodsy with maybe some coconut and ginger, and something else that must be just him. I wish I hadn't stuck out my tongue at him in the diner last night. But I doubt he even remembers me; I don't stand out in a crowd. Anyway, his cheeks are flushed now and he's definitely not anemic, and he's just said something I didn't hear.

"Are you up to date on tetanus?" he repeats.

"Um … probably. My mother—" Another clench in my gut.

He waits, his expression questioning. I don't explain, so he just dries my foot and wraps the cut in gauze, then tapes it all together. "I'm pretty sure this doesn't need stitches. And I'll find you some flip-flops. But you might—"

The entrance bell jangles. We both turn to see the waitress from the diner hurrying toward us.

"Thank heavens you came here!" she cries. "Are you all right?"

I look to my rescuer, dumbfounded.

"Stupid question, of course you're not," the woman corrects herself. Her name's Cassie, I remember. "I'm so sorry about your mom, what terrible news! But I've spoken to your father—"

"*What?*" Any illusion of privacy with the blondish guy is gone. "How did—"

"Our friend Sandro is a fireman, and last night he used the jaws to cut a girl out of a car with New York plates. I hoped it wasn't you, but when Will—"

"Wait, time out!" I raise my voice. "What jaws, and who's Will?"

A pause. "Uh, that would be me. And she means the Jaws of Life." My rescuer's tone is apologetic. "I recognized you from the diner. And I called Cassie, and she told me about the accident. I'm sorry, too."

"But you called *her*?" I jerk my thumb at the waitress. "Why?"

He flushes, but answers readily. "You obviously needed help—"

I raise a palm to silence him and whirl to face the waitress. "And how did you find my father? You don't even know his name!" My voice shrills with fear and anger. And, yes, paranoia.

Will gathers the basin and first-aid stuff. "You needed help," he says again. "But Cassie can explain." He disappears into the back room, and the waitress perches on his stool and takes my hands. I jerk away, unnerved.

"Just spit it out," I say. "I'm having a *rotten* day."

"Dear," she says. "Once two and two made four, and I realized your family were the ones in the accident, and you'd found Will—well, it was obvious where your father was. *Is.* I didn't call myself, of course. They wouldn't have put me through. So I got our pastor to do it."

"But why?" I clench my teeth. "My family's problems are none of your business."

"Why, to explain my offer!"

Silence descends. I've got a really, really bad feeling about this.

"Dear," Cassie says again, setting my nerves on edge. I hate endearments. Not that I hear many, I mean directed at me. My friends' moms have no problem calling their kids sweetie, or honey, or even doll-face. Okay, the last one's weird, but the feeling behind it is what counts. "It's obvious your dad can't care for you properly right now. And he understands that, so you're coming home with me."

I leap to my feet and yowl in pain, hopping on my good foot. "Are you *nuts*?"

"Just for a few days," Cassie says. "Until your mom—"

"Don't call her that, you don't even know her. Not in a trillion years would my father let some perfect stranger take—on the say-so of some crazy priest? Where's a phone, I need a phone."

Cassie digs through her bag, her hair hanging in her face. "Besides our pastor ..." she mumbles, "... a policeman friend, Sergeant Thompson, spoke with your dad. So, he's got two character references. And we're not total strangers, are we?" She holds out her cell phone, coaxing, as if she's offering a saucer of milk to a stray cat.

Ignoring her, I snatch the phone, punch in two numbers, and stop. Is the next number three or four? I pretty much just call my parents on speed dial, for rides. I push the cell at Cassie. "You talked to him, you must have the number." She scrolls, presses buttons, and hands back the phone.

"Dad!" I say when he picks up. "You know that waitress from the diner? The one you tipped twice? She says—"

He's barely gotten out a few phrases, how he's got-to-stay-with-Mom and these-are-fine-people, when I move the phone away from my ear and let his tiny voice squeak words a daughter ought never to hear. My father's thrown me under the bus again. But this time, the bus is full of strangers.

I turn slowly and face Cassie, appalled.

8

I'm squashed between Will and Cassie in the front seat of her tired Plymouth. The back seat is crammed with stuff that looks like it's from, or headed to, a thrift shop. A battered fan, some baskets, a faded roller shade, a blanket. On my lap I clutch a plastic bag of toiletries from the apothecary, courtesy of Will: toothbrush, toothpaste, comb and brush, shampoo. Even floss. My toes straddle the thongs of the flip-flops he'd promised me, yellow with white plastic daisies on the straps. They're hideous.

We pass a grove of tall pines sheltering some picnic tables and rumble onto a causeway across glittering water. A sign flashes by: Welcome to South Hero. I frown.

"South Hero's the southernmost town on the Champlain Islands," Cassie says. "There's a whole chain, right to the north end of the lake. It's called Vermont's West Coast. Have you ever been here?"

I ignore her. Somewhere nearby is where my family would have spent our so-called vacation. My mother—I probe the word, the way I would an aching tooth—said she'd rented a cottage, but that didn't mean a modest one.

Her choice would be spacious, architect-designed and shingled, with wraparound porches out of *House Beautiful*, maybe a turret or two, and phenomenal water views. And, of course, sunsets. Inside would have been equally upscale, either beach chic or with the mountain ambience of Hammacher Schlemmer, L.L. Bean and Eddie Bauer.

The water's gorgeous, and this might be the same island, but somehow I'm sure Cassie's place won't resemble my imaginings. She and Will don't have that vibe, even if Will does wear collared shirts and a braided belt. These people are more suited to be Benny's hick cousins.

We rattle off the causeway onto the island's two-lane main road. South Hero is tiny and rural, with just the basics—town buildings, an ice cream stand, a bank. And a pharmacy, a pizza place, even a minuscule ambulance garage. Without warning, Cassie swings the car onto a country lane. *Uh-oh.* I peer backward to memorize the intersection. These people are total strangers, and the whole pastor thing could be a decoy. My father should have called Grammy and Grampy Warner, his parents in New Jersey. I make a mental note to phone them first chance I get … assuming I have one.

That sounds dramatic, but the farther we drive from the main road, the more I have to restrain myself from chewing the sides of my nails. Will seems nice, but so do some serial killers.

"You'd better not be axe murderers," I say. Not that they'd admit it if they were. On the other hand, a twisted mind can justify anything, the way Wallace Shawn's character Vizzini tries to outsmart the Man in Black in *The Princess Bride*, one of my favorite flicks. Pure escapism, and I love how Wally drops dead, poisoned by his own cleverness. *Pay attention, Britt. This is real, and your life could be at stake.*

Will fumbles inside his shirt. I stiffen, but he just brings out the leather cord from around his neck. Hanging from it is a wooden cross, maybe an inch high and half-gilded diagonally with what looks like real gold. He raises it almost into my face, so close my eyes blur.

Now I'm really creeped out. I don't know anyone seriously religious—New York isn't exactly the Bible Belt—so I'd have no clue what to expect. And this too could be a trick. *What was my father thinking, handing me over to these people?*

"There's no need to be afraid," Will says simply.

"Seriously, how can anyone believe in God? The world's a disaster, don't you people watch the news?" *Keep talking, maybe he won't pull anything.*

We round a bend. "Two years ago, I *was* the news," he answers. "I'll take this any day."

"That's clear as mud in a frog pond." Sarcasm may not prevent a crime, but it calms me. A bit. And was that pain in his voice?

"Here we are."

Arching across the lane above the car is a ranch sign like the ones on black-and-white Westerns and vintage TV shows. *Bonanza*, incredibly, is still on cable. Whenever I'm sick in bed, I love to suspend my regular life and sink into another time and place. Two-foot-high letters made from branches read NARROWGATE FARM. We pass beneath the sign. To either side stretch lush pastures edged by white triple-board fences. A dozen horses graze peacefully. At the end of the lane are a picturesque barn with paddocks, a farmhouse, a new, raw-wood bunkhouse, and a riding ring.

I stifle an exclamation. The buildings and fences could use paint, but other than that? It's perfect.

"What are you, secret cousins to Bill Gates?" I demand.

"Do you like horses?" Will says. "Maybe we could …"

His words fade. I was nine or ten, perched on a low stool by my mother's knee with my socks sagging to my ankles. She sat under a hairdryer at her beauty salon, reading a magazine while I scratched my mosquito bites. When they were nice and bloody, I touched her leg timidly.

"Please, Mom. Dad said to ask you."

Her knee twitched. I removed my hand.

"Why a horse?" she said loudly, above the noise of the hair dryer. "Can't you settle for something simple? A turtle, maybe?" The salmonella scare hadn't hit the front pages yet.

All the ladies were snickering. I flushed, but I'd gone too far to stop.

"I want … to take care of something bigger than me. We can afford it! Janine Cameron owns a horse, and our house is twice the size of hers. Please?"

My mother smiled into her magazine. "I'm bigger. You can take care of me."

Grimacing, revolted—avoiding her was half the point—I retreated to the waiting area. When I looked back, she was absorbed by hot air and full-page jewelry ads.

Will has stopped talking, I realize with a jolt. "What?" I say.

"Do you ride, I said."

I hesitate. "I'm actually not keen on horses. But yeah, sure."

"That's great. Tomorrow after church I'll give you a tour, and we'll put you on a horse. Maybe even do a trail ride if the weather holds."

"But—"

"I mean, if your foot's okay."

It won't be. I'll make sure of that.

Cassie pulls up to the farmhouse. Will climbs out and I slide along the seat after him, but he shuts the car door before I can get out and leans in the open window. Again his face is inches away, and I flush.

"Catch you later." He taps his fingers on the door-frame and moves off.

"You're leaving me?" I blurt before I can stop myself. Nothing dire has happened, but—

"So long, Will." Cassie backs the car in a half-circle and drives back down the lane.

My alarm bells go off again, even louder when the ranch sign re-appears in the distance. "You don't live here?"

"Not exactly." In another fifty yards, just before the sign, she veers onto a different lane. It's overgrown, but ahead of us water sparkles through the lower limbs of a grove of trees. We bump toward it.

"I don't get it." My voice is high, nervous. "You're too young to be his mother, too old for his girlfriend—"

She laughs. "Priscilla and Luke Easton own the farm. I rent the original cottage on the water, for a few years now. I'm very blessed, 'cause we're close friends. Like family."

I ignore the pang her last words bring and inspect her cottage. It sits at an angle, with the front porch facing the lake. Cassie parks by the steps. A few yards away, a magnificent willow trails its fronds into the water. There's a mossy bench, too, where she probably watches the sun set. Or rise? I've lost track of which way we're facing. Northeast, I think. But the cottage itself is old, even dilapidated. And the three-speed bike propped against the porch sports a wire basket that would look great on an upscale catalog cover, holding a pot of flowers—but the shiny chrome light on the handlebars suggests that Cassie actually rides the thing.

"Home sweet home," she says. "Isn't the view fantastic?" She catches me eyeing the peeling paint of the porch spindles and laughs. "Don't worry, inside's better." She exits the car and mounts the stairs. I lag behind, dangling the bag of toiletries.

"Isn't it funny Will's family wouldn't offer to have me?" I say cautiously. "Their house looks more, um, roomy."

She gives me a sharp look as she struggles to unlock the front door. "Will is a foster kid. Along with his two sisters, though one of them's aged out of the system and soon he will, too. So Priscilla and Luke have their hands full, which is why I haven't told Luke about this silly ..." She rattles the lock, until at last the door opens.

I wrinkle my nose. *A foster kid.* My father might not have let me come if he'd known, not to be snobby, what kind of people these are. I've heard most foster parents take kids in for the money, and as for the rug rats themselves ... 'nuff said.

Then it hits me. I, Brittany Warner, whose mother only yesterday was strategizing my admission to the Ivy League, have been farmed out to a waitress. In a sense, I'm a foster kid too.

It's true, what homeless people say in interviews. One

false move, and the life you had is over. I can blame no one but myself, and the guilt is crushing.

Who knew my safety net was so fragile?

Cassie's kitchen is cramped and grotty, with flaking varnished paneling. A teakettle perches on a stove burner, with boxes of tea stacked nearby on the counter. Rusty metal canisters, an olive-green blender, and a row of stained cookbooks crammed with index cards stretches along the chipped Formica. It's dismal, the only bright spots being a ceramic bowl brimming with tomatoes and another full of apples and unripe bananas. Beyond a pass-through between the upper and lower cabinets is a living area with a maple kitchen set and a couch draped with colorful afghans and some unfinished knitting. In the corner are a tall rocking chair and a vintage TV topped by a tiny, cheap antenna like they sell on QVC. Along the front wall, opposite the kitchen, is a bay window crammed with blooming plants, some hanging and others catching the sun on a deep windowsill. A breeze stirs the leaves, and the sweet scent of flowers tickles my nose.

The afghans and bay window full of plants are the only decent things in the place. The rest of it's a dreary disaster.

"Let's show you your room." Cassie leads me to a tiny hall at the far end of the room and around the corner into a doorway. I peer in at more dated décor: a twin bed with a faded floral quilt, a wooden dresser with peeling varnish, a vintage PC on a desk that matches the dresser. I toss the bag of toiletries onto the bed from the threshold.

"I guess you're unpacked," Cassie says. Is she joking

or being dry? The latter, I decide. No one could be that earnest. "You must be hungry. Are you ready for lunch? I've got ham, tuna, or I could heat up some soup."

Immediately I conjure Benny, eating Condensed Cream of Mushroom soup straight from the can. *Lovely.* Cassie will at least heat hers, being a waitress and all. I slip past her toward the bay window.

"Whatever. But, um … I really need my cell phone. To call home."

I don't mean my actual house, of course. No one's there. But she gives me a funny look and heads for the kitchen.

"We'll ring the police later and ask if they found it. Your clothes, too. Make yourself at home, Brittany."

Settling in is the last thing I want to do. I wander to the bay window and finger one of the babies on a huge spider plant. It breaks off, so I poke a tiny hole in the dirt and hide it. I'm clueless about plant care. Some hired service tends ours when I'm at school. This baby spider is doomed.

"Like my window?" Cassie calls. "Luke installed it last summer. The breezes off the lake are marvelous, and in winter it's weather-tight. Come in here, I'll show you this year's project."

Reluctantly, I return to the kitchen. In the midst of opening a can of tuna, she stops to hook a pinky around a drawer knob and open and shut it—*kerthunk*—and beams like a little kid on Christmas morning.

So …

My puzzlement must be obvious. "I'm in drawer hardware heaven!" she says. "The slides were so sticky, my fingers always got jammed. Never again, thanks to Luke."

She opens and shuts the drawer again, and sure

enough it's smooth like, well, every drawer in our whole house. Since our kitchen was renovated, we don't even boil water for tea any more. We just push a button on the built-in cappuccino maker beneath the granite counter, *et voila*. And the granite's always warm, which is great to lean on in winter even if it is terrible for the planet. I mean, we recycle, but nobody's perfect. I bet every single resident of Westchester County hides some dirty little secret about their energy use or recycling habits.

So I can't imagine my mother—*quiet, stomach!*—getting excited about something as ordinary as drawer hardware. When she got her latest Lexus last year she kept smiling, trailing her fingers across the gleaming, platinum engine hood.

"Heaven!" she trilled.

My father grinned. "Ag, when I was a kid we celebrated a new car by going out for ice cream. What say?"

Her fingers stilled. "Sure. Fine," she said. "But if we're baptizing a car with ice cream, let's take yours."

His face darkened. "I'll find my keys," he said, pretending she hadn't just crushed him. He rumpled my already-messy hair. "What's your favorite flavor, pooch?"

I winced. Even my mother knew—knows, I mean—it's always been butter pecan. So does Harriet, who's usually the one to buy it for me even though she's really just our twice-a-week cleaning lady.

Now, at Cassie's dining table, I pull the crust off a tuna sandwich and nibble the center. It's delicious, with celery and some sort of seasoning. I take a real bite.

"So, how soon do I get my phone?" I say again, chewing. "I'll find somewhere to stay back home. The sooner I'm out of here, the better, right?"

"Not exactly," Cassie says. "You think any of us

would let you ride a bus to New York by yourself? Don't you see your folks can't worry about you now? Your dad was so exhausted when we talked that he called my offer an answer to prayer."

I snort. "That's just an expression. He's no believer."

Her face sags in dismay. "Oh. Well … forget it." She dials a number on a plastic wall phone, the kind you see in movies and on old TV sitcoms. "Tommy? Hi, it's Cassie Parker." She explains the situation, dripping sincerity and obviously determined to help. I mentally cross being murdered off my list of immediate worries.

She hangs up. "Some of your family's stuff was brought to the station. But Tommy—Sergeant Thompson—doesn't remember any phones. We'll go into town, I mean Burlington, when you're finished eating." She eyes the clock on the counter. "I was supposed to work this afternoon, but I'll call and see if anyone can take my shift."

"Whatever." I take a last nibble and push away my food. "I'm done."

Her eyebrows draw into a single line, but she takes the plate. "Give me a few minutes."

9

Sergeant Tommy Thompson is a muscle-bound guy without an ounce of fat, and blond hair so short that his scalp shows through. It's easy to picture him with mirrored sunglasses and a wide-brimmed hat, brandishing a nightstick and intimidating lawbreakers on Vermont's highways. But Cassie's at ease with him—they went through elementary school together, she told me on the way over—and when she asks, he brings me a paper cup of water. We huddle by his desk opposite him, she and I, in metal chairs with vinyl seats and rubber cups on the legs.

"So," the Sarge says. "We've got to find out what caused this crash. And you, young lady, are here to tell us."

My eyes pop open. *What an idiot I am. I walked right into this.* I shoot Cassie a mute, furious, panicky appeal.

"Can't you ask Brittany's dad?" she says. "Surely—"

"Well, that's a sensible idea." Sergeant Thompson's gaze bores through me. "But apparently, Mr. Warner doesn't remember what happened."

I knock over my paper cup. Cassie dabs the spill with a tissue, while a tiny hope fizzes within me. If my mother's in a coma, and my father has amnesia … *no one knows what I did.*

Except me. My ears seem to hum and I sit as still as possible.

"The driver of the semi says you were in his lane when he rounded the bend," the Sergeant says. "That true?"

My fingers crush the empty cup. *"So, you love this bag?"* I'd taunted, dangling the stupid Prada bag out the window. Then came the blare of the horn, the silver cylinder rushing at us, the swerve of our car … I'll wear this hair shirt forever. But 'fessing up is impossible; it would only make things worse.

"It's … hazy," I hedge. "The other driver—is he okay?"

The cop peers at me. "Doctors say he will be." He turns to Cassie. "Did she black out too?"

"They said not. But, Tommy—"

"I did!" I pipe up, and they both regard me uncertainly.

Finally, the Sarge sighs. "Cass, I've got a report to write. If someone or something distracted Mrs. Warner, whether inside the car or out of it, I need—"

"I'm sure my dad wouldn't have—" I say in a tiny voice.

But the cop talks over me. "Three of you in the car. And no one can say what happened." He scowls at a bulletin board plastered with WANTED posters of scrungy felons. If it's meant to intimidate, it's working.

I get to my feet, my legs wobbly, and grab the edge of the desk. "I … I might've been asleep. There was this loud smash, and I heard sirens and a chainsaw thingy." My blood pulses in my temples in the silence. *What if he doesn't believe me?*

The Sarge drums his fingers on the metal desk. It sounds exactly like nailing a lid onto a coffin and I realize, horrified, that I've just contradicted myself. If I were asleep, how could I know if I'd passed out?

"Ask about my phone," I hiss to Cassie.

She stretches her arm along the Sergeant's desk. "The thing is, Brittany's real anxious to—"

"Cassie. Let me handle this," he interrupts.

My stomach muscles clench as I perch on the edge of the seat again. But I'm rescued. A cop with a horsey jaw and buzz cut lugs in my dad's duffel and a tray full of our stuff. My cell phone and iPad are right on top. *Yea!* I grab them both and freeze. Underneath lies my mother's Prada bag, its side gashed and the red fabric lining pooling through like blood. Nausea overwhelms me and I feel like bawling.

"Your mom can buy another, honey," says clueless Cassie. "Tommy, isn't that enough for now?"

The Sergeant leans back and crosses his arms behind his head, studying me through slitted lids. Ovals of perspiration darken his armpits. In one fluid motion he leans forward, raps his knuckles on the desk, and stands.

"Cassie's right," he says in an almost kindly tone. "Go home with her. Settle in, unwind, let her pamper you. She's a terrific gal, oughta have kids of her own. And don't mind if I seem tough. It's just part of the job."

I will my stomach to settle. *If I can keep it together a few more minutes ...*

"But don't leave town," he says. "And"—he leans forward and plucks my phone from my grasp—"We've got to keep this. It's against state law to use a cell phone while driving."

"But—that's mine!" I shoot a panicky glance at Cassie. "I don't drive, and my mother wouldn't—"

"She might if her battery were dead." He pauses. "Ring any bells?"

Silence.

"No." I eye my phone hopelessly. It's my lifeline, not so much for contacting anyone—long story—but for being able to Google stuff. The virtual world at my fingertips, that's part of me.

Was. No longer.

"… one of those pay-as-you-go phones," the Sergeant tells Cassie. "Walmart sells 'em. Save your receipt, and I'll make sure you're reimbursed. Now, let's see." He unzips the duffel and lifts out a long pair of khakis.

"Guess you'll need some clothes too," he says. "The other bags were destroyed. And we'll have to bring these to your dad before whatever he's wearing falls apart on him." He laughs at his own joke, which for me has always been a sign of limited intelligence. "Well, Walmart's the place."

I muster a sick smile. On a normal day, I wouldn't be caught dead wearing anything from a discount store. They reek of petroleum from the greasy plastic goods they sell. But I wouldn't say so here if my life depended on it.

In a way, it does.

Cassie drives while I set preferences on my new el cheapo cell phone. Which isn't even a smartphone. It's prehistoric not to be able to Google stuff 24-7, not to mention access my social media. I hope her cottage is equipped with decent, high-speed internet, so at least I can use my iPad.

For the second time today, I clutch a plastic bag on my lap. My new clothes consist of jeans, a couple of pairs of cutoffs and gym shorts, and a bunch of T-shirts including two oversized ones to sleep in. All pretty flimsy, compared to my usual duds. And cheapo sneakers and a denim jacket no designer would touch. Cassie says that even in summer, nights here are cold—it's what gives northern apples their snap. Did I know Vermont is the home of the McIntosh, and there are orchards right here on South Hero? *No, and I don't care.* We checked out knapsacks too, after I said I hate purses. It's a brand-new aversion, but she doesn't have to know that. But she was anxious about the cost of it all, even when I assured her my father would pay her back, and insisted she'd lend me something. He'd told me, during our awful call, that he'd reimburse Cassie for my keep.

I'm being boarded, like a pet at a kennel. I can't help but wonder, will my daily tab be more or less than a springer spaniel's or Abyssinian cat's?

"We did real good," Cassie says. "Where else can you buy a whole wardrobe for seventy-two bucks?"

I experiment with the phone. "So, I have zero contacts on this thing. How am I supposed to call anyone?"

She gropes in her purse and hands me her cell. "In here's your dad's, Will's, and my numbers. Your dad must have some of your friends', right? Staying in touch with kids is part of parenting. Why don't you call him and put your number in my Contacts too, so I can reach you when I need to."

Mentally I groan. What misadventures could I possibly have on an island in Vermont? Cassie's not even forty, I'd guess, but she seems like an overprotective old maid. She's probably overwhelmed, having a kid under her roof for the first time. If I weren't hideously aware that being here is my own fault, I'd be tempted to really give her a hard time.

But I'm too busy not-thinking about the accident.

Cassie's made a pork roast, complete with mashed potatoes and some carroty vegetables called parsnips. I nibble one. It's sweet, somewhere between a carrot and a chestnut, and why I've never heard of it is a mystery. There's a rhubarb pie too, which I haven't tasted either. Just five hours from home, it's another culinary world. I bet my hostess has never eaten edamame, or a California or shrimp tempura roll, or pumpkin-stuffed ravioli, which I've only had twice but practically swooned over. Not that Burlington wouldn't offer them—I've heard the city's pretty cosmopolitan—but the diner where she works is old-style, and South Hero seems somewhat remote. I'm no foodie either, though. At home, if we don't eat out, we basically live on rotisserie chickens and roasted veggies. And salad. Lots of Caesar salad. It's boring, and I live for the days when we get Thai takeout and I can eat my way down the sushi menu. Followed by a square of dark chocolate, doled out by my mother to each of us for its health benefits. Heaven forbid a real dessert should enter our house.

"You didn't reach *anyone*?" Cassie spreads a napkin on her lap. Today she's wearing a faded T-shirt and baggy leggings, both forest green, and I'm reminded she took off work for me. She should include her lost pay on my tab to my father, but I bet she won't. She'd feel guilty.

"It's summer. People go away," I fib. The sad truth is that there's virtually no one back home to call. Jeff

Cox and Benny are history, and I sure won't call Chelsea or Marissa. I'm not close to any of the girls from track, and that's awkward anyway since my mother snuffed my athletic career. Which still gives me a pang, on top of everything else.

"What about family?" Cassie says. "You must have grandparents, aunts, uncles?" She spears a parsnip disk.

I do have grandparents. Three, actually, and I called them all once my father texted me their numbers. Grammy and Grampy Warner are two elderly clones who always echo each other's words. They match each other perfectly, right out of a commercial for a retirement community, but tonight they weren't what I needed. For one thing, my father hadn't even told them about the accident. So I was forced to, and listened to their my-how-terribles and what-a-shames 'til I wanted to roar. When at last I broached the idea of maybe coming to stay:

"Honey, you know Grampy has diabetes," said Grammy. "And high blood pressure."

Grampy added, "And Grammy's A-fib gets worse when she's under stress. But we're so sorry, honey. And tell your dad to call us."

A pause. *Don't hold your breath,* I longed to say. *It took him two hours just to text me your number.* Which makes me ashamed. According to Cassie, he confers with dozens of doctors each day.

"My dad's parents aren't well," I finally tell Cassie. "And my other grandfather died ages ago. Both my parents were only children, so that's pretty much it."

"But what about your—"

Grandma Audrey. I sigh. "I did call my other grandmother. She said"—I imitate—"'As I told your father, I'll come when Agatha wakes. No point coming sooner, or you coming to Vegas.'" I stab a chunk of meat and nibble the edges off my fork.

"Vegas?" Cassie says faintly.

"Yeah. I think she was playing the slots. I heard *ka-ching, ka-ching* in the background a few times."

Cassie frowns and drags the saltshaker along the wooden table, one of the most irritating sounds in the world.

"I'm sorry," she says finally. "Families are supposed to support each other in times like this."

Not mine. "I guess you're stuck with me."

Her hand presses mine, so briefly there's no time to pull away. "That's okay by me. You see any husband here, Brittany? Kids? I'm alone in the world, no kin at all."

I snort. "Well, a family's not all it's—"

"No parents, sibs, cousins, grammy or grampy," Cassie goes on, gentle and dreamy. "I've never had a husband … or a child."

Whoa. But still … "You've got Will," I say.

She laughs so hard her snaggletooth shows.

"And he is handsome as the dickens, isn't he? All-around terrific, too. I about busted with pride at his GED graduation a month ago. Thanks to Luke and Priscilla and his scholarship, he'll take classes at UVM this fall. And he's not even eighteen. So he's not my Romeo, I'd be robbing the cradle."

She pauses, her expression more sober. "If only—" She stops, but my curiosity's piqued.

"If only what?"

"Nothing. He just hasn't had the easiest time, that's all."

I almost snort. From where I sit, Will lives in paradise, even if he is a foster kid. How bad could his life be? Suddenly I hear Benny's voice in my head, "You live in a mansion, my heart bleeds." And *he* didn't understand.

"But you're right," Cassie goes on. "Luke and Priscilla and Will and his sisters are my family. I can't wait for you to—"

"I won't be here long enough," I remind her, feeling that same odd twinge at the closeness she's describing. Almost a yearning, that I mentally squash. "And you don't have to babysit me. I'm kind of a YouTube addict, actually, so if you don't mind me using the computer in your—I mean my—bedroom, I'll be happy just to hang out—"

Her expression stops me mid-sentence. "Uh … I'm afraid I don't have internet. Or even cable TV, any more. I'm saving my pennies for … for now."

No. I'm stranded in Vermont, in a grungy cottage with a woman whose baggy leggings and T-shirt seem to be part of her, and now I can't get online? No how-to articles, no YouTube, no Angora Flatline to cheer me up … I scowl, my good will incinerated to ashes and my lips, to my horror, trembling.

"Well, you'll find I'm a barrel of laughs, Cassie," I say shakily. "By the time I leave, you'll want to throw me in the lake." I leap to my feet and head for my room, my eyes burning with unshed tears.

"You didn't try the rhubarb pie," she wails behind me. "And I bought ice cream."

So what. Cassie may have worked hard on our dinner, but it's like I'm stranded on a desert—*Earth to Brittany.* South Hero *is* an island. And I'm every bit as marooned as if I did fall off a ship, somewhere in the South Pacific.

But nowhere near Hawaii.

Later, I fiddle with my iPad on the window seat in Cassie's guest room. I've got a few videos downloaded, but the battery is low and … my charger was in my duffel. *Grrr.* No way can I return to the police station and be chummy with that Sarge. I'm cursing the whole situation under my breath when someone knocks on the door.

"Yeah," I say.

Cassie comes in, awash in motherly concern. She's so eager to please, it's pathetic. In another lifetime, my better self—assuming I have one—might reassure her. But right now, I don't have it in me.

"You're welcome to borrow this, for as long as you like." She hands me the kind of vintage, leather knapsack that certain upscale companies try to imitate. But this one's the real thing, and way cool.

"Thanks," I mutter and lift one of the pocket flaps. "Was it your parents'?"

Her face shutters. "It's from a thrift shop."

I slam shut the flap of the pocket. This thing might harbor anything: spiders, germs … *anthrax.* First chance I get, I'll search for signs of chalky powder and sanitize the whole thing. Cassie chews her lip, obviously wanting to say something. I set aside the knapsack and wait.

"Your dad called."

My whole body stiffens. She lowers herself onto the afghan at the end of the bed and pats the bed beside her. When I don't move, she sighs.

"He says your mom's holding her own. But …" My anxiety about the knapsack drains away and I press my arms to my side. "The first few days of a brain injury can be … risky." She plays with the fringes of the afghan.

"Your father was so upset that I didn't ask how much he told you. But her brain may begin to, um, bleed. If it does, the doctors might have to drill a hole in her skull—"

Oh, no. No, no, no. "Stop!" I practically shout before I jam my fingers into my ears. And go numb all over. Blank out my brain. *Breathe in, breathe out.*

"My mother should be moved to New York," I say after a moment, only slightly less loudly.

Cassie raises her voice, too. "The hospital's a Level One trauma center. They're well equipped to treat head injuries, since the area's loaded with ski resorts. Now, I've asked our church to pray for your family. People do that on their own, of course, but there are meetings every Wednesday, too. Maybe you'll join us sometime?" She looks hopeful.

Not happening. Was it just this morning that Will showed me the cross he wears? It seems like three months. "I already told you, we're atheists."

She walks to the doorway and turns. "You can always change your mind, you know."

"If the hospital's as great as you say, I won't have to." I raise the volume of my iPad.

Her smile disappears, and I smirk with satisfaction. This is probably how my mother feels when she scores a point in court. Not that we're alike, of course—that would be horrible, because she's downright mean. Still, a gossamer thread of guilt wafts by and settles on my shoulders. Maybe I hurt Cassie?

But my hostess just says, "Let's settle you in," and opens the top bureau drawer and pulls out a stack of sweatshirts. I'd bet this is her winter wardrobe, and that the next drawer is full of sweatpants as baggy as her leggings. At least she's not a hoarder. That would send me over the edge.

I move past her and empty my Walmart bag onto the dresser top. "This is fine."

After a moment, she returns the sweatshirts to the drawer. Her sleeve brushes a piece of paper off the desk beside her. She snatches it up—I glimpse a computer photo of a small girl in a pink dress—and grabs another sheaf of papers and presses them against her middle.

She's hiding something.

"I'll just move all this out of your way," she says brightly. "Now, is there anything you need?"

"Um … maybe I'll take a shower."

"Of course. I put out some towels, to the right of mine. Actually, they're new. I just cut off the tags. They're"—to my surprise, she blushes—"pink."

Pink towels, pink dresses, pink cheeks. What's the deal? I nod and pick up my iPad again.

She still lingers in the doorway. "Well, guess I'll say nighty-night," she says. "Don't hesitate to ask if you do need something. And Brittany …"

Finally, I look up. She's holding up her hands in praying position. I look down, so she can't see me roll my eyes. At last she leaves, pulling the door shut behind her with a soft click.

The Big Ben alarm ticking loudly on the nightstand says it's only eight-thirty. It's still light out, and I've been put to bed as if I'm five. Not that I really want to go outside anyway; the place is probably rampant with mosquitoes. I decide to allow myself three YouTube videos before my shower.

I need my fix of Angora.

Hot water streams over my head and down my body. I reach for the cheap shampoo Will bought me. My iPad died in the middle of the third video, on how to clean the bottom of a saucepan with lemon juice. Somehow, it's the last straw in a messy barn. I wanted—no, I needed—to see the tarnish disappear from that copper bottom, leaving the pan penny-fresh and reassuring me that *something* can still be made right in this world. Miserable, I work shampoo into my hair and let the spray rinse it out. The shower door is fogged, like my car window was right before the accident. My mind flashes to my own taunting smirk when I dangled my mother's bag out the car window. And how the semi's horn blared … I can't dwell on the driver, but sheesh, I hope he'll be okay. And that my family won't get sued, or any of us put in jail.

I cross my arms over my ribs, slump against the shower wall, and slide to the floor. The hot water beats against my shoulders, and to my horror, a sound that's half-groan and half-sob escapes my mouth. I want to bawl like a little kid. But if I do, I might not be able to stop.

"Why, why, *why?*" I moan instead, through gritted teeth so Cassie won't hear. "Why did this have to *happen?*" There's no answer, of course. I'm alone. Friendless. Unloved. And today I lied to a cop.

How many prisoners are at the Burlington police station, or wherever they're kept? I'm a virtual captive myself here at Cassie's, but things might get even worse. Today I committed perjury, which could get me arrested. That's bad enough. But now the most nightmarish thought I can imagine penetrates my dripping head.

If my mother dies, I'm a murderer.

10

The next morning, Cassie makes us both waffles and eggs. Breakfast isn't part of my normal day, except for maybe a granola bar, but my helicopter hostess insists I ate nothing yesterday. I won't let her pull this again, but it's my first taste of real maple syrup. *Wow.* How incredible that it comes from a tree. I'll have it again sometime, when … everything isn't so awful. Because as I swallow my last bite of waffle, Cassie says my mother's still in the coma, but holding her own. We're halfway through the three-day, high-risk period for a brain bleed.

It's a relief. But mentally, I'm keeping the whole thing at arm's length. If I didn't, I'd go berserk.

Today is Sunday. But when I tell Cassie I hardly slept, which is mostly true, she surprises me by saying church will still be there next week, and hands me a book of crossword puzzles. If I'm still here, I'll have to break the news to her that I won't be darkening the door of any house of worship, in Vermont or not, any time. As if it would really help my mother! If God were real, the world wouldn't be such a mess. Also, I'll make it clear that except for something huge like my mother waking up, she has to spare me the medical details. Whether it's from some childhood trauma or another reason, I don't know—but I don't do death, illness, injury, or deformity. Not in books, movies, or on TV. They make me feel weak, even faint. Not that it's any of Cassie's business.

When she returns from church all chipper and reheats some homemade minestrone, though, I eat that too and decide to save serious discussions for later. I sure misjudged her on the canned soup. Her menu may not be the most cosmopolitan, but she's a majorly good cook. At this rate, I'll put on serious weight if I'm not care-ful—though my pediatrician says I'm underweight for my height, five-five.

After lunch, Will arrives to show me the horse farm. He holds out a thick, peeled stick about four feet long with a crook at the top and eyes me uncertainly. Like he's handing me a weapon, and isn't sure what I'll do with it. "For your foot," he says.

I'd forgotten all about the cut in my arch. It hardly hurts at all, and I've got so many bigger problems. But I take the stick from his hand with a brusque nod, and we hike along Cassie's driveway. He says it'd be best if we didn't ride today, so for now I'm saved from setting him straight about me and horses. I limp a bit just the same, though I use the "cane" mostly to lop the heads off the waist-high wildflowers we pass. It's oddly satisfying.

We round the bend in the lane, and the horse farm stretches in front of us. And what can I say? It's perfectly gorgeous. Next to the rambling farmhouse is the barn, picturesque and inviting. Nestled around them both are a riding ring with six or seven jumps, more fenced pastures, and a tall, circular pen made of metal piping. A pang shoots through me and I feel as hollow as if I hadn't just gorged on waffles. *I wish I'd always lived here.*

"You sure landed on your feet," I mutter.

"Believe me, I know," Will says. "It's my favorite spot on earth. How's the pain?"

"Okay."

We approach the riding ring. At the far end, a slender blonde wearing a helmet and tall boots canters a huge pale-gray horse over a triple jump. The end posts are freshly painted in red and white spirals, like barbershop poles. The girl reins the horse to a trot, posting perfectly, and waves to Will. She's about my age, and I instantly dislike her.

"Lookin' good, Jess," he calls.

"Hey, Will. He's going so well!" She slows the horse, slides her feet from the stirrups, and lets the horse amble toward us with the reins draped loosely on his neck.

Show-off.

Will goes to meet her. I follow. Avoiding this kind of barn brat is partly why I quit riding after just one lesson back home. Who'd want to let some snotty chick bring me a horse she'd brushed and saddled herself and later would feed, hug, and talk to like he belonged to her? Riding wasn't enough for me. I wanted—needed—a horse of my own, that would nicker when I arrived to feed him and nuzzle my pockets for an apple.

And love me.

The girl vaults lightly to the ground, removes her helmet, and shakes out her ponytail. Our eyes meet, and she gives a quick nod.

"You should've seen him when he got a load of the new stripes!" she tells Will, jerking her thumb at the barbershop poles. "He ran out on me once, shied twice, popped it once … but now they're no big deal, are they, buddy." She rubs the horse's damp neck, high under his mane. "But the crossbars need to be farther apart. Got a minute to lend a hand?"

"Sure," Will says. "Hey, Jess, this is Brittany." To me he says, "Jessica is Pastor Dave's daughter. She's in training for a three-day event in August. So, wait. It's jumping, dressage, and—" He scrunches his face, concentrating.

The girl snickers. "Cross-country. I should tattoo it on your brain, you always forget." She turns to me, easy-mannered if not exactly warm. "Hey, Brittany. Meet Captain. He's an Arab, and he's seven."

I nod, surveying the horse. He's gorgeous, with a pale, speckled coat and liquidy brown eyes, and groomed to perfection. His saddle and bridle gleam with some sort of polish. It's clear his owner dotes on him. Who wouldn't? I'd kill for a horse like that.

"Be right back," Will says. Jessica ties Captain to a fence post, obviously not trusting me to hold him. Which is fine by me, even though it's slightly insulting. They walk to the triple jump, lower the crossbars to the ground, and move the three sets of posts farther apart.

I watch, my arms crossed against my chest and my mouth sour. *Some people have all the—*

"Are you my brother's new friend?" pipes a voice beside me. I jump. It's a little girl, maybe eight or so. Long dark braids, thick lashes, chubby cheeks … what most people would call adorable, except that a pretty big part of her left cheek is red and shiny. *Scarred.* Weakness washes through me and I clench my teeth, averting my gaze.

"Priscilla, she's here!" the girl calls. To me she says, "I'm Meghan. And you're Brittany, but I'm going to call you Britt."

A stocky, middle-aged woman pushes a wheelbarrow full of dirty shavings from the barn and parks it along a low retaining wall. Brushing off her palms, she limps toward us. Her brown eyes, chestnut hair, and freckled pug nose remind me of a teddy bear—but her expression is closed, almost cool.

"So, you're staying with Cassie," she says. "Pleasure."

Her tone and the right hand that stays in her rear jeans pocket say the opposite. But I jerk my chin again.

"Will says you know about horses, Britt. Could you help me bring in Tiny?" Meghan asks.

I catch my breath and glance at Priscilla, but she's already turned away.

"Um … uh. I guess." I can hardly claim my wounded foot as an excuse, since I told Will I was fine *and* hiked here from Cassie's cottage.

"Great!" Meghan grabs a lead line off a hook in the barn doorway and we clomp out to a pasture, where she slips through a gap in the fence by the gate. It's wide enough for a person, but too narrow for a horse. *Clever.* I follow her through and stop short.

A few yards away, the most ginormous horse I've ever seen chomps on grass. Caramel-colored, he's got a massive head, a flowing, creamy mane, and thick tufts of hair—or fur?—at the backs of his ankles. He raises his head and sees us, his jaws working. His teeth are the size of cigarette lighters.

My feet are rooted to the ground. "This … is Tiny?"

"He hates to be caught," Meghan says. "Are you coming?"

My heart does a blippety-blip. She goes to the horse, but he ambles away. She follows, trying to move close. He trots away a few paces, his huge feet thudding against the ground … then stops and rips out more grass, eyeing her while he chews. This happens three or four times, until finally she parks her fists on her narrow hips and faces me, indignant.

"Britt, I told you I need help!"

Here's the thing. Much as I love horses, and have longed for one practically my whole life, they … well, they terrify me. The one riding lesson I took a few years ago left me traumatized, and my mother saw her chance to make me quit. But I'm darned if I'll admit this to a pipsqueak with muddy knees.

I grit my teeth and circle to Tiny's other side, giving him a wide berth. Whoever named this animal had a sick sense of humor. Feeling like an idiot, I wave my arms in great circles.

"Shoo!" I say desperately, hoping he'll move toward Meghan. Or the gate. Anywhere away from me. "Shoo, blast it."

The horse swings around and heads straight toward me. I'm about to flee when Meghan, taking advantage of his distraction, dashes in and jumps up to grab his halter. She pulls his head down and clips on the lead line, scurries back, and hauls on the rope with her whole weight. Dreading yet more spillage of blood, I wait for the horse to rear and stomp on her. But to my astonishment he wheels slowly, like a great ship, and plods toward the gate with his great whiskery jaw practically on her shoulder.

My knees almost buckle with relief.

"We got him! Thanks, Britt," the kid squeaks.

Will is standing by the gate. He opens it for the horse and girl to pass through, and waits patiently for me too. It's sickening, how obliging he is—after abandoning me.

"Why'd you go off?" I hiss. "I was almost trampled!"

He raises an eyebrow, his lips quirked. Meghan, who obviously overheard, turns and gives an exaggerated shrug, palms-up. The kid's a born comic.

Back at the barn, she hooks up Tiny in the wide doorway. Two ropes run from his halter to metal rings on either side of the doorframe, so he's standing in the center and can't nibble anything. Or anyone. She drags over a stool, climbs on, and applies herself to his massive neck with an oval rubber brush.

Will and I move on. "So, how 'bout the truth," he says easily. "Have you ever even been on a horse?"

Um. I sigh. And peek back at Meghan, but the horse is apparently behaving himself. She's scrubbing his back now, with total concentration. "Once. It spooked the moment I got on and I fell off, right in front of some snotty barn brat. Speaking of which, is that ... blonde girl ... your girlfriend?" I say with distaste.

"So, you're scared." He ignores my question. "But Jess is no snob, she must've mucked out ten stalls today. And she's a hundred percent sold on the ministry."

I snort. "Her, a minister? That's rich."

The dimple in his left cheek deepens in amusement. "No— Luke and Priscilla are setting up a horse ministry to help troubled teens. Next summer."

Ministry, minister ... who knew there was a difference? *I hate looking stupid.* "I suppose you qualify?" I ask sweetly. "Jessie would enjoy teaching you a few things, I bet. Or maybe she already has?"

He frowns. "Jessica's a good person. If you asked nicely, she might even give you lessons."

"On flirting with hot guys? No, thanks." I walk ahead, resisting the urge to check his reaction to my backhanded compliment. But when he catches up to me, he still looks troubled. Maybe insulting his female friend wasn't such a good idea. *So what, I'm only here a few days.*

We watch in silence as two horses chase each other in the next paddock. They run, buck, rear, snort. Their hooves strike the earth so hard that the bottoms of my sneakers vibrate.

"Meet Genesis and Midnight," Will finally says. "And old Saratoga over there hung up his victory wreath to be a nanny to this filly. She's two." A drowsy swayback in a third paddock guards a spindly young horse with bangs splayed over her forehead, right down to her eyelashes. Her locks glint orange in the sunlight, as if they've been highlighted with peroxide.

Like mine. My hair's a wild mess of curls, which I attempt to contain in a braid, but secretly I don't mind its coppery color. Both my parents deny it's from their side of the family, and they can't both be right. But my father's Irish-German-Russian ancestry is a more probable genetic source than my mother's Scandinavian heritage. Which may explain her coldness … I mean, those Viking types lived by the Arctic Circle. And our name "Warner" is German for an officer who oversees game in a park, which is hysterical for two reasons: first, my mother does the managing and tending in our family, such as it is. But when our house becomes zoo-like, the female inhabitants hissing and spitting at each other, my dad does "watch the game"—as a spectator, his head swinging back and forth as if he's at a tennis match. A protector he is not.

Either way, the irony slays me.

But now I clutch the top rail of the fence and, my irritation forgotten, practically drool over the filly. "Oh, she's darling! And those bangs—she can't even see!"

Will doesn't answer, so I turn and peer at him. He's gazing at me oddly. "You love them!" he says, like he's discovered the Pacific. "Don't you. Why are you hiding it? If you're afraid, Luke can help you."

Oh, no. I start to deny it—all of it—but why bother? Plus, my nose is prickling, so I turn back to the scene before me. But the old nag looks so sweet and protective that I feel even worse.

"I've always wanted a horse." My voice trembles. "It's all I ever asked for. If I'd gotten one, my life would be—" I clear my throat. *Why am I telling him this?*

"Different?" he says softly. He runs his fingers through that thick hair, the sun glinting golden on it. "That's how I felt about getting a motorcycle. I wanted it in the worst way, thought it would solve all my problems. I pictured myself real cool, you know? *Vroom-vroom*, tooling along some open road with sagebrush in Arizona—"

"I'm not trying to *escape*," I say. "It's not like I've got fantasies of galloping on a beach in France." Which isn't exactly true, but that's not the point. I'm not sure of my point, actually. I click my tongue at the filly, but she ignores me.

"Anyway, then I got one," Will goes on.

"And?" Finally, I face him.

A pause. "I can't say it wasn't fun in the beginning, though I never made it to Arizona. Or anywhere worth mentioning. But after a while, I still felt ... numb. It didn't change anything—"

"Why would it?" I interrupt. "A horse is different, it will—well, love you back."

He shakes his head slowly. "Never enough. I had an empty place inside me, Britt, and no way to fill it. You name it, I tried it. Every addiction you can think of."

He fingers the cross hanging from his neck, seemingly unaware.

Ugh. I know where he's going. "Yeah, well, any empty place in me is shaped like a horse," I retort. How perfect and complete Jessica appeared, flying over that fence in her cool, tall boots and helmet, hunched like a jockey high on Captain's gleaming neck. *You can't tell me she lacks anything.* Envy streaks through me like poison, and suddenly I long to wound Will, or at least shock him. "But right now I'd settle for a joint, or a shot of something. Got anything?"

His expression doesn't change, but I sense some sort of emotion. "No. But hear me out? My dad was gone, my mom was … hurting. All I thought of was myself. But when I did get my bike, a heap of trouble came with it."

"And that was the bike's fault?"

He flinches and looks away. When he turns back to me, his expression's almost sad. "Of course not. I just meant I did all kinds of things with it that I shouldn't have. Like skipping school, drinking, and … worse. Bad stuff. So, two years ago I got locked up in juvie. After a while, Luke came to see me. And—"

"Wait. Was he your foster dad then?"

"No, we'd never met. But there I was, I'd hit bottom. Everything was wrong, I'd been sh—I was dead inside, thought I was worthless. And he told me it didn't have to be that way. My life could be different."

Right. From what I've seen, things left to their own devices pretty much go downhill. Nothing gets better by itself. But he's speaking faster now, the sadness gone, and *something* obviously changed Will from burned-out loser to … an easygoing guy who seems more at home in his skin than anyone I ever met. Right now, if I'm honest, he's thrumming with some sort of special energy. Curiosity flickers inside me.

"Like …?" I ask casually.

The kindness in his face brings a lump to my throat. Those eyes are riveting, with depths like the rich greens and blues of bottom-of-the-ocean photographs. They seem to see everything, yet not to judge. I picture myself tumbling in and swaying, like seaweed in a watery hammock.

"For one thing, he told me how much God loves me—"

The vision ends. "And you caved," I groan. "Aw, Will, you were a sitting duck, a captive audience. Don't you get it?"

"It wasn't like that," he says defensively. "I'm not explaining it well. But Luke is awesome. It sounds trite, but if it weren't for him, who knows where I'd be today? He's the real deal, Brittany. He trains horses, but now he leads our Youth Group and is studying to be a pastor."

Sheesh. This is the man Will practically idolizes? But I'm saved from answering when a green pickup rattles down the lane toward the farmhouse. He brightens. "That's Luke now! Want to say hi?"

Um. "Don't you work today or something?"

"Never mind," he says. "It'll keep."

Forever, I hope. Even if Luke does have the most awesome job in the world. Meaning horse trainer, of course, not his crazy idea of being a pastor. Aloud I say, "I don't need anyone putting the fear of God into me."

Will's expression softens to an unbearable gentleness. "Not fear, Britt. Love."

For once, I have no snappy comeback.

11

Cassie's stretched out on her living room sofa, a mass of pastel yarn spilling over her legs. I get the feeling I woke her. "Oh, my," she says. "Tour all done?"

"Yep." I plunk myself on a threadbare floral easy chair. Beside me is a teddy bear with its tags still on, sporting a bandaged head and a crutch under its arm. I stiffen. *If this is her idea of a joke ....*

"What's this?" I demand.

"Just a bit of encouragement," she says. "From Vermont's very own Teddy Bear Factory—"

I toss the bear onto the braided rug by my feet. It tumbles to a stop upside down against a leg of the coffee table, its glassy eyes unfazed by indignity. "You seriously think I need reminding that my mother's head is bashed in?" I burst out. "Don't you think I live with it every bloody, waking second?"

She leans over, scoops the teddy onto her lap, and stares at me, her eyes as round as the bear's. I glare at them both.

"And I'm too old for stuffed animals." *And have been for years.* When I entered kindergarten, my mother came into my room and, to my horror, swept my bunnies and teddies and my stuffed lioness off my shelves and into a garbage bag. She was going to let me keep a pink bear named Snoddy who wore a party hat and carried a tiny glass of Coke, but I followed her to the door and stuffed him into the bag myself, stifling sobs. If I couldn't keep all my animals, I didn't want any. I cried myself to sleep a few nights, but I got past it.

Kids can adjust to anything.

Now Cassie thrusts the bear at me. "You're never too old for a teddy. Or too young for a latte. It's too early in the season for pumpkin, so maybe a nice caramel latte? My annual picnic is next weekend, to celebrate the Fourth. I invited your dad, by the way. And I've got a ton of stuff to buy, no perishables yet, but whatever won't spoil in the meantime. Paper goods and whatnot. Why don't you come along? Afterward we'll hit Starbucks and visit your mom. Everyone's thrilled that she's hanging in there!"

Who is "everyone"? And talk about seeing the glass half full. I drop the bear onto the couch. "I'll come. And have a latte. But I won't go to the hospital."

Because the very idea of facing my mother makes me feel ill. I've got to make Cassie understand.

She sets aside her knitting with a frown.

We sip iced caramel lattes on a bench outside Starbucks. Burlington's got an awesome outdoor pedestrian mall— the city really is quite sophisticated—and since it's a gorgeous summer day, people are everywhere. Not to mention their collies, labradoodles, chihuahuas ... so we've been window-shopping *and* observing various life forms. I slurp the last of my latte, gather my strength … and toss my grenade.

"So. You may as well know, Cassie. I won't be visiting my mother 'til she wakes."

Cassie raises shocked eyes above the rim of her cup. "You don't mean that."

"I do. It's better that way. And I don't want to talk about it." Suddenly I spot the dark guy from the diner coming toward us, with the same two dudes in tow. "Cassie." I lower my voice. "Who's that guy? He was in the diner."

She peeks behind her. "That's Manny Sligh, a snake dipped in testosterone. And his goons. Buck Forrest, the stocky one, he's local … but the other's called Z, and he's new to town. Stay clear of them." As they pass, she says loudly, "And they better stay clear of you."

Manny spins around, his gaze sharp. He taps his brow in a mock salute and slinks on with panther grace.

"Cassie Higgins!" A white-haired woman with a hearing aid and cane approaches. "You're just who I was going to call!"

"Mrs. Marino." Cassie beams like the woman's her long-lost friend.

While she and the old lady talk, I get up and carry my empty cup to the nearest trash bin. Nearby, Manny and his doughy sidekick—Buck, was it?—bend over a smartphone held by the skinny one. Z, Cassie said. *What a name.* Manny glances at me, reaches into his pocket, and holds something up. I squint. A pill. Behind me, the two women are still gassing away, so I catch Manny's eye and mime smoking a joint. His eyebrows arch, and that magnetic grin spreads across his face. I shiver, again sensing his incredible charisma. And if I'm honest, maybe something else. Something hidden, and darker.

Back with Cassie, I perch on the edge of the bench. The beefy Buck strolls by and drops a packet by my leg. I grab it so my hostess won't see and peek in. It's two joints and some pills: a care package. A tension within me eases. I'm not one to self-medicate, as I've said, but I'm desperate for a break from this horrid alternative reality. Telling myself none of this will matter in a hundred years isn't much comfort while my mother—*can it, Britt.* I glance at Manny. He winks and parks some shades on his nose, either Gucci or a darn good knockoff. Drugs pay; no surprise there.

Cassie's elderly friend leaves, thanking her loudly for some kind of help involving a reunion. *Whatever.* At the end of the pedestrian mall, Manny and his pals climb into a black SUV with tinted windows. They roll away, as majestic as if they're visiting dignitaries riding in a limo. My hostess stands and lifts her bag, smiling ... until she sees where I'm looking and stiffens.

"Let's go shopping," she says.

Something earsplitting trills in the yard while I rock on Cassie's porch glider. Through the open kitchen window, her head is visible above the stove, and a pot lid clangs. I slouch, light a joint in the opening of the baggie, and take a deep drag. Then I tamp out the joint and seal the bag. Straightening again, still holding my breath, I twist and peer in the window. Cassie lifts her nose and sniffs, uncertain. I lean almost all the way to the paint-flaked porch floor and exhale.

She pokes her head out the door, startling me. "Dinner," she announces, then withdraws. I stand and stretch my legs and arms, waving them around a bit so no cannabis particles follow me inside. Because that single hit has given me amazing mental clarity. This is the home of a saint. If Cassie knew who's occupying her guest room, she'd kick me out.

I'm a fish out of holy water here. But I can't leave. Suddenly I envision the little mare at the farm, with her sweet peroxide bangs. Visiting her would kill time and get me out from under Cassie's feet. *I'll go soon.* This decision, and the pot, take the edge off my mood. So during dinner, just burgers and store-bought coleslaw since we were out so long, I'm pleasant to my hostess. None of this is her fault, and she's so grateful that I'm almost sorry I haven't been nicer.

But I've only been here two days. Once my mother's out of danger, she'll be moved to New York. And we'll go home, and the worst of this will be over for all of us.

In my sweet cannabis glow, I almost believe it.

At six the next morning, I peer into the filly's stall, making kissing noises the way Meghan did to Tiny. The little horse backs away and bobs her head vigorously, the rims of her eyes flashing white.

"Ha! Caught you." Will comes from behind me, his arms full of hay, and drops a clump over the half-door. The mare attacks it as if she's starving, her delicate legs splayed apart in the bedding.

"I was just visiting," I say. "Do you have a carrot or something? I forgot to ask Cassie."

He pulls out a toothpick and holds it up. "Just my fake ciggies. But Meghan would," he says. "She puts cut-up carrot sticks in her pocket every morning, then forgets about them. And Priscilla finds soggy orange bits all through our laundry. Drives her nuts."

The horse still gobbles frantically, shifting her weight from side to side. "What's her name?" I ask.

"Joy. But I wouldn't get too attached, if I were you. Luke might sell her. Horses here have to be kid-friendly, and this one's not too keen on people. Better to keep your distance."

Bummer. The young mare raises her head and eyes me suspiciously, as if she's thinks I'll steal her hay. "That could be a sign of intelligence," I say, but inside I'm disappointed. I'd hoped we might be friends.

Will crosses the aisle and throws the last bunch of hay to Saratoga. The old fellow nickers, that wonderful, deep *hnn-hnn-hnn* horses make, as if he's saying thanks. He chews slowly, like he's got a hundred years to live, though his gray whiskers say he's headed for the glue factory sooner than any living thing on the farm.

Will dusts off his palms. "Not sure they've established a connection." He walks away, whistling through his lower teeth.

"Not sure they've established a connection," I mimic to myself. Who does he think he is, sounding so pompous? Meanwhile, Joy's still chewing frenetically. We're both outcasts, but somehow it's comforting that I'm not alone. "Two roads diverged in a wood," Robert Frost wrote in a poem we read at school. One path's better than the other ... but is it the least or most travelled? Either way, I'm too far along the least used path to return. No matter how bumpy it gets.

I'm glad I ran into Manny in town, and wouldn't mind if it happened again before I leave Vermont. We two seem to be travelling the same by-way, at least for now.

This isn't real life.

I'm dreaming, and can't wake myself. Finally, I do—I think—and roll over in Cassie's guest bed. The shrubs outside my window thrash in the wind as if invisible animals inside are battling for their lives. A few yards beyond them, within the grove of trees on the shore, some large animal—a fisher cat, or a bobcat?—writhes and plunges in circles. Over and over. Its insane eyes gleam at me in the moonlight. Then it bares hideous, sharp teeth and gives a guttural hiss.

I gasp and bolt upright, shaking. *It was a nightmare.* I lie down again and curl on my side, trying to get comfortable. But the pillow is lumpy, and being awake is torture too. In my mind, the ventilator that keeps my mother alive in the ICU rasps endlessly, trapped like a fly between a windowpane and its screen. You might ignore the buzzing by day, but at night its frantic dartings and crawlings torment you.

Cat or fly, both are horrid.

My mother makes it through the three-day, high-risk period without a brain bleed. I guess that's a good sign. I don't talk to my father much, but he updates Cassie by phone morning and night. Once when I heard her discussing embolisms, strokes, and infarctions, I went weak all over, and told her again to spare me that stuff. So now she just reminds me how many people at church are praying for us. Which is weird. How can you pray for someone you haven't met? My hostess is also coming home from work earlier, either by letting go of shifts or cutting her hours. But I can't think about that. She's too bloody sweet for her own good, and I'm too crabby and guilt-ridden to be nice back. Even if I wanted to.

Like today. She came home from work and made chicken parm. Afterward she said, "By the way …" and dropped a paper sack on my lap with something squishy inside. I pulled out a silk-screened nightshirt with a giant moose on the front, surrounded by smaller moose and pine trees. All of them are dancing, even the trees.

"It's done by a Vermont artist," she said. "I saw it yesterday in a boutique in town and thought you might like it. You can wear those other shirts with a swimsuit or something."

I folded it carefully. "Gee, thanks, Cassie."

She nodded, but a line appeared between her brows. I guess I didn't hide my reaction very well. The shirt wasn't cheap. The cotton is actually a thick weave, of high qual-ity. But no power on earth could make me sleep with a moose on my shirt, no matter how—okay, how adorable he is. If Cassie's disappointed, too bad. I mean, I'm sorry she spent her money, but she should know better than to expect anything from a kid in crisis.

The whole scene is a hurry-and-wait deal, that's for sure. This week in particular is lasting forever, with long empty stretches where I almost wish *anything* would happen. Before school ended, I was worried I'd be bored at home this summer. But now I'd give anything to rewind my life to before the accident. And the scene at Benny's. And having to kill my fish. And hearing I'm off the track team. I'd re-live all of those again willingly if only I could pull that Prada bag back inside our car and tell my mother I was joking.

But with this coma, no news is good news. Everything could still turn bad in an instant, I gather from monitoring Cassie's conversations with my father. Like seizures and clots ... so I'm relieved when one day follows another without anything dire occurring. And I don't let my mind roam ahead, though it's impossible to ignore the Fourth of July picnic she's hosting this coming Saturday. Almost every afternoon someone from the church drops off banquet tables, or grills, or a volleyball net. It means nothing to me. I'm hoping to be gone by the end of the week and no longer care about this year's fireworks. My dreams of Waikiki seem eons ago. But as Will pounds in posts to set up the net, I can't help but wonder what kind of boyfriend he'd make. We'd have no future, of course. He's a hayseed and I'm, well, from New York. No matter how I fight it. I dig Broadway musicals and classic movies, and follow an Aussie influencer on YouTube. He likes Youth Group and bowling, and probably isn't even online. I like salmon, he's Burger City.

He goes to church. I don't.

We both like trees, though. And he's definitely a helpful guy, which I think people take advantage of. I mean, does Jessica really need to re-arrange her jumps every single day? It irks me that he doesn't see through her flirting, though maybe he does but is flattered. For all I know, he could have had a crush on her since third grade. They probably knew each other then.

Meanwhile, I've started to ration Manny's joints and pills. The teeny portions aren't enough to make me high. They just take the edge off the days.

Nights are the worst, though. If I do run into Manny again, though I won't go out of my way to do it, I'll ask what else he's got. I dream of that silver cylinder hurtling toward us, of Chelsea and Marissa taunting me, of Benny giggling on the couch with a stupid brassiere on his head. The worst is when my mother haunts me, furious. I wake shaking and drenched in sweat, my skin sticking to Cassie's sheets. The sight of the lake sparkling through the trees on the shore eases my breathing and slows my pulse.

Will stops by sometimes, usually on his way to work. One day he pulls up in his Escort and climbs the porch steps to where I'm sprawled on Cassie's glider. Before I can react, I'm holding a thick maroon … Bible. I almost drop it—the weight's so unexpected—but my fingertips recognize real leather. Though the cover's not buttery soft like my mother's Prada—*stop, Britt!* Thoughts of the accident still ambush me, every day if I let them. This must be what PTSD is like.

"What's this for?" I say.

He shrugs. "You're going through a lot. And the Psalms can be a real comfort. I especially love 37 and 142."

"Hike," I quip, hoping to divert him. The guy needs a life.

But he takes the Bible again and flips through the pages. "Here's another great one," he says earnestly. "Psalm 46, verse 1."

He points to the open page.

I glance up instead. Holding my gaze, he quotes softly, "God is our refuge and strength, a very present help in trouble."

A real love letter. So forget the idea of Will ever being a boyfriend, not that I'm even sure I'm interested. I run a finger along the edges of the gilded pages. They're sharp as tiny knife blades and I recoil, feeling tricked.

"If I got into this," I say sharply, "I'd be a religious nut like—" I stop just short of saying you.

To my surprise, he laughs. "Maybe. But living by faith is a wild ride, Britt, the greatest adventure on earth. I never could have imagined coming to this place. It saved my life. The first time Luke drove me under that Narrowgate Farm sign, that he built himself from trees around here, I got chills. I mean, there I was, the scum of the earth, just sprung from reform school, and now … well, anything's possible. Not that I want to scale Annapurna, but my options have … expanded. And you never know what yours could be."

Strategizing for the future, my favorite topic. I set the volume aside. "Cassie asked me to peel potatoes." This happens to be true—the picnic's tomorrow, and she needs gallons of potato salad. But then curiosity gets hold of me. "Hey. Why is that cross you wear half-gold?"

He pulls the carving from inside his shirt. "Gold in the Scriptures can represent God. Wood symbolizes man. His Son was both."

All Greek to me. "It's just paint, though, right?"

He gives a gentle smile. "Gold leaf, actually. Many of the holy objects in the original Tabernacle—the tent where the Israelites worshipped while they roamed the desert—were pure gold."

"Oh. Here endeth the first week," is all I can think to say.

"Yep," he agrees. But his eyes are soft, and that always makes me sort of quiver inside. I can't decide if I like it.

12

Saturday arrives at last, and with it, Cassie's picnic. I slouch on her top porch step, yawning. By Manhattan standards it's early for a party, just eleven in the morning. But her place is a madhouse, people everywhere doing old-timey stuff I've only seen in movies. Three guys grilling burgers and dogs are no surprise, or the guy setting up a guitar and amp; but there's also croquet, horseshoes, and even a fiddler. With the mountains all around, I could almost imagine myself in the Appalachians. And Mrs. Marino and a bunch of chirpy ladies in flowery shirts have set out five kinds of pasta salad. Seriously. It's a far cry from catered events at home, where skinny young hotties in black and white—of any sex, and sometimes it's hard to tell which—offer trays of chevre, portabella mushrooms, radicchio, and marinated thises and thats. The recollection makes me a tad homesick, not that I've gone to many of those events. Just a few weddings and bar mitzvahs.

Three girls husk corn at a picnic table. The one with her back to me has a striking cloud of black hair. She pushes a stray lock behind her ear, revealing an enormous hoop earring. Curious to see her face, I inch down the porch steps—and some teen trips over me. Then, "Excuse me!" someone practically shouts in my ear, and a woman wearing a bib apron slides past carrying a tray of pies, and sets them out on a picnic table covered in plastic gingham. Clearly, I'm in the way. I stand and dust off my backside just in time to catch Will giving the black-haired girl a warm hug. He even rubs her back. Cassie comes from behind me and stops, balancing a platter of watermelon wedges on her hip.

"Who's that?" I aim to sound casual.

"Where?"

I jerk my thumb.

"Oh, that's Kara. Will's older sister, she's nineteen." Cassie's expression changes subtly.

"Oh." I blush. His *sister*. The black-haired girl pushes herself away from the picnic table and stands, her body profile visible. And—

"She's pregnant!" I blurt. Several women stop what they're doing and stare … at me.

Cassie's lips tighten. "Yes. Kara's made some poor choices … though not what you're thinking."

"Only one way I know of to get preggo. Outside a lab."

"Careful, Britt. Everyone makes mistakes." Her unusual edginess and emphasis alarm me. *Does she suspect something about the accident? Maybe that cop gave her ideas.*

Or she's just protecting a girl she obviously cares for. My nose prickles, and I walk away. Much as I loathe being here, I don't want Cassie to hate me. But I can't seem to help acting obnoxious. I'm not the person I was, and that Brittany wasn't so hot either.

My crabbiness and I wander through the picnic. I'm a pillar of grit amidst one of those picnic scenes by Renoir, or maybe more like Pigpen in the Peanuts cartoons, enveloped in a smutty cloud. A laughing, foot-tapping audience surrounds two men playing banjos in a seeming competition, though their pieces, oddly, go together. Old Mrs. Marino sets out paper plates and plastic silverware and ketchup and stuff, joking with other women grouped around the tables. A sudden, sharp *snap* makes me jump. Beyond the trees, some men cluster together in a grassy meadow. One, a graying, goateed guy in cowboy boots, lowers a rifle—a *rifle,* like you'd find in some backwoods hick town—and does a victory jig. The other guys laugh, including a Hispanic-looking guy who looks vaguely familiar.

A bunch of teens are playing volleyball in a cleared area by the driveway. Will and Jessica are on the same team, and even though he didn't say she's his girlfriend, it's obvious she's got a thing for him. Pathetically, she tries to assist him with a set-up—but he's not where she expected him to be. He makes a grand leap for the ball anyway, misses, and tucks his shoulder just in time to roll like a gymnast and break his fall. Jessica wails laughing apologies and helps him up, even brushing off the seat of his pants, which to my mind takes nerve. He catches my eye and beckons me to join them. But I want no part of their lollipop flirtation. Or the game.

The thing is, I'm a complete klutz when it comes to any sport involving a ball. I discovered this on my tenth birthday, when I tripped on my brand-new soccer ball and sprained my ankle so severely I ended up on crutches.

Phys Ed became a torment, since most of the class had witnessed my fall and teased me mercilessly. Luckily, one day in junior high I made the fastest time in a special qualifying race, and the JV coach cornered me for girls' track. It worked out okay, getting me out of the house, and no one minds an occasional pat on the back.

But I've sworn off games with balls, at least when I have a choice, so now I sit by myself at a picnic table. At the other end, a little girl with inch-long pigtails on either side of her head sits in front of—I count them— four desserts. Blueberry pie, a lemon square the size of my palm, a block of brownie ... and a huge wedge of watermelon. While her mother tucks a napkin into the kid's shirt neckline, her father hurries over clutching three drinks. He skids to a halt at her side.

"I wasn't sure which you'd like best, sweetie, so I got them all," he explains. The girl beams at both her parents, flirty and coy. She's got them wrapped around her little finger, which bugs me because she's nothing special. On the other hand, she probably won't have my so-called advantages or go to a selective college, if she goes at all. If those pearly teeth grow in crooked, chances are they'll stay that way. For all I know, being served four desserts might be the high point of her whole life, and everything after today will be downhill.

So why should I mind if her parents dote on her? I sound like a brat, even to myself.

Years ago, my mother threw me a ball at the play-ground. I fumbled, it rolled away, and I tried to chase it, but tripped on a tree root. Something gashed my knee; blood flowed. My mother snatched a stroller from a woman she'd just met and practically threw me into it. The woman protested, and my parent snapped, "Keep your shirt on, I'll return it." To me, she said, "If you'd looked where you were going, you wouldn't be riding like a baby." On the way to the doctor's office, her stinging words were outweighed by the astonishing privilege of riding in—on, actually, with my legs hooked over the bar—a stroller as if I *were* still a baby. Because babies are cared for, even when the baby was me. Growing up changed everything.

I have no clue why.

Who's to say this kid's life won't be happier than mine? She's already ahead of me by two adoring parents and four desserts. I rub my eyes and find my fingertips damp. The girl stops mid-bite, her cheeks smeared with blueberry, and gawks at me.

"Keep your peepers to yourself," I snap. Her face crumples and her father scowls, apparently incredulous that anyone would insult his darling.

"Try the brownie, Cyndi." He stuffs a chocolatey morsel into the kid's mouth.

Unbelievable.

I jump to my feet and collide with Meghan, right beside me. She pulls herself onto tiptoes, clutching my arm for balance, and whispers into my ear. "You know, Britt, Will would like you better if you weren't so mean."

Huh? "Ever hear of MYOB? Mind. Your. Own. Business." I jerk free and stride all the way to the barbecue area before I peek back.

She's still standing where I left her, palm against her scarred cheek as if I'd slapped her.

Sheesh. I hope she won't tell Will. I'm not quite sure how I feel about him, but insulting both his sisters—though hopefully Cassie won't tell him what I said about Kara—won't win me any favors. Maybe I should bring the kid a hot dog or some watermelon. But before I can do anything, a bellow drowns out the whole picnic.

"Watch your children, folks!" Sudden silence, as a few people draw their kids to their sides. "Okay, ready!" the same man shouts in a Hispanic accent. *It's Sandro*, I suddenly realize. Cassie's fireman pal, who comforted me through the car window the night of the accident.

A chainsaw roars. Something massive crashes onto the shore. I whirl around. The entire top third of Cassie's willow lies across the rocks, its fronds trailing in the water like the hair of some fallen warrior queen. Sandro and Will steady a ladder that reaches high into the tree's remaining foliage. Above them the saw roars again, operated by an unseen hand.

Half-choking, I sprint toward the willow. Another heavy limb falls, almost hitting me. A woman shrieks.

"Stop. *Stop!*" I scream. My pounding heart threatens to burst from my ribcage. I push Sandro aside and start to climb the ladder. Will grabs my elbow and pulls me off, while Sandro recovers his balance and seizes the ladder. Whoever's in the tree scrambles partway to the ground and braces the saw blade on his knee. He's wearing heavy safety glasses and spiked boots. When he lifts the glasses, the whites of his eyes gleam against his tan.

"Let me go!" I shout, drumming Will's shins with my heels. His forearm is hard against my ribs. "You ignorant … hicks! W–what in Hades are you doing, killing this tree? Haven't you heard of *green*? What gives you—"

"Cut it out, Britt," he pants, his breath warm in my ear. "He's not killing the willow, he's just topping it."

I go limp in his arms. He lets me go and helps me to my feet when he's sure I won't belt him one. I pull my shirt over my stomach—it had hitched way up. To my horror, the whole picnic's gone quiet and is staring. Even the banjo players' fingers have stilled on their strings.

"*W—what?*" I hiss.

The guy in the tree climbs to the ground. He's older than my father, in his late forties or early fifties, but lean and rugged and fit. He comes toward me, and I register far-seeing gray eyes with a thrill of dread through my fury.

"Topping a willow is just a way of pruning it," he says. "To cut out the rot. It'll grow back, stronger and healthier than ever. In a summer or two you won't be able to tell this ever happened. But I'm sorry to scare you."

He sticks out a strong hand. "I'm Luke. And you must be Brittany."

A sinkhole, that's what I need. An honest-to-goodness sinkhole like you see on the news, just big enough for me to disappear into. Ignoring him, I head for Cassie's driveway. Two women at a picnic table along the way munch through ears of corn on the cob, their fingers greasy with butter.

"Well, it's obvious she's troubled." The plumper one picks corn from her teeth.

"Cassie can't keep her forever," the other agrees.

My eyes blur. I bolt down Cassie's driveway, avoiding the ruts. I'm so done with this place, I'll hitch home if it kills me. But would my death be such a loss to the world? For the first time in a week, I remember my go-to creed: in the long run, nothing matters. My mother's coma has overshadowed everything, made me forget the big picture. Now, as I flee unpleasantness yet again, my favorite philosophy calms me, the way lucky rabbit's feet protect people in spaghetti Westerns. *Nothing matters. Listen and repeat, Britt: nothing matters. In a hundred years, we'll all be dead.*

13

Hundred years or not, I don't make it very far. I've only gone a few yards when a strange car bumps toward me on the narrow lane and I'm forced to move aside. The window nearest me rolls down.

"Hey, stranger," says a familiar voice. I run to the front passenger seat and jump in beside my father. When the car starts moving, I grab the wheel to force the car around. But the passageway is too narrow, and the fender flattens some bushes.

He wrests the wheel away. "Whoa, whoa, *whoa*. Careful, this is a rental."

"Get me out of here!"

"What? But Cassie invited me, I've got to—"

I open the door and start to climb out. "You go. I'm leaving."

He grabs my arm. "What's wrong? Now, I mean."

Someone giggles nearby. Two girls burst through a gap in the bushes, batting a balloon between them.

"There." I point, glaring at him. "Check out their idea of fun. This place is a loony bin—"

"I just see kids being kids." His tone is mild. "Look, Britt, I realize this is hard on you, but we both have to be patient—"

"It's been seven days! How much longer?" I demand.

He sighs and switches off the ignition. From the picnic come some guitar strums and a screech of electronic feedback from the amp. Someone hoots in delight, and there's a burst of applause.

"The thing is," he says. "The first weeks of a coma—"

"Weeks? Did you say *weeks*?"

"—tell a lot. But I've got fantastic news: Mom's breathing on her own!"

I've successfully blocked my memories of the hospital. Now the awful sight—and sound—of that rasping ventilator pushing air into my mother's unresponsive lungs comes to mind again, more horrible than ever.

"Is she awake? Can we go home?"

"No, and no," my father says. "Her doctors say that for now, she's better off staying put." He starts the car again.

"*What?* Get a second opinion! From Manhattan—"

"I have. Several, actually. Mom's own internist, Dr. Reynolds, and a couple of specialists have reviewed her scans. All three agreed to keep her here. And start another medication."

"But—"

"You can't force-quit a coma, Britt. Mom will wake when she's ready, not a moment sooner, and that can happen here as well as"—his voice cracks, and he clears his throat—"anywhere. And you have no idea how exhausting it is to spend entire days in a hospital. Talking with so many doctors, waiting on all her tests …."

Suddenly I recall the bandage he'd worn in the ICU, and his mild concussion. The bandage is gone, but he does seem tired, though he's still talking. "So are you coming or not?" he finishes.

I pull the car door shut and we roll down Cassie's driveway. People are drifting to the picnic tables now, carrying paper plates heaped with food. The volleyball's over, too, the teens bunched around a cooler, chugging sodas. At home there'd be vodka in them, but this is a church group.

"We're lucky in a way," my father says. "Mom's got her own nurse with special training in head injuries. Her name's Sharonda, from Jamaica, and she's fantastic. She's really taken to Mom."

"What about your concussion?"

"I'm okay. Matter of fact, this woman keeps asking when you're coming. It's, uh, kind of embarrassing."

"Coming?" I'm scanning the picnic for Will, but don't see him.

My father gives me a sharp look. "To see Mom. Families do visit their loved ones in the hospital, you know. Especially when it's a parent."

A peculiar feeling comes over me. "Loved one" is not how I think of my mother, no matter how awful I feel about her coma. We have too much painful history. "She wouldn't even know I was there, Dad. And you—"

He interrupts. "Sharonda says hearing your voice could help wake Mom. At the least, it might comfort her."

Seriously? I suppress a bitter laugh. When I was small, I loved to scribble in a coloring book while my mother worked in her study at home. A typical kid, I babbled and sang and asked questions. But one day she took off her glasses, rubbed the bridge of her nose, and said in a rush, "Brittany Warner, one more interruption and I'll tape your mouth shut."

Okay, so she didn't do it. And if she had, people have endured far worse. But multiply the incident by a lifetime, and a picture forms of a small girl who took a wrong turn somewhere in her parent's mind and heart. And I have no idea when, or what I did.

What I do know: if my mother did hear my voice, she'd probably be annoyed.

"Let Sharonda comfort her," I say harshly.

My father parks by a row of cars near Cassie's porch. He removes the keys from the ignition and fingers them. "Britt. I know you've had your issues with Mom, but she's always wanted the best for you." He drops the keys on the console. "That cop keeps calling, you know. The Sergeant. You better call him, or me, if you remember anything else about the accident. Do you?"

My mind races to invent a suitable answer, but then Cassie saves me. "Mr. Warner," she calls. "You came! I'm so glad. Apple or blueberry? Pie, I mean."

He opens the car door and climbs out. "Call me Steven, please." He strolls toward her, hands in the pockets of the tangerine cargo shorts he bought when he and my mother went to the Bahamas. His legs are long and tan, his feet encased in sandals I haven't seen. He's not spending *every* minute at the hospital, unless they've got a sun deck. But his shirt's rumpled, so he's not taking great care of himself either.

"How 'bout some of both?" he says, and Cassie beams.

My skin breaks into a cold sweat, and I slump against the seat. *Close call.* Something's wedged in the crack of his seat, though. Leaning over, I pull out a nip bottle of booze, the kind they sell on airplanes and by the cash registers in convenience stores. But what's it doing here? He doesn't drink, to my knowledge. My parents don't keep booze in the house, except the occasional bottle of wine to bring somewhere as a hostess gift. While he talks with Cassie, I twist off the tiny cap and sniff. The pungent fumes sear my nostrils … pleasantly. I take a sip and savor the taste, which reminds me of vanilla extract. I replace the cap and peer at the label. Bourbon. *Nice.* I dive under the steering wheel, grope beneath the driver's seat—and pull out seven more bottles.

Seven? I eye the pile, disturbed. I've deliberately shut down thoughts of my father this week. In addition to our whole situation, he abandoned me. But this may be the first time in my parents' marriage that he's made decisions on his own, and I figured he threw me to Cassie because I'd be a bother to have around.

I never dreamed that maybe he just couldn't cope. It's mind-boggling, and terrifying. But my world's falling apart too, and right now these nips—and Manny's stash— seem heaven-sent. Though what deity would bless a kid with booze and drugs, I shudder to imagine. I tuck the bottles into my waistband, climb out the driver's side door, and sneak behind Cassie's cottage. Luckily my bedroom window's unlocked, so I crawl in with my stash.

Outside are the sound of pounding feet, the smack of bodies colliding, shrieks of laughter. The party's still going, but for me?

It's moved indoors.

A car engine wakes me. I'm lying on my bed at Cassie's, facing the bandaged teddy bear on the desk. It's still dark out; the alarm clock says it's ten. The party guests took off for the fireworks in Burlington before dusk, but I told her through my closed door that my head hurt. She made me swear I'd take the aspirin and water she set out in the kitchen, before she'd leave me alone. For a while I listened to the muffled pop-pop of nearby bottle rockets—the whole island must not have gone into the city—but I'd slept so poorly the past few nights that I dropped off.

Wide awake now, I retrieve the booze nips and Manny's stash from beneath the clothes heaped on the dresser top and plop onto the bed again. I twist open a nip bottle and chug a mouthful. It burns my throat, making me cough.

Rapid footsteps sound outside my door, then a knock. "Britt? Okay to come in?"

Will! I bolt to sit up, yank an afghan over my stash, and tuck the open nip against my leg. No time to find the lid. He cracks the door, and enters when he sees I'm not lounging around in risqué underwear. Left that at Benny's. Still, he leaves the door wide open. Light streams through the dark living room from the kitchen, and I hear Cassie filling the coffee pot for tomorrow morning. They must have returned together.

"Hey," he says. "Why'd you run off earlier?"

"Seriously? Um, let's see. I was a jerk in front of the whole picnic, I stink at sports, I don't swim, and to top it off, I was rude—" I catch myself. Maybe Meghan won't tell anyone what I said.

He frowns. "Going to fireworks isn't a sport. I figured you'd gone with your dad, but when we got there, Cassie said he left and you weren't well. I feel terrible we left you alone."

"Whatever." I rub my forehead. Whether it's the teeny bit of booze or Will being here or the whole dumb picnic, I'm not sure, but now I do have a headache. A whopper.

"What are you doing here, anyway?" I ask. In the kitchen, Cassie starts to sing, a tuneless tra-la-la.

Will takes the teddy and tosses it in the air. The plastic cast falls off and bounces on the braided rug. "Oops." He retrieves the cast and fits it onto the bear's leg. "The kids all want to know you better," he says softly.

I snort. "Only because they don't."

Suddenly he plunks himself onto the end of my bed, making the mattress bounce. Too late, I grab for the nip leaning against my thigh. It spills onto the quilt, and now the room reeks of bourbon. Will sniffs, sees the spreading brown blot.

"Where'd you get this?" He scowls so hard his sandy eyebrows meet over his nose.

"None of your business," I say. Now his lips are pressed together, making them appear bloodless. He's ticked off, a side of him I've never seen. *But why?*

He plucks the nip away from my leg and holds out his palm. I deposit the tiny lid in it, feeling like a kid about to get her knuckles rapped with a ruler by some nineteenth-century schoolmaster. He screws on the cap, glances at the wastebasket, and—I read him like a book—reconsiders leaving alcohol within fifty feet of me. He stuffs the nip into his jeans pocket, darts into the bathroom, and comes back with a dark brown towel. Cassie's, but I don't enlighten him.

"I picked the darkest one," he says, and presses the towel onto the stain. He changes to a fresh section of towel and does it again. By the time he's finished, the stain is almost gone and the towel no worse for wear. He rinses it out in the bathroom and returns. "I think it'll be okay," he says, and I don't know whether he means the quilt or that Cassie won't smell the alcohol. Is he actually covering for me?

Maybe not. He sits on the bed again and gazes at my hands. I get the feeling he wants to hold them, but is worried I'll think it's romantic. Obviously, that's the furthest thing from his mind. Sure enough, when he begins to talk, his voice is so strained and low I have to lean forward to hear. Cassie's now clanging pots and pans in the kitchen *and* singing, but they'd both freak if I got up and shut the door.

"… whether to tell you," he mumbles, raking his fingers through his hair. "Look, Britt. My mother was a drunk. One night she passed out with a lit cigarette and our house burned down."

I smother an exclamation. "Meghan got … hurt," he goes on. "It just about ruined our lives, and it's why the three of us wound up here. Booze isn't cool, Britt, it's lethal."

Suddenly I snap. Yeah, what he's saying is awful, but the day's events have shaved my nerves raw. And he's not even my boyfriend. I raise both palms like a school traffic cop.

"Not that it's your business, but you've warned me off Joy and booze. What's next, sex?"

Instantly he averts his face. "Look," he says. "You're going through a horrible time. But there are no accidents, Britt. Even bad stuff happens for a reason."

"You got that right," I say bitterly. "I dangle a stupid—" Suddenly I freeze. Will doesn't know what I did. No one does, and it has to stay that way. But when I peek at him, he's still looking away, and doesn't seem to have noticed my slip.

"I mean a *good* reason," he says.

I almost laugh. When I was nine, my grandfather died of a stroke. My mother and I traveled to his funeral at some humongous church in Michigan, complete with a dozen warbling, crimson-robed sopranos. All around us were gorgeous, stained-glass windows. I couldn't take my eyes off their jeweled colors.

My mother hissed in my ear, "Don't think Grandpa's frolicking with any angels. We're a few bucks' worth of chemicals, from ape to dust. Anyone who says otherwise is a fool. This life is all there is. You've just got to grab it while you can."

"Seriously?" I say to Will now. "My mother's in a coma. What's good about that?"

He takes the teddy and adjusts its bandage. His eyelashes are ridiculously long, and when he looks up again to meet my gaze, I'm stirred in some way I can't identify.

"God didn't put your mom in that coma, Britt."

Panic rips through me. "What are people saying?" I demand.

His eyebrows shoot up. "Nothing. I just meant— look, not even a sparrow can fall without his say-so. Like when that bull—it's just, we don't always know the reasons."

Bull? Who knows what he's talking about, but it doesn't matter. "Look, I don't need—"

Will sets the teddy aside, leans forward, and takes my hands in his. My anger evaporates. His palms are warm and solid, and to actually touch someone feels so good that I just want to rest against his chest and feel his arms around me. The patchwork quilt between us is full of stars, intertwined in a complicated design. Whoever made it was a true artist, just like whoever made those stained-glass windows. But the idea that there's some silver lining to this hideous situation that I myself caused? I can't buy it.

My nose prickles, and I swallow hard. "It's no mystery, Will. I'm … bad," I whisper.

"We all are," he whispers back. "No one's perfect. I've done plenty wrong in my life, Britt. Like—I knew my mom wasn't fit to care for Meghan that night, but I left them anyway." His anguished eyes bore into mine. "You hear what I'm saying? Because I had other … plans, my little sister almost died and will carry the scars forever. So will I, you just can't see them." His hands rub my knuckles.

Will's memories are etched with horror like mine. We do have something in common. Even so … "I still don't see how the fire was your fault," I say. "From what you're saying, your mom was the one who … who drank, and fell asleep. Does Meghan blame you?"

He sighs. "Of course not. She doesn't even know the full story. But she essentially lost her mother that night and worships me, irony of all ironies. My leaving that night was just a tiny part of my life pattern then. I was completely off track, Britt. And every time I see Meghan's scar, I remember. Though it doesn't seem to bother her much. Her problem is nightmares. Sometimes she wakes up screaming, and Priscilla has to bring her hot milk and sit with her until she falls asleep again."

Nightmares, I can relate to. And Meghan seems such a happy kid, if a bit precocious. But you never really know what someone's dealing with, I guess.

Will's expression clears, even becomes hopeful. "But Priscilla got her some good counseling, and I've had some amazing talks with Luke. He helped me understand that there's … grace. Forgiveness. For anyone who asks, no matter what they've done."

I can't speak as Will searches my eyes for what seems an eternity. A few more seconds, and I might even blurt out my guilt—which would be my second-worst decision ever. But finally, he releases my hands and sets the teddy on the desk, arranging the crutch carefully. Then he turns to me. "So, listen. Tomorrow morning there's church, but later a bunch of us are going to play Kick the Can and have a campfire. Want to come?"

The moment's gone. I force myself into sassy mode. "Kick the Can, huh? That ended in the fifties, but South Hero probably has its own version, passed on for generations …"

He smirks and holds up his iPhone. "Not exactly. We Googled the rules. Should be a blast."

"Oh, you do use the internet!"

"What?"

"Never mind. You people sure party a lot." *And I'm objecting? Benny would bust a gut laughing.*

Will shrugs. "It's summer. So, will you come?"

"Maybe the campfire," I say. "Ixnay on the church."

He gives a puzzled glance. "Uh, about that … I'm pretty sure your dad and Cassie made some kind of deal. About a few things, actually."

I groan. "Let me guess. No booze, no drugs, no sex. Cut off at every pass. Aww …" I mime a passionate hug, but he pulls back slightly, his brows drawn together in that frown again. And I'm stung. I *cannot* make this guy laugh. He stands up and nods at me.

"Well, see you." He leaves the room, closing the door gently. The kitchen grows quiet except for his and Cassie's murmuring voices.

I'm hollow to my toes, like some cartoon character being erased off the page except for its outline. What a loser, and Will's not helping one bit. I didn't dare ask for my nip bottle back, and to finish washing out the quilt without Cassie seeing is out of the question. Maybe she won't notice the stain until I'm gone.

Which better be soon. I'm hanging by a thread.

14

I'm in church, being preached to by a guy in cowboy boots. Part of me is gnashing my teeth to have been dragged here. Will was right, blast him. Cassie put her foot down with my father, insisting I attend, and he can count himself a hypocrite since he himself wouldn't be caught dead in this place. But mostly I'm just relieved it's finally daylight, after my horrid dream last night. This time a giant hawk flew over me, screeching with claws extended. Below, little, field-mouse me zigzagged over an open field with nowhere to hide, eyeballs bugged out in panic and tiny lungs bursting with exhaustion. By comparison I feel safe now, even peaceful. For one thing, this is no ordinary church. Exhibit A: the preacher, Pastor Dave—aka dad of Perfect Jessica—is wearing the same jeans and boots he wore skeet shooting at Cassie's picnic. Yep, the gray-haired goateed guy turned out to be the leader of this tribe. He ditched the Texas hat and added a sport coat, but I've never seen a minister without a robe, not even on TV. It's a shock.

The building's not very churchlike, either. There are no stained-glass windows or pulpit, just a wooden podium with a carved cross on the front. What Cassie called a sanctuary is actually an auditorium with about a hundred portable chairs. It wouldn't surprise me to see basketball hoops at either end of the room.

Meghan sits next to me, against a wall. On my other side, extending to the aisle, are Cassie, Will, Luke, Priscilla, and Will's sister Kara, her forearms crossed over her bulging belly. Secretly, I'm shocked she's here. I mean, even I know most religions frown on sex outside of marriage, much less becoming preggo. Obviously, she's got no shame, and these people are hypocrites to let her in.

Up front, at the other extreme, Jessica poses at a keyboard behind her preacher dad, blonde hair curling over her shoulders as if she's in a shampoo ad. Instead of hymns, though, she and the guitarist and drummer belted out some soft rock before the sermon. To my surprise, she has a decent voice and even goofs around a bit while performing. *Go figure.* Everyone obviously loves her, present company excluded of course—though as her father preaches, she keeps her eyes glued to his back, with an expression I can't decipher.

Nightmares aside, I'm not too happy to be here. As I've said. I shift around in my seat while the cowboy pastor paces back and forth, trailing the cord of his handheld mic.

"Anyone here think you're perfect?" he asks, all folksy and confiding. "Without sin, no darkness in your hearts and minds? Turn with me, please, to Romans 3:23."

The air comes alive with rustling. People thumb through pages like he's timing them with a stopwatch. Meghan eyes my empty lap and passes me her Bible. It's got a pink cover, with pictures inside. *Seriously?* I flip through, just for show, but she reaches over, finds the page easily, and points to the verse. Eight years old, she's an honest-to-goodness biblical whiz.

"Scripture tells us, 'All have sinned and fall short of the glory of God.' *All*, folks," Pastor Dave emphasizes. "That means you and it means me. Whatever I say, believe you me, I've got one finger pointed at you and three more back at myself. No one's perfect, and that includes yours truly. Just ask my wife over there. Trudy, you got anything you want to tell everyone?"

That's just what Will said, I realize as everyone laughs and a big-haired, grinning woman in the front row shakes her head firmly. He and Pastor Dave must have talked about me. My cell phone beeps. Mortified, I grab it and hit Mute. I can't read a text with eagle-eyed Meghan perched right next to me, but my stomach flips when I recognize my friend Chelsea's number. *Um, I mean my ex-friend.* I shove the phone into my knapsack—actually Cassie's, which further inspection did reveal to be free of visible signs of anthrax. The phone clinks against one of my dad's nip bottles. *Oops.* Meghan eyes me, not quite accusing, but definitely suspicious.

What is it about this pipsqueak? I'm tempted to stick out my tongue, but try to outstare her instead. She meets my gaze steadily, though, and in the end I'm the one who turns away. *Man, I'm off my game.*

"So let me ask," the pastor goes on. "Moms and dads, you love your kids, right? Course you do. But would you let them in your house with … these?" He reaches down and holds up a small pair of muddy barn boots. I recognize the green and yellow daisy pattern immediately, as they usually sit just inside the Narrowgate barn. They're Meghan's.

"I'd hose 'em off first," Priscilla calls. The whole congregation laughs, including Pastor Dave.

"Thank-you Priscilla!" he says, and I'm even more dumbfounded. Who ever heard of someone talking out during a sermon and the preacher answering back? Not to mention that she'll be a pastor's wife one day.

"'Cause that's just what God does," he goes on. "He loves us, but he can't let us into his heavenly home with our boots all dirty with sin. Our pride, our greed, our lust … by which I don't mean just sex, folks, I mean anything in this beautiful world we value more than we do our heavenly Father. So … he needed a way to wash us off." He sets the boots on a chair, wipes his palms on his jeans, and surveys the congregation like a hawk in a field full of mice.

"And that's where his Son comes in. The one and only way to get right with God, folks, is by confessing our sin and placing our faith in him. Jesus died on that cross willingly, so we who are muddy from wrongdoing will never be punished. He's the Lamb of God; he sacrificed his life just like a lamb on an altar, for all who believe. And when we trust him, God doesn't just clean us up. He welcomes us into his own family as precious sons and daughters, and blesses us with eternal life in heaven. Ever hear of a greater gift? It's his perfect plan, friends, for anyone who hears and believes. And so simple, a child can understand."

Meghan takes my hand. Her dark hair spills over her brow, and Will's hoarse words echo in my head. "I left Meghan with my mom …."

Suddenly it hits me. Might their mother, and Kara's, still be alive? Her kids got fostered. But Will didn't say she'd died, just that Meghan got hurt. *Burned.* I can't bear to think of it. It's comforting to know he did something awful, too. We're not as different as he imagines, even if he does follow Jesus. Whatever that means. But—and it's a huge but—Will didn't burn Meghan on purpose. I dangled my mother's bag deliberately, even if I didn't mean to cause the accident.

I'm not just bad, like I told Will. I'm evil. For the first time, I admit it to myself. No one needs to preach it to me; I *feel* the darkness inside, through every cell and tissue. It's horrible, but I'm not convinced it's spiritual. This is plain old, garden-variety guilt.

All my life, I was told this world is all there is. It upset me as a kid, but my parents aren't fools. I mean, they've both got advanced degrees. And if God were real, he wouldn't forgive people who get their sisters burned and put their mothers into comas. So I'm ninety-nine-point-nine percent sure that these people are deluded.

Which means Will's wrong.

Meghan slips her hand from mine and slides past me. Probably going to the bathroom. Why they didn't make her sit on the aisle, I don't know. *Maybe she wanted to sit by me?* Unlikely. Anyway, now that she's gone, I peek at my text message. "This U Britt? Got your number from yr dad. U R right Jeff's a jerk. xo Chelse" Instantly my mood lifts. *She's still my friend.* Maybe I'm not a total loser. I did one horrible thing, but I bet everyone does something bad at some point in their lives. And one day soon, hopefully, my mother will wake up and be just fine.

The pastor's still talking, and my gaze roams the room. Some of these people, complete strangers, pray for my family. A bunch of teens who look familiar from the volleyball game fill the last row of the section opposite us. If the pastor's right, they're sinners too. But if they're here, they probably pray. What makes them think anyone's up there listening? Yet these kids seem ordinary, not like I'd imagine religious nuts to look. One guy has thick, shiny hair; another must wrestle or lift weights because his abs are gorgeous, which I notice him noticing me noticing. He winks at me, and I quickly look away. *As if.* A couple of others are cute in a generic way, and the girls just look … like girls back home. But I'd bet their skinny jeans aren't designer, and their flimsy flats aren't from Nordstrom.

Speaking of abs, just beyond Cassie, Will sits leaning forward, elbows on his knees, concentrating on the sermon. His profile is nice, with a straight nose that's the perfect length. He's better-looking than I thought when we first met, and I compared him to Manny. Meanwhile, Jessica has sat immobile at the piano behind her father since the music ended. Her eyes meet mine. My arrival may have upset her applecart, because Will's been watching out for me. But so what if Jessica hates me? No one can have it all, and she's got that gorgeous Arab. Her horse, I mean.

I'm not sure about me and Will, though. He's friendly and easy to be around, but does he *like* me? Or is he always that way, no matter who he's with? Plus, he's so serious, and his religion's a deal breaker—but his lips are nice and full, I've noticed, and I bet he's a wonderful kisser. An imp seems to whisper in my ear, *You'll be gone soon. Have some fun.* I agree. Meghan slides past me again, and I decide that first chance I get, I'm going to shake things up.

He's not the only one around here with a nice mouth. Even stupid Jeff Cox said I was a good kisser, though he sort of swore when he said it, like he hated to admit it.

I impale two marshmallows on a peeled twig and thrust them in with a dozen others roasting over a campfire. The kids jostle marshmallows in a mock duel and roar in mingled delight and dismay when a couple of them—marshmallows, not kids—fall into the flames and sizzle. You'd think playing Kick the Can would have provided enough roughhousing. That was actually more fun than I expected. Running and darting and being captured while sneaking to home base was sort of thrilling, like hide-and-seek on steroids, and I'm still sweaty. I remove my marshmallows from the twig, slap them onto squares of chocolate between graham crackers, and carry them carefully to where Will leans against a rock, stargazing. With no free hands, I elbow his arm.

"Thanks," he says, surprised. Like I've never done anything nice for anyone.

I plop down beside him and bite into my s'more. *Yikes.* White sugary goo squishes onto my fingers and scalds the roof of my mouth. He bites into his two-fisted, as if it's a sandwich. His mouth must be made of Teflon.

Even my feet are hot now. I shuck off my sneakers and let the air cool my sweaty toes. We nibble our s'mores in silence. Finally, I pop the last bite into my mouth and lick my fingers, psyching myself for my next move. Luckily—is it fate?—right then a huge shooting star flashes across the sky and he grins at me. *Carpe diem,* I think. *You only go around once.*

I scooch closer. Our eyes meet, even closer than when he told me about his house burning down.

"Did you ever read what Juliet said about Romeo?" My voice squeaks unexpectedly.

"Uh, no …" His tone is deep, questioning.

"Well, she wanted to cut Romeo into stars so he'd make the sky beautiful and the world would fall in love with the night." I never saw the play, but last year at school we had to memorize selections of Shakespeare.

Will gives me a look. "Which would achieve what, exactly?"

I slap his arm lightly. "Don't be so practical! She meant it to happen once he was dead. Or maybe after she died, I forget."

"Weird."

"Girls in love say crazy things," I say, cribbing a line from somewhere, and swiftly lean in to kiss him. Will's lips are warm and smooth and chocolatey, and we're just warming up when he stiffens and pulls away.

"Sorry, I can't do this," he mumbles.

I frown. "Didn't take you for a prude."

"I'm not. But—"

"Life goes by like *that*, Will." I snap my fingers. "You've got to grab your fun while you can." I reach around him sideways, to pull him toward me. But he holds himself away, and I flush. *He doesn't want to kiss me. He's not even attracted.* We're only hanging out because my mother's in a coma, my father's ignoring me, and Cassie's probably egging him on.

They just want to save my soul. I jam my feet into my sneakers without untying them.

"Britt. There are a dozen reasons this can't happen," Will says soberly.

The back of my left sneaker folds, jabbing my arch. I fix the problem and shove my foot in again. I can't wait to get out of here, but—"Name one," I snap, trying to ignore the tiny hope that's flamed within me. *Not wanting to kiss me would only be one reason.*

"You're fifteen."

"Almost sixteen, actually. So? I've done plenty already."

"I'm sorry to hear that," he says, half to himself. "But that's even—for crying out loud, Britt, your mom's in the ICU. And …" He hugs his knees and eyes the stones at our feet. I look down too, as a huge black beetle crawls across a jagged gray rock.

"It's Jessica, isn't it. You like her, why don't you just admit it." I extract an annoying pebble from the toe of my right sneaker and hurl it into the bushes. Something small scurries away, probably a chipmunk. I'm Brittany Warner, Scourge of the North Kingdom.

"It's not what you think," Will mumbles behind me. "I prom—"

"Whatever it is, keep it to yourself." I stalk away, ignoring his pained expression. But I whirl and face him again. "By the way, I don't appreciate your telling your pastor my personal business."

"Huh?" His surprise appears genuine, but I'm not fooled.

"You and him, that no-one's-perfect line. Twice in twenty-four hours is no coincidence."

He brightens. "You're right. But I haven't talked with Pastor Dave, Britt. Like I said, there are no accidents. Maybe someone's trying to get through to you."

I glare at him. *Right.*

15

I cross Cassie's porch, my clothes reeking of campfire smoke. Luckily, she's busy at the stove, so I sneak past. In my room, I punch in my father's cell and perch on the edge of the bed.

"When are we going home?" I demand when he answers.

"Brittany." His tone is uneasy. "I was going to call you tonight. There's, um, something I need to tell you."

Every nerve in me zaps on alert. "Is Mom—"

"No, no, nothing like that. But I've taken a room here in Burlington, a little while ago."

Dead silence. My lungs feel frozen, like I've forgotten how to breathe.

"A little while," I finally echo. "Are we talking hours, days, or a week? What room? In a motel?"

"No, no, today. Just a few hours ago." He actually sounds indignant, like I've questioned his good intentions. "And it's not a motel room, more of a short-term rental."

"You rented an *apartment*?"

"No, no—well, yes, but just a studio, so you'll have to sit tight at Cassie's awhile longer. Do you understand, sweetheart? The space is too small for both of us. You'd have to sleep in the medicine chest with the cotton balls, heh heh."

Not enough room is a simple concept, and cracking a joke means he's fully aware he's ditching me. Again.

"Couldn't you rent a bigger place?" I press my trembling lips together. *Don't cry.*

"I didn't even try. You'd be bored stiff with me gone all day, and I don't have time to keep an eye on you. But, wonderful news!" he says. "Mom's out of the ICU. She's on a Neuro Med floor now."

I clear my throat. "Is she awake?"

"Well, no. But her doctors—"

Quietly I press End. What a rotten day. First church, then Will pushing me away when I kissed him, which is mortifying even when the guy's a hayseed, and now … another betrayal by my so-called dad. I jam my fists into my cutoff pockets and feel something plastic and squishy in one of them.

Manny's pill packet. Ha, someone *is* looking out for me.

The water glass by my bed is partly full. I fish out a pill from the baggie and swig it down in a single gulp. Moments later, or maybe it's an hour, my father's call and the whole horrible day slide into oblivion.

My peace doesn't last. I dream yet another horrible nightmare. But this time, instead of hurling threats, my mother is neck-deep in quicksand, so deep that struggling is pointless. Her expression is broken, sorrowful, and her vulnerability more terrifying than if she were waving a butcher's knife. She tilts her head, mute, her eyes begging me to save her. But I can't, and it's my fault she's going to die. Then a whole school of Siamese fighting fish swarms over her head, attacking her. She whips her head helplessly to evade them, but it's useless.

"Mommy, I'm sorry," I shriek again and again until I wake, my cheeks damp. But tears shed while sleeping don't count as crying, at least not in my book. Does she dream in her coma? What happens if she wants to cry and can't? The idea is horrifying.

"Honey?" Cassie's voice floats through the door. "Did you have a nightmare?"

"Beat it," I mumble. No point in prettying my words with no parent around.

A pause. "I'll pray for you," she whispers. Her slippers swish away, and I flip onto my back. Light flickers on the ceiling, and I realize it's no longer pitch-dark outside my window. Orange and violet streak the horizon, and a cool breeze flows off the lake. I remember the horses sleeping in the barn and suddenly crave their comforting presence and the smell of horseflesh.

I pull on a T-shirt, shorts, and sneakers, and tiptoe through the living room to the kitchen. Quietly I open the fridge and remove the fattest carrot from the veggie drawer. Outside, I tiptoe down the porch steps and wheel Cassie's bike to the driveway. I brush a spider web off the handlebars, but the tiny builder is nowhere in sight. *He'd better not crawl on my neck.*

The bicycle bumps along the rutted lane, the seat coils squeaking beneath me. Sleepy birds twitter in the grasses and shrubs to either side, and a rabbit hops in front of me, nose twitching. He dashes away as I wobble toward him. The ground's slippery with dewy sand and pebbles, and twice I almost fall. Once I slap at a mosquito whining at my ear; if I do this again, I'll nick Cassie's repellent. But when I round the bend onto the farm road and the barn comes into view, I picture Joy's delicate filly-face, her peroxide bangs mingling with her eyelashes, and am glad I came. Will warned me to keep my distance, but bringing her a carrot can't do any harm.

The same breeze off the lake wafts through the barn as I walk toward Joy, but now I inhale deeply. The smell of horse manure wouldn't be most people's cup of tea, but for me it's heaven. And I love being alone with the horses, as long as they're safely contained inside their stalls. Captain, Genesis, Midnight, Aloha, Lady … I read their nameplates aloud as I pass and thrill to the sound of their whickering, that deep, wonderful *hnn hnn hnn.* I should have brought the whole bag of carrots from Cassie's fridge, so they could each have a treat. *Next time.*

Joy scrambles to her feet with a snort when I peer through the bars into the last stall on the left. "Hey, sweetie, I came to see you." I offer the carrot. But she flattens her ears and backs away to the far wall. Her brown eyes flash rims of white in the dimness.

Normally, I wouldn't dream of going into a stall with a horse in it. But Joy's so petite, and acts even more frightened than me. And I really, really want to give her the carrot. So I slide the bolt on the stall door and shove the door sideways, just enough to slip inside. She tosses her head—once, twice—and a shiver of alarm goes through me. *Maybe this isn't smart.* But I ease one foot forward, in case I need to beat a retreat, and hold out the carrot again.

I don't know what happens next. But I'm sprawled against the side of the stall, my arm throbbing, and Joy is rearing high above me with a shrill whinny. The stall door rumbles open on its tracks and Luke's iron hand grips my arm. He hauls me out of there, waving his other arm wildly in Joy's face. She retreats, squealing, and her hooves ring against the wooden wall.

He rams the door shut along its tracks and faces me, his face white. "What on earth do you think you're doing? You should never go into a stall with a strange horse, especially this one! I told Will to warn you …."

He's shouting. I'm trembling, fighting tears. Luke bites off his words. He rubs his chin and looks away. After a moment he clasps my wrist gently and leads me to some bales of hay outside a stall. We each perch on one, just in time because my legs are about to collapse.

"Look, I'm sorry," he says, and I'm flabbergasted. *A grown-up just apologized to me.* Even though the shoe is on the other foot: I'm the trespasser, and this is the second stupid, dangerous thing I've done on his property in less than forty-eight hours. "It's just that you scared me half to death. You might have been seriously hurt," he says. He lifts a hand, as if to touch my arm, but lowers it. "Do you understand?"

It's the same question my father asked last night, but the way Luke says it is utterly different. My father sets me away from himself, both in words and physically, but Luke's actions almost make me feel like he cares. Even though he hardly knows me. I nod and wipe my eyes with the heel of my hand. I will *not* cry in front of him.

Now he stands up and presses my shoulder briefly. "Are you okay? I should have asked that first."

"Yes."

He moves away and exhales. "Thank God," he mutters.

"Luke," I say shakily. "Have you ever considered m-maybe Joy's just scared? M-maybe someone was mean to her."

He raises his eyebrows and nods, slantwise. "Good call, you've hit it dead-on. But when you're talking about horses, scared can be as dangerous as mean. Even then"—he rubs the back of his head—"well, I don't believe any horses are born bad."

I digest this. "Did you ever find a horse you couldn't train?"

"Once or twice. But it's rare. There's almost always a concrete reason, like a problem with the pituitary. Fact is, Joy's training is going slower than I'd like. Speaking of which—" He checks his watch. "Is there anywhere you have to be this morning?"

The sky is light now. And I don't want this to end. "Not exactly. But Cassie thinks I'm in bed," I confess.

"Why don't I call her. After that, if you're willing, you can help me move this little gal to the round pen."

"*What?*"

"That tall metal pen outside is called a round pen," Luke says. "It's for training."

"But—"

"Don't worry, you'll be safe. Sometimes, working with a new horse, it's good to have someone watching. Priscilla's not always available." His gray eyes crinkle at the corners.

I nod, and Luke calls Cassie. Her dismay shrills right through his phone when she hears I'm gone, but he assures her I'm safe. We walk to the end of the barn aisle, and he takes a long nylon line off a nail on the wall. Cautiously, he slips just inside Joy's stall, snaps the clip onto her halter in a lightning move, and attempts to get the line over her nose. But she snorts and rears, and he scoots back into the aisle. I stand well back, my fingernails digging into my palms. He opens the stall door all the way, steps aside, and—

Joy explodes out of her stall, skidding to a halt an inch from the stall across the aisle. Inside, old Saratoga squeals and shies backward, hitting the back wall with a thud. Luke moves to the rear door of the barn, light on his feet as a lion tamer. Joy bolts past him into the outdoors, and they seesaw back and forth all the way to the round pen. First one dashes ahead, then the other, the green nylon line taut between them like a tightrope … and she bucks and rears the whole way. I follow at a very safe distance, clenching and unclenching my fists and trying to still my hammering heart.

At the round pen, Luke opens the gate, swiftly unhooks the line from Joy's halter, and again stands aside as she plunges past him. He slips into the pen, clangs the gate shut, and grabs a rope hanging over the gatepost. Mid-ring, he faces her and snaps the rope behind her butt. She snorts and rears. But he does it again and again, making loud kissing noises, until finally she moves to the rail and starts running.

Nothing I've ever seen compares with what happens next. Outside of the movies, I mean. At first Joy races in panicky circles, her mane flying. But after a few laps, she slows to a trot and flicks an ear toward Luke. The other ear follows. A couple more circles, and her head tilts toward him. Luke waves the rope again, and somehow, she changes direction. She comes so near I'm afraid she'll run him over, but she doesn't. He makes her go left, and right, then left again. At last when she's starting to look toward him, he lets her stop and face him, her sides heaving and slick with sweat. And he walks up to her and rubs her nose! Quietly he attaches the green line on her halter again and, a few seconds later, walks away to unlatch the gate. Meek as a kitten, practically nosing his shoulder like Tiny did with Meghan, Joy follows him out of the round pen and into a paddock nearby, where he drops the line on the ground and lets her graze.

"That was awesome!" I shout from outside the rail of the pen.

Luke shuts the gate and grins. "Natural horsemanship. She did well." He narrows his gaze, considering. "What you did this morning, Britt, wasn't totally wrong. Bringing her carrots is fine. Just don't go in the stall. Break them up and throw the pieces through the bars. Deal?" He thrusts out a hand.

"Wild horses couldn't drag me in," I say dryly, and we shake on it. Joy eyes us as she frantically pulls up clumps of grass. *She's tense again.* I decide to bring her a carrot every day. When someone does that in the movies, the crazy horse is always tamed, without losing his spirit of course, and they canter off into the sunset with gorgeous lens flares.

Easy-peasy, right? But Luke's face is shadowy beneath the brim of his cowboy hat, and I have a niggling suspicion this won't be so simple.

16

For the rest of that week and into the next, I set my alarm and bring Joy a carrot early each morning. Cassie buys a jumbo bag just for her, which I somehow keep forgetting to thank her for. Sometimes I stay while Luke works with Joy. It's not as scary as the first time, but bringing her to the round pen is still a challenge. Then after each session she follows him back to the barn, docile as Mary's little lamb—but the next time, is awful all over again. I can't imagine anyone riding her. Ever. Luke himself says her training isn't carrying over to the rest of her behavior. His frown as he says it worries me.

I don't dare ask what happens if she's not trainable.

The rest of each day still needs filling. I wonder briefly who might be around back home, but that life's a million miles away. I didn't even answer Chelsea's text. So, I just hang with Cassie in her off hours. We might drop in on someone like Mrs. Marino, who talks nonstop about the family reunion she's planning. Or we run errands. One day we drop by the church, and Cassie returns serving dishes to people who brought food for the picnic. While I wait outside, who comes along but Sandro, who I've met twice now under awful circumstances.

"Miss Brittany," he says. "I hope you and your family are recovering from your terrible accident. We are praying, you know. All the church, every day. How do you find this beautiful area of ours?"

I shrug. "It's okay." That sounds ungracious, so I add, "People are friendly. Um, were you born here?"

He laughs. "No. I'm from Puerto Rico. Two years ago, I came here."

"With your family?"

"No … my mother and father still live at home. With my brother and sister."

"Doesn't it feel weird to be here? So far from them?"

His face lights up. "The snow and cold were a shock, yes. *Brr.* But my home is here now. I have new family."

Sheesh, he sounds like Cassie. She joins us now, and Sandro excuses himself and goes into the church office.

"Is he the janitor?" I say. "I thought he drove an ambulance."

She eyes me oddly. "Sandro's a firefighter, who is sometimes called to use the Jaws of Life … but he's also one of our elders. A fine one, as it happens."

"Oh! Doesn't an elder have to be—I don't know, maybe a lawyer or something?"

"No." She tries, but fails, to hide a smile. "Just a mature man of God, and by mature I don't mean his age. Now, I have a shift today at four. Will you be all right if I drop you home?"

"Sure." And I mean it. When Cassie works, I've developed a special routine, since Manny's joints and pills are gone. I'll replenish the stash if I find him … but anyway, usually I slouch against my pillows and mentally run through my favorite YouTube videos as if I'm watching them. Angora Flatline telling how to remove red wine and other stains with seltzer would have come in handy to clean the bourbon off Cassie's quilt, if I'd thought of it. And if Cassie had any seltzer, which she doesn't like. But I enjoy seeing stains disappear like magic. And it's kind of neat I can quote almost everything Angora said, including her cute Aussie signoff. Being an oral learner has perks sometimes, even if it does make me a sitting duck for those sermons every Sunday. Sometimes during the week, I catch myself pondering something I heard without even meaning to. *Blech.*

Without my techie toys, I'm learning to entertain myself, which makes me kind of proud. I mean, the pioneers who settled this country didn't have smartphones or Apple watches or iPods. They made their own music, sometimes even their own instruments. Okay, so parroting a video I've watched a dozen times isn't in the same league as carving a dulcimer. But I don't need any fluff in my watchspring now to remind me not to speed through life. The days pass so slowly, the movement's virtually stopped.

So I'm not sorry one afternoon when Will's Escort pulls up outside Cassie's and the engine cuts off. I sit up, anticipating a visit. But the kitchen door slams and I hear Meghan squeal in delight and skip down the porch steps. I'd thought I was alone, but Cassie must have brought her home without my hearing them. She and Priscilla swap favors almost daily; I swear, they do act like family. I crane my neck out my bedroom window, almost dislodging the Bible Will gave me, which still props it open. Meghan's got him in a bear hug, and I can't help but notice he doesn't push *her* away. Of course, she's his sister, therefore no threat to his precious virtue, or whatever.

Neither of them wants to see me, though. I'd bet on it. The church kids must think I'm a snob, even though they say hi when Cassie and I run into them. South Hero's a small town, and Jessica's prejudiced them against me, I suspect, not that I care. So I plop onto my bed, flat on my back, staring at the ceiling of my Vermont bedroom. At least the breeze off the lake is cool.

A short while later, there's a knock on my door. Cassie pokes her head in. "You *are* here. I figured you were at the barn, but Will just stopped by and said you weren't there. I'm going to make popcorn and put on a movie. Interested?"

I cut my eyes at her. "With him and Meghan?"

She frowns. "No, they've gone swimming. I'm sure they'd be glad—"

"No. Do the popcorn." I swing my legs to the floor.

So another pattern is established. But Cassie's movies, I learn, are Hallmark presentations she recorded one long-ago Christmas when she still had cable—on extra-slow speed, so three movies fit on a single VHS tape. Talk about vintage. They're grainy, with wide, pale streaks through some scenes—but mostly, they're so syrupy I want to gag. Interchangeable chicks with long wavy hair, square-jawed guys with sculpted cheekbones. And abs. Lots of abs. One male lead reminds me of Will in a cute way, which appalls me. *What are my tastes coming to?* The movies are full of elves, Santas, sleigh rides, castles, and the same smarmy endings as the ones aired every year around Christmas. I've caught a few by mistake, and exactly five minutes before the end, like clockwork, there's always a kiss. But watching movies with Cassie fills these otherwise-empty evenings. Plus, she makes popcorn the old-fashioned way, with real butter. Another revelation. Her cooking is spoiling me. It'll be tough to go back to rotisserie chickens, Caesar salads, and granola bars.

Days follow nights, nights follow days. Woven through them, electric as the sizzle of egg-yellow yarn in Cassie's pastel knitting project, my father's repeated phone calls nag me to "visit Mom." I don't get why it's so important, I mean she's in a *coma*, but he says my absence is embarrassing. In front of who, her Jamaican nurse? But people's opinions have always mattered a ton to both my parents.

I'm still not ready to hit the hospital. Maybe I won't be until my mother wakes, when I'll find out how much trouble I'm really in. If the cottage had internet, I'd Google comas and amnesia and find out how much she might remember. But it's probably just as well that I can't. Whatever I read might terrify me even more than I already am.

I'm also scared to learn the maximum sentence for a teenage girl who ruined someone's life. Even in the best-case scenario, Agatha Warner will *not* be happy when she wakes and sees that dent in her cheek. Even if New York does have wonderful plastic surgeons.

The second week stretches into a third. My father calls me less often. He's finally gotten the message about me not visiting the hospital, and seems content to rely on Cassie for news of his only child. Meanwhile, she feeds me tidbits about my mother's condition, like that her muscles are contracting and there's a concern about bedsores.

Nothing too serious, though, and I cross my fingers that she'll wake up soon and we can all go home. I still bring Joy carrots each morning, but Luke's often somewhere else or cleaning stalls. Hopefully, he won't give up on Joy. He *can't*.

Meanwhile, I suspect Meghan and Will are avoiding me. They could have invited me to go swimming with them last week. Except Luke says Will is working extra to save for college, so maybe not. Which is ironic. Here this guy is dying to go, but needs loans. I'm not sure I want to, but won't need to worry about money if I do. Does anyone ever get what they want? The way things are doesn't exactly prove God exists.

Once or twice I watch from a distance while Perfect Jessica trains her gorgeous Captain on the jump course. He really is poetry in motion. And she's patient and persistent, I'll give her that. I can't imagine working so hard toward a goal. Even if I weren't afraid of horses, the disciplines of dressage and jumping would drive me mad. If I ever did manage to do anything horse-related, I'd want to ride and go camping out West, maybe in Montana. Or gallop on a beach in Barbados, the waves rolling in all foamy and frothy. No goals, just a great time.

Something's driving Jessica, but I have no idea what. She seems to have everything a girl could want, and watching her lean close over Captain's neck before a jump fills me with envy. Not that I'd want to trade places with her, of course, not if it meant practically living at church.

One day as she's cantering Captain toward a jump, hooves thud in a nearby paddock and a horse squeals in distress. I whirl around in time to see Saratoga gallop to the end of the corral he shares with Joy and skid to a stop by the fence. Luke runs out from the barn, but I reach them first. Thin streams of blood run down Saratoga's leg, and he's trembling. Luke takes one look and takes off for the house. While he's gone, I croon to the wounded horse from a few feet away, averting my eyes from his injury. His large, liquid eyes fasten on mine, and his ears perk forward. "Itsy Bitsy Spider" is all I can think of to sing, but he doesn't seem to mind.

Luke comes back, sloshing a bucket of warm water and a sponge. He leads Saratoga out of the corral and ties him to a fence post. "Ssh, boy, it's okay," he murmurs. He sponges the wound, and the horse flinches. I wish I dared rub its neck. Luke dips the sponge and dabs again. A few yards away, Joy paws the ground impatiently, and I get the feeling she'd like to charge us right through the fence. But he ignores her and just squeezes bloody water from the sponge, his expression grim.

Priscilla hobbles over. "What happened?"

"Dang mare just kicked her nanny," he says. "There, fella, you'll be fine."

His wife limps away, muttering.

Luke rubs ointment into Saratoga's wound, straightens, and rubs the old horse's ears. They look so soft.

"Um, Luke?" I say. He looks down at me, so sternly I feel I'm the culprit. I long to ask what he's thinking, but am terrified he'll say Joy's got to go. Which would be awful. Somehow this young horse has come to seem my kindred spirit, an equine counterpart or extension of my own being. If there's no hope for her … there isn't for me, either.

I shake off my gloom. "Is it okay if I, um, pet him?"

Those gray eyes see everything. He gestures for me to go ahead, and my stomach flip-flops. But I inch forward and lay my palm against Saratoga's nose. It's the first time I've been close to a horse without being thrown or almost trampled. The old fellow's muzzle is cool and rubbery, and his whiskers ticklish. I laugh, and Luke's grim expression softens.

Something inside me unknots, for the first time in a long time.

Friday evening rolls around again. I nibble popcorn in Cassie's living room while she knits away at the mass of yarn on the coffee table. She doesn't want grease on her project, so I eat most of the bowl myself. The movie she put on is almost over, so we fast-forward past many commercials. Arthritis medicine, car insurance, long-term medical care … adulthood viewed from this angle sure isn't very appealing.

"Who's the knitting for?" I mute a white-coated doctor lecturing a smiling, perfectly coiffed woman perched on an examining table.

Cassie shifts uncomfortably. "Um, it's crochet. See?" She raises the single needle to show me and resumes her repetitive motion. It's such a trivial point that I suspect she's stalling, and her next words confirm it. "It's a blanket, for Kara's baby. But don't tell her, okay?"

"For *her* to use? You don't mean she's keeping it!"

Cassie's hands still. "I thought you might not approve. But she's still praying about it, and it's got to be her decision. So, I'd appreciate it if you wouldn't mention this. Either way, the blanket's for the baby." She rests her hands on her lap.

There's plenty I could say. But for once, I hesitate. Cassie's the only person who offered to keep me here. If I offend her, my father might very well put me on a plane to Las Vegas. It would be simpler than sending me home, where there's no one to care for me. I picture myself playing slots with Grandma Audrey in a casino on the Strip, my grandmother slamming the knobs—levers, whatever—enraged at having her selfish life interrupted.

No way.

Now my hostess gives me a sharp look. "Why aren't you bowling with the Youth Group? Will said he'd invite you. I sure hope he didn't forget."

A vision of Will laughing flashes into my mind. Annoyed by my own disappointment—I don't mind bowling, and am nowhere near ready for bed—I get to my feet and dump the popcorn kernels into the kitchen trash. One advantage to a cottage: everything's more or less within reach.

"It doesn't matter," I say. "Those kids and I have nothing in common."

She considers a moment and resumes her crocheting. Then she says, real casual, "I don't know when you last talked to your dad, but your mom's got an important consult coming up."

Hope flares inside me. "Will they move her to New York?" *I could leave this whole scene behind.*

"That's up to the doctors. But— listen, Britt, it's obvious something's wrong between the two of you. If you ever want to talk about it—"

"I don't." My tone is curt, even though I'm not sure which "two" she's talking about. I've got problems with both my parents.

"Hang on, I didn't mean with me," Cassie says. "I know a woman who works with teens, and—"

"I bet she's from your church, right? Did you hear

anything I said? If I—"

"You could do worse." She pokes at a stitch with her needle. "Especially if … well, your mom's condition is still pretty serious. If she doesn't improve the way we—"

"Cassie," I cut her off in an icy tone worthy of my mother. "Listen up. There is no 'we' when it comes to you and my family."

One of her eyelids twitches, and she turns pale.

I will *not* apologize. Instead, I sling my knapsack against my side. "Where's the bowling alley?" I say through clenched teeth.

"On the main drag. At the end of town." She clears her throat. "Listen, Britt—"

But I'm gone, the door banging shut behind me. I wheel her bike away from the house and am swinging my leg across the seat when she pokes her head outside.

"Take my—oh good, you are. Use the light," she says and shuts the door. Not quite a slam, but hard enough.

I just lost my best friend in Vermont. And I don't care.

17

I pedal off. Once I'm past the bushes near the cottage, the sun's rays slant across the tops of the tall grasses to either side of the lane. The whole field seems lit with candles. There's plenty of light for riding a bike, and I remind myself that Cassie isn't my mother.

Ten minutes later, I'm tooling along the main road of South Hero. Cars whoosh by, too many to be local. The out-of-state plates confirm that people really do vacation here. Or at least pass through, maybe on their way to Montreal or Quebec. By the time I pass a pizza place and a bistro that actually looks worth checking out, the sky's a deep midnight blue. Rick's Bowling Bar is at the northern end of town, where I've never been. I swing into the lot, lean the bike against the building, and stop short at the sight of Manny's SUV. Its tinted windows appear almost menacing in the dim light, yet I long to crawl into it and sleep. But of course, the doors are locked when I try them; even in this little community, a drug dealer wouldn't be so trusting. So I move on and slip inside Rick's place.

The bowling alley assaults my senses. Neon signs and blinking numbers, balls thundering down blond wood alleys, the crash of pins, the pungent odor of sweaty shoes and—I sniff again—pepperoni pizza. The Youth Group, twenty strong, occupies several lanes by the door. Luke's in a serious pow-wow with a kid with acne. Will watches, fists loosely knuckled on his hips, as Perfect Jessica bowls a strike. She whoops, he applauds, they high-five. *Gag me.* Ignoring them, I stride toward the back.

Manny's lean silhouette drapes over the bar, one booted foot braced on the rung of a stool. He's bent over the outstretched palm of the bartender, a hard-looking brunette with a hooked nose and an inch of silver hair along her center part. Pretending to read it, it looks like, and before I can duck away, he glances over and sees me.

"Princess!" He drops the woman's hand. It thuds against the bar and she winces, nursing it. "Where's your entourage?"

"Ha ha," I say. He peers past me at the Youth Group. Close up, he's still that peculiar combination of foxy and homely—until he grins and becomes wickedly devastating. "What've you got?" I demand, rattled by his flirtation with the bartender but determined to hide it. "And nothing … aromatic. The woman I'm staying with is a bloodhound."

Manny snaps his fingers at his skinny pal Z, who's somehow dozing amidst the din. He startles awake, smoothly lifts Cassie's knapsack off the back of my bar stool, and disappears into the hallway leading to the restrooms. A moment later he reappears and brushes past me, dropping the knapsack at my feet. I retrieve it and peek inside. There's a baggie of about ten pills, with a cell number scrawled in black marker across the plastic. I settle the knapsack on my lap, tuck my arm through Manny's, and lean against him. Gazing into those pale amber irises, I detect the faint aroma of the patchouli they sell in hippie stores, along with incense, dream catchers, silver jewelry, and scarves from places like Guatemala and Bolivia.

The dregs of a martini sit on the counter in front of Manny. I nab the olive and pop it in my mouth. It's salty and delicious, and I immediately want another.

"Got one for me?" I say.

Manny's eyelid twitches. "We'll party another time, hey, princess? Looky … your knight in shining armor."

Will bears down on us, his expression grim. I cross my arms against my ribs and face him.

He doesn't even greet me. "Manny Sligh's bad news."

Involuntarily I glance sideways, but Manny must have ducked out a back exit. Near the front door, Jessica shoulders her purse and glances around. She squints toward where Will and I stand in semi-darkness.

I tilt my chin toward her. "Did someone weave you awl awone?" I say in a baby falsetto.

Will's eyes are soft and pleading. "If you ignore everything else I say, trust me now, Britt. *Please*. We've got history."

"You and little Miss Perfect? I knew there was a reason you didn't invite me tonight."

He rubs the back of his neck and leans over. His breath warms my ear when he speaks, so quietly I barely hear him over the crash of bowling balls.

"You're so hard on Jess, when you have no idea what she—never mind. Look, running with Manny Sligh is what got me on probation. I was so broken, my life was one bad choice after another. At this point, if I ever got arrested again—which, believe me, I'm not planning on—I'd be tried as an adult. You don't know who you're dealing with, Britt."

Instinctively, I hide my shock. None of my friends was ever in serious trouble. *But Will's not my friend,* I remember. *I'm just his summer project.* I poke his chest with two fingers.

"So I'm to stay away from the big bad wolf," I say lightly.

He grabs my arm. "What can I say to convince you?" If I didn't know better, I might think he cared.

"Nothing," I say. "If you'd invited me here tonight, like Cassie wanted you to, you might have grounds for your interest. As it is—" I nod toward Jessica, who's tapping a foot. "Your dream girl awaits." I pull away, stifling a pang of envy. The two of them will ride home shoulder to shoulder and knee to knee. *She's already got a horse and wants Will, too.*

"I'm giving her a ride home," he says tightly. "But the reason I didn't tell you about tonight—" He stops and rubs his palm across his mouth, and I'm puzzled because he looks almost shamefaced.

Finally, he says, "I just needed a break, if you must know. From trying to help you. Now please, for heaven's sake, let me take you home."

How can one body feel such different emotions all at once? Even as rage threatens to steam from my ears, I feel I've been knifed in the gut. I glance toward the bar. Still no Manny.

"I never asked for your help," I spit. "But home for me is New York, Will. If you really want to help, drive me there. Tonight."

"You know I can't do that," he says quietly. "You need to stay with your mother."

"Fine. I've got Cassie's bike here. I'll ride back." I head toward the front of the bowling alley. He ducks around me, arrives there first, and holds the door open. I pass beneath his outstretched arm, so near I feel the warmth of his body. A slight whiff of fabric softener and perspiration wafts toward me. Even his sweat smells enticing, and I furiously resist the impulse to fake-trip and land against his chest.

"Let me give you a ride," he says again. "South Hero's safe, but it's dark out."

He's obviously concerned for my safety, and I almost give in. But then I envision Jessica's pale face in the front seat of his Escort a few yards away—*an Escort for an escort, ha*—and I wouldn't get in that car if it were the last space-ship leaving a doomed earth. So I shake my head in a final no, swing myself onto the bike, and pump hard.

But as I pedal along, the four cars carrying the Youth Group pass me. They're doing a sedate thirty, and even their exhaust seems sanctimonious. "Ho-ly rollers," I mutter to myself. But as the taillights of Will's Escort shrink to pinpoints far ahead, I wish I'd accepted his offer. I wish he could like me for who I am, without trying to help or change me. I wish ... oh, so many things. And if wishes were horses, beggars could ride ... I don't know where that saying came from, but it fits.

The next evening, I'm munching a burger at Cassie's. She's even got me liking onions now and has acted normal today, so I guess I didn't permanently offend her last night.

There's a knock at the porch door, and a masculine voice calls out, asking if anyone's home.

The tone is familiar. But when my father walks in, my whole body jolts and goes rubbery, like my elbow does when I bang my funny bone. *I haven't seen this man in ages,* I think, then am shocked. When did I get so alienated?

He takes in my stunned expression and immediately assures me my mother's okay. But his next words floor me. He's going *home* for a few days, and—the one, two punch—Cassie's happy to have me stay on.

She won't meet my eye. *This is not happening.*

A thin dread spirals inside me. I want to burrow into my childhood blankie and wail, but the battle's already here.

"You're *leaving* us? Mom too? When?" I demand.

"Tomorrow morning. I wanted to tell you in person," he says. "And say goodbye, of course. Hey, you'll both be fine. Mom's stable, and it's just a few days. Cassie's so kind-hearted, she's fine with you staying on. And I've got to deal with stuff that's … uh … piling up."

My hostess's face is expressionless. Something's up, and I'm about to press him when the front door opens again and Will slips in. He senses the tension right away and scans our faces, jiggling his keys.

"Well, I'm c–coming with you. No way am I rotting here alone!" My voice is shrill. Doesn't Cassie realize he's taking advantage of her? Not to mention abandoning me yet again. I throw the burger on the table, spattering ketchup droplets like blood, and rush to my bedroom.

Voices murmur behind me. "I'll find her a duffel," Cassie says dully. She plods into our tiny, shared hallway and I tense, willing her not to come into my room. But she passes my door.

In the kitchen, my father babbles—to Will!—what he wouldn't tell me. I make out snatches: "… may be longer … got an appointment … might check on a project …."

My teeth chatter. I get it. He might be gone for weeks. Leaving me high and dry, as if Cassie's cottage is some church camp where you drop off kiddies to sing songs about letting their little lights shine. *Think again, Dad.* I shut the door and start to pile my belongings onto the bed. I've worn the same few clothes all summer, so it's simple: some T-shirts, cut-offs, jeans, toiletries … and the moose nightshirt Cassie bought me, its tags still on. I won't leave the gift unworn for her to find, no matter how betrayed I feel. There's a soft knock, and my door opens. A strained Cassie sets a faded army duffel just inside the doorway and withdraws without a word. *She* gets it. I calm down a bit.

By the time I'm packed, my mind is even jumping ahead to who might be around back home. Chelsea spends every summer in Nantucket. In fact, this week she texted me again: "WHOA, FINALLY HEARD!! WHERE R U?" I haven't answered, partly because this phone's such a pain. But Marissa bops around to different places, including the Hamptons and some Adirondack island her family's owned for three generations. *Ha.* I've got a few thoughts of my own about islands now, but she won't hear them because we're still not talking.

Another rap at the door interrupts my thoughts. Will enters, unsmiling.

"I'm going home, Will!" I announce.

"So I hear. Well, that fits."

"Huh?"

"With how you've been acting ever since you arrived."

My fists gravitate to my hips. "Why don't you tell me your real opinion? Don't hold back."

He flushes. "Okay. I will. I know you're going through a hard time, Brittany, but that's no excuse. Truth is, you're being a brat."

A flash of red fills my vision. Literally. A split second later, without my consciously deciding it, my palm arcs through the air toward his cheek. But he grabs my wrist and holds me off.

"Forget the part about hurting Cassie," he says. "One of the kindest people on the planet, and with everything she's done for you, you don't even—" He pushes my hand away and faces me, his legs planted squarely apart. "But what I really don't get is why you haven't been to the hospital once in, what is it, three weeks? What kind of person are you, Brittany Warner? I'm beginning to think I know—the most selfish girl I've ever met!"

"How often do you visit *your* mother?" I snap. "Wherever she is?"

He flinches. "I can't. She died four months ago in a homeless shelter. From alcohol," he says tonelessly. "Her esophagus burst."

Whoa. My legs give way, and I collapse onto the bed. "Oh, *Will.* I don't … that's … wow."

He's silent for a few moments, then sits beside me, leaning forward with his elbows on his knees. "Yeah. Well. You have no idea. We all assumed she was just off doing her usual, and sooner or later she'd turn up again … but she couldn't outrun it this time, Britt. Her demons got her, and I do mean demons. I've been over it a thousand times, we all have. But I was locked up in juvie when she left, dealing with my own stuff … and you can't force someone to want to get better."

I touch his shoulder lightly. "I've heard that."

He looks up at me, his eyes bleak. "It's not much comfort. But it's not too late for you, Brittany Warner. Go see your mom."

"She doesn't need me, she hates me!"

Will blinks and sits up straight. "Is that what you think? Then go to the hospital and deal with it. While you still can."

"While I—what's that supposed to mean?"

He moistens his lips. "I just meant ... ah, shoot. It's just—your dad's checking out a place in ... well, somewhere near Hartford."

"*What?* My mother works in Manhattan. We can't move to Connecticut!"

"Not you. It's for her, a ..." He tugs his earlobe.

"What? Tell me!"

He sighs. "It's a long-term care facility. There are a bunch of them between here and New York, and this is one of the best. Your dad was just saying, if she doesn't wake in the next week or so, her chances of a complete recovery are ... well, not great. Like, they're bad. In any case the hospital can't keep her forever, which is how long her coma could last."

My heart seems to stop beating. My head hums. My mouth gapes open and shut in slow motion, like a fish's. Will watches in concern and adds softly, "I thought you knew."

Knew? I whirl and stumble from the room. "Dad!" I shout, my breath catching in my throat. But he's not there. "Dad?" I run to the kitchen door and look out. The rental car's gone.

Cassie's alone at her dining table. She lifts her head slowly, her face wretched and blotchy.

"Where's my father?" I croak.

"He'll pick you up in the morning." Her voice is hoarse, too. *With everything she's done* ... Will's right, I've hurt her deeply. But I can't dwell on that now.

A large, glossy booklet lies on the table in front of her. I walk over and bend to inspect the cover, my hands knotted behind my back. A rose garden. Bright-eyed seniors in wheelchairs beam at smiling aides in full color, a pristine azure sky studded with fluffy white clouds above them.

The truth pierces me.

My father is giving up on my mother. I can't tell if her condition is worse than he's let on, or if he's being his usual passive self.

Will comes to stand by Cassie, kind of protectively, and rests his forearm across her shoulder. She grabs one of his fingers, like a baby needing comfort. Something twists inside me.

"Can I borrow this?" I say. She nods. I take the booklet and head toward my bedroom.

"You shouldn't have done that," Cassie tells Will quietly, and I stop in the hallway to listen.

His voice is low, miserable. "I know. I just—lost it. But it's been coming on awhile, and Cassie, I just can't stand how she's been treating everyone I care about. You, most of all." Cassie says something I don't catch, then Will says, "She doesn't ... *mumble* ... what her dad's dealing with ... *mumble* ... guy's falling apart ...."

I'm out of their sight, straining to hear.

"Will." Her voice is gentle. "Walking in faith means loving people even when they act badly."

He groans. "Ugh. You're right. That's what you all did for me, just poured out love, and I was way worse than Britt—" His voice breaks, and I stop myself from peeking at them. "I failed her, Cassie."

"Tell her, not me," Cassie says softly. "And we all mess up, I can think of half a dozen major things I wish I'd done differently, starting with … well. Let's just say I never planned to end up in a rental cottage, depending on my friends' kindness and good tips. But there's always grace." I picture her stroking his hair, like a mom would, and my throat tightens. "Britt hasn't made it easy, Will. She's broken inside. But God loves her same as he loves you."

"I know. I just never thought it would be this hard," he says.

"We've got to trust, is all. And keep praying."

I tiptoe to my bedroom and ease the door shut. They say religion's a crutch, and now I get it. These people live in la-la land. Wish I could move there, too. But the enormity of what's happened hits me in the face, the way the reality of death did when I was a little girl. And like then, I can't stop thinking.

My mother will probably live out her days in some sort of institution. In a coma forever, stashed in some back room with her hair gone gray and her teeth rotted out from lack of saliva … and with who-knows-what wrong inside her. What seemed just an inconvenience before—being forced to spend a whole summer in Vermont, with her making a full recovery, instead of basking in Hawaii and honing my track times for the fall season—has escalated beyond my worst nightmare.

I throw myself onto my bed, hug my pillow, and bury my face in the soft down as if it could save my life.

My bedside alarm reads three-eighteen. That's a.m. And I haven't slept, only endured an infinity of hellish moments since my head hit Cassie's flowered pillowcase. My eyelids are dry and gritty. I slide out of bed and onto the window seat, where Will's Bible still props the window open. The waves are crashing on the shore, rolling the pebbles, and the wind off the lake whips through the trees and plasters my T-shirt against me. The air is mostly warm, but a tiny stinging on my skin warns me October's coming. And November, and December.

Where will my mother be at Christmas? Where will I? Might Cassie and I still be watching scratchy VHS movies? My father's a wild card, I can't count on him to—

What a horrible thought. This isn't about me. I clamp my eyes shut. In the past few hours, I've re-lived again and again the moment I clutched the leather strap of her Prada bag, the wind threatening to take it from me. Images of that awful day in the ICU have bombarded my inner lids: my mother's bruised cheek, her pale, still hands on the blanket, the rasping ventilator. But now I hear, too, my father's voice from long ago when I was a small girl so petrified of death: "And when you're very old, you'll have done so many wonderful things, you'll be ready for a nice long—"

And before I can stop myself, I see my mother's pale form slip away, into oblivion, where she'll stay forev—

"No-oo-oo!" I shriek, and bolt out of the room and across the tiny hall to Cassie's bedroom.

A soft knock, and I push the door open. The room is dark, her sleeping form hidden beneath the covers. The air smells of lavender, the way I imagine an old-fashioned grammy's home would.

"Cassie?" I whisper.

She bolts to a sitting position. "What? What is it?"

I inch my way across a braided rug. Cassie switches on a lamp, sees me, and scooches sideways a few inches. Her nightgown's a short-sleeved, flowered, pilly knit that's seen better days, like most of her belongings. She pats the bed beside her. I perch on the edge and clamp my hands between my knees to stop my shivering. I'm not cold, I just—

"What is it?" she says again. "What's wrong?"

I swallow hard. Even in the dim light, it's obvious her lids are swollen. "I keep thinking … if I'd gone every day, she'd be awake now."

She touches my hair. "Your mom? No, no, don't say that. Your dad's been there all along. It's why he let you stay with me, remember? So you wouldn't—"

"He's leaving, Cassie. I—I owe her. I've got to wake her up!"

She presses her lips together. "That may be out of your—"

"If I don't try, I won't be able to live—"

"Ssh. Don't talk nonsense," she says. "Will shouldn't have called you selfish."

"But it's true."

She's quiet.

"So, Cass—is it really okay if I stay?"

Dark, mothy wings seem to settle over my words. Finally, she answers, her voice thick. "It's okay."

A pause. "Without you," I say. "Without you, Cassie, I'd have drowned in some hotel pool by now. Late at night, all alone, wearing my stupid chartreuse bikini—"

She claps her hand over her mouth, stifling a noise that's part laugh, part sob. A tear glistens on her face as she leans forward and puts her arms around me. Her skin is warm and feels strange. Except for my father's unexpected embrace in the ICU, it's been forever since anyone hugged me. I mean a real hug, not from a horny jerk of a boyfriend or worse, an unwilling one. My hands creep to her back. Her cheek is damp, wetting mine too. Her tears, never mine.

"Ssh," she says again. "It'll all work out. You'll see."

"Why would it?" I gulp.

"Because God is good," Cassie says. "And he loves us."

Right. "Will says that too, all the time. But what makes you so *sure?*"

She twists and points to a two-foot-high wooden cross on the wall over her bed. "Check out his logo."

I gape.

"He didn't come to judge us, Britt. He came to save us. From ourselves."

18

Will drives me to the hospital in silence. He swings into the circular drive by the soaring atrium at the main entrance and pulls over by the revolving doors. Three stories of glass tower above me, glittering in the sun but with odd, angular shadows creating an ominous effect. Somewhere in these buildings is the shell of my mother, and I wish I were anywhere but here.

"I'm glad you stayed," Will says. "And … I'm sorry. For calling you a brat and, well, judging you." He tugs at my sleeve. "Forgive? Unless maybe you want to hit me?"

I really do. Want to, I mean. But I'm hoarding my energy to deal with what awaits me inside. So, I make an upward chopping motion with the side of my hand.

"Right. I consider myself slapped," he says. This guy might deserve more credit than I give him. I grimace my agreement.

"Well. Are you, uh, okay going in there?" he asks. "My shift ends at two. Maybe—"

"I'd r–rather swallow knives," I croak. "But you being there won't change anything." I climb out of the car, my knapsack loaded with fairy charms, magic potions, and … *not*. If only it were.

I need a miracle.

My belly hurts.

A guard points me to an information desk. There, a thin, middle-aged woman with close-set eyes points me to a bank of elevators at the far end of the pavilion. On the sixth floor, an orderly guides me to a nurse's station. There, the person in charge gestures toward a corridor and says, "Room 685." I set off again, dodging meal carts, orderlies, and another nurse whose arms bristle with blood pressure cuffs. She reminds me of the picture of Medusa in my sixth-grade mythology book, snakes sticking out from her head in every direction. And I'm some unnamed Greek hero, preparing to face a giant. Or not.

At last I spot it, 685 on a plaque outside a room. In slow motion I read the name on the sign beneath it: A-g-a-t-h-a W-a-r-n-e-r. My stomach churns, and I command my nausea to subside.

I push the door open.

An oxygen plug pinches the underside of her nostrils like a tiny crab. The silver roots framing her blonde hair almost suggest a tiara. To either side of the bed, banks of machines still beep and monitors still scribble green lines. A tall IV pole still guards her. But the dent in her cheekbone is much improved with the swelling gone and, to my surprise, my mother looks more or less like her usual self. Except that she's eerily still, and seems at peace.

I'm the one who's hyperventilating, my palms sweaty. I inch toward the hospital bed. "M–mom? It's me."

She doesn't answer, of course, so I perch on the edge of a brown vinyl chair and check out the room. Typical for a hospital, I guess. Autumn foliage prints on the wall, an easy chair by the windows, and mountain views wasted on someone in a coma, but which I bet the staff and visitors appreciate. On the nightstand sit a box of tissues and a hairbrush, glinting blonde hairs tangled in its bristles.

"Someone's taking good care of you. You're as beautiful as ever," I say.

A monitor starts beeping. Maybe I should call a nurse? But no wild-eyed staff rush in all panicky, so I remind myself why I'm here. "Mom, I didn't w–want to come here. If you remember anything about the acci— about that day—well, if it makes you feel any better, I hate myself. But shouldn't mothers … forget it." I take a tissue, blow my nose, and start over.

"I'm here to wake you," I say. "So you'll have your life back, even if you never f–forgive me." I rummage in my knapsack, pull out the teddy bear with the crutch and bandaged head and set him on the nightstand. "Now, don't gag. But Cassie—um, remember the diner waitress we met the night of the accident? She says you're never too old for a teddy." Just thinking of my friend calms me, especially her reaction this morning when I came to breakfast wearing the moose nightshirt. She stopped midway through pouring our coffee and brightened, her worry lines wreathing into a smile.

"Sweet," someone says behind me, and I jump. A familiar-looking nurse, stunning with dark skin and coral lipstick, sets two full IV bags on a table by the pole. "We have met, have we not? In Intensive Care. I am Sharonda.

And you are Mrs. Warner's daughter Brittany, correct? It is good you are here."

I nod, ignoring her unspoken *finally*. "I've got to wake her up, Sharonda. Please, tell me what to do?"

The nurse moves to my mother's side and smooths her hair. "Isn't she lovely? Actually, any stimulation will benefit her. You might sing, for instance. My GranMa used to love for me to sing hymns."

It's obvious why. Her voice is musical, with a lilting accent, though her speech is oddly formal. She's Jamaican, my father said. But I set her straight.

"No hymns. What else?"

For a moment she seems taken aback, but recovers. "Mm, let me see. You could rub her hands. And feet. That would stimulate her circulation, you know, her blood flow."

Now I notice. My mother's hands are folded across her middle, as if—*stop, Britt*. I reach out and trail a finger along her forearm.

"Don't be afraid. She's your mama," Sharonda says. "And there's lotion you can use. Even smells can help, pleasant or not." She moves around the foot of the bed to the nightstand, reaches into the drawer, and hands me a plastic bottle. I squeeze out a few drops and rub them gingerly into my mother's skin. "That's it, that's it," she says, drawing out her a's. "But you know, the best thing you can do is to talk to her. She may be able to hear, has anyone told you that? Sometimes a patient will wake from a coma and remember everything that happened in their presence. For years, even."

Appalled, I snatch away my hand. "She can hear us? That's … creepy!"

The nurse rounds the bed again and removes an empty IV bag from the pole. "I said may. But I would think it might encourage you. She may be closer than you think."

I shudder. This is *so* not comforting. I never dreamed my mother might actually be able to understand speech. "How do I tell if she's waking? Will she just start yakking away?"

"There would probably be signs before that. You might find her watching you. She does open her eyes sometimes; she's a bit higher on the coma scale than some. Or she'll move her fingers or toes, or an arm or a leg. Perhaps she would grimace, or even say a few words." Sharonda represses a smile, forming a perfect dimple in her left cheek. "That may be a bit of a shock. One gentleman awoke after three years in a coma, and can you guess his first words?"

Nope. I shrug. "Hi, honey?"

She stifles a laugh, no longer so dignified. "No … he said to his wife, *'What the heck did you do to your hair?'*"

There's a pause, as she waits for me to respond. But I'm appalled. *Three years?* She's friendly, though, and unlike my sandy-haired friend on the farm, evidently not holding a grudge about my staying away. I relax a bit.

"Or," she adds, "her brainwaves might change." She points to a monitor.

I lean over the bed. "Don't worry, Mom, you'll be in the courtroom again. I promise!" To Sharonda I say, "She's a brilliant attorney."

The nurse attaches a full IV bag and fiddles with the flexible tubing. "And there's no reason she can't be again. Someday. But … you do realize your mother is wearing a corset?"

"What? I thought they went out with hoop skirts."

This time she stays serious. "You are speaking of corset, the woman's underwear. This corset is a special medical vest. To stabilize your mother's neck and spine."

I lift the top sheet and peer under it. A puffy thing is wrapped around my mother's middle. It's connected to a belt-like band that encircles her head, which in turn is supported by four stakes.

"Her spine is fractured in two places," Sharonda says. "She may not walk again."

For a moment I'm positive I heard wrong. I swivel my head in slow motion toward the nurse, and time rolls backward.

When I was about ten, my mother and I were ambling through Central Park in Manhattan, eating lemon ices. I'd been to the orthodontist, and was forbidden to chew gum.

"Lemon's a terrific hair rinse," she said. "It could lighten the mousiness you got from your father's side of the family. His Aunt Miranda was a real carrot-top, you know. Or maybe you don't. I guess you never met her. But lemon will bring out the highlights, and once your braces come off, you'll have nothing to complain about." I scowled and chomped into my ice so hard my teeth hurt. All I heard was, "You'll never be beautiful like me."

A moment later she stopped short, and I bumped into her so hard my lemon ice fell to the pavement. I hopped aside to avoid stepping in it and looked up, expecting a rebuke. But my mother's attention was focused on a graying, disheveled woman in a wheelchair who was tossing breadcrumbs to a flock of pigeons. Beside her, a bored caretaker betrayed no expression.

"Look at that," my mother said, low and intense. "She's half a person. If I'm ever like that, Brittany, for any reason? Shoot me." Her cobalt eyes glittered.

"She'd rather d—die," I tell the nurse now. "She told me."

Sharonda tilts her head. "People often say that, but when the situation arises—"

"No!" I practically shout. "She meant it."

The nurse frowns, rummages again in the nightstand drawer, and hands me a brown leather notebook. The soft cover is cool and smooth, and my fingers recognize top-quality leather even as I remember pulling it from the tote bag holding my test prep books the night of the accident. And my mother's odd reaction, like she didn't want my father or me to see it.

"That may be true. But Mr. Warner reads this to her when he is here," she says. "Perhaps you would continue while he is away. This may help to keep her dreams alive."

I clutch the journal to my stomach. "And d—dreams are all she's got, that's w—what you're saying. But you're wrong. My mother will be fine. You'll see."

Sharonda regards me with sympathy. I stuff the journal into my knapsack and rush from the room.

At the end of the hall I stop by a water fountain, gasping, and grope in my pocket for Manny's pills. No one is near, so I bite off half a pill and peer in the baggie. Nine left. I pop the other part in my mouth too. I should have done this earlier, but wanted to be alert.

I bend to drink. The icy water feels like a divine healing, a purification. Outside the hospital a few minutes later, I head down Colchester Ave toward where Will works, retracing my route from the morning after the accident. I was even more of a mess then, but today the dry, fine air—and the pill—soothe my tortured mind.

But it's not enough, and for the first time I bite a second pill in two and swallow another half. So by the time I spot the gilded BENNETT'S lettering across the glass storefront, I'm a lifeboat bobbing on a sea of peace. My family's problems seem an ocean away, as if I'm viewing them through the wrong end of a telescope.

Except I'm not even doing that. I'm gazing upward, marveling at how beautiful the puffy white clouds look against the beautiful blue dome of the sky.

I push open the apothecary door too hard. The overhead bell jangles, and a row of faces like emoticons swings toward me when I approach the counter and climb onto a stool. I make a goofy face, they're all so stodgy-looking, but no one reacts. *Vermonters.* Will comes from the back room, wiping his hands on a dishtowel. He raises his eyebrows when I grin at him.

"Hail, most excellent William," I say. "Allow me to honor you with my presence—" I stop. A few seats away, a man slides off his stool and claps a policeman's hat on his head.

"Thought that was you," Sergeant Thompson says. "I expected a call from you by now. Or Cassie." He peels a couple of bills from his wallet and slaps them onto the counter. The wallet gapes open, loose in his meaty palms. One finger is encased in a bandage. Even cops bleed, apparently.

Instantly I'm cold all over and stone sober. It never occurred to me I might run into Cassie's cop buddy outside the station. His hair's even shorter than when we first met, and brown spots pepper his scalp even though I don't think he's very old.

An impossible silence stretches between us. "Well, at least you're keeping good company with young Will. Tell Cassie and your dad I said hello. Oh, and in case you've forgotten where to reach me—" He pulls a business card from his wallet and hands it to me with a smirk. "The accident file's still open, we don't sign off on anything 'til we're sure we know the truth. Got to do right by your mama." He pockets the wallet, jerks his chin toward Will, and strides out, his cop shoes squeaking on the black-and-white-checkered linoleum floor.

My cheeks and lips tingle. I touch my face.

"You okay?" Will asks.

"Huh? Sure," I squeak. My heart is hammering.

He spreads the dishcloth on a rack to dry. "Give me five and we're out of here."

I sink onto the stool and force myself to breathe slowly. In, out. In, out.

That was close. Next time won't be so easy.

19

Sprawled on Cassie's porch glider, I open the leather journal above me. The first page is blank. The second contains initials, A.F.W., and a cell number. Very proper, even understated—but beneath it, heavy printing warns, "PRIVATE—DO NOT READ UNDER PENALTY OF PROSECUTION."

I sit up, uneasy. I've defied my mother a million ways, mostly minor. This feels different, an invasion of her privacy … but I want to know. Have to know. And my father's already read these pages, setting a precedent—another legal principle she swears by. So, he'd be first in line for her wrath. Unless … *what if he ignored her warning because he knows she won't find out?* I squelch this terrible thought and flip the page, balancing the journal on my knee. Seeing her perfect script jars me. She's always used a fountain pen, and the sweetish aroma of sepia ink is one of my earliest memories. Now it rises off the page and into my nostrils, and I want to sob.

"March 10," I read aloud past the lump in my throat. But what year? I flip through the pages. Fewer than half are filled, and the last entry is May 23 … right when the Hartwell trial began. That occupied her for weeks, and she brought the journal to Vermont … so, it's this year. I smirk. *Well done, Sherlock.*

"Everything's falling apart," I read to myself now. "I'm hanging by the sheerest thread. One snip of a scissors, and I'd plummet over a cliff."

Whoa. Automatically I flip to the front page again, to double-check the signature. Yes, Agatha Warner wrote this. I read on, my insides in turmoil.

> Where to start? Maybe with my moment of infamy, that affected my whole life—but why did even that happen? Can it ever be undone, or am I stuck forever with that awful night—and who I've become? It's far too late to redress that wrong, but I have to find a way through if I'm to go on.

If? I read on.

> Heaven help me, I've shunned journal-keeping all my life—always pitied those poor souls who spend their days navel-gazing—but Dr. Friedman says it's either this or write each of my parents a letter. Ix-nay on that, I'm done with both of them. So first, a recap for the shrink. Then we'll see how much progress I make with my so-called "pivotal" experiences.

My mother was seeing a counselor. A *shrink.* Everything she wrote shocks me; it's so unlike her normal, invincible self. Far from reflecting on the past, she rushes at the future headlong, like the frantic headmistress Miss

Clavell in the *Madeline* books my babysitter Maxine used to read to me. Frowning, I slouch against the glider cushions and read on.

> I was raised quasi-poor in Michigan, and my father was scary. When I was small, I learned to stay out of his way. And my mom fed our cat Trixie out by the garage. She'd been a stray, and Papa didn't even know she was ours, because we didn't dare let Trixie in …

Footsteps wake me. Cassie's crossing the porch, laden with grocery bags. She jumps at seeing me and drops her burdens with a *thunk*.

"Hey. What a day, the diner was slammed. What's that?" She eyes the journal.

"It's my mother's. Her nurse gave it to me. My father read it aloud in the hospital, and now she says I should."

Cassie tilts her head. "Read to your mom? Then why bring it here?"

I'd hoped she wouldn't ask. "Um … I want to find out why she's the way she is."

Seeing her puzzled look, I add hastily, "I mean even before the accident. You met her, Cassie. In the diner. Wasn't it pretty obvious something was … off?"

She leans against the porch post and purses her lips.

"She's always on me about college and stuff." I'm aware how lame that sounds.

"Britt, every mom wants her child to have the best life they—"

Right. She'll never get it. In Cassie's book, my mother's actions are reasonable and appropriate. Even that she made me take violin lessons for two whole years, knowing the screechiness of the bow on the strings drove me mad. And my hostess definitely wouldn't approve of how I fired the instructor with a note, saying, "Brittany is unfortunately unable to continue her lessons." To her, forging my parent's name would be a sin.

But pain is pain, isn't it? And to convey the essence of my family to Cassie—the accumulated hurts, the lack of affection, above all the profound absence of any loving sentiment—is impossible. Cheesy as her movies are, some of those people grinning at each other like fools have choked me up a bit. Not that I let her see.

I'm empty inside. Have been all my life, and never even realized it. But why? It's much more than not ever getting a horse. My aching, cosmic inner vacuum threatens to overwhelm me.

Weren't my parents supposed to fill my emotional cup, at least when I was small? Make sure I got the love I needed, and felt secure?

"Cassie," I finally say. "My mother was rude to you that night we met. Admit it, please?"

She sighs. "Maybe. I guess. But I offended her by suggesting the Buffalo wings. The way she ordered for you all, I figured maybe you didn't know there was any other kind of food. It kind of hit me wrong, but it was none of my business and I shouldn't have reacted that way. Anyway, what have you found out?"

"Well. She said she grew up in Michigan, but ... not how it was. I mean, she didn't go hungry, but listen:"

When I was maybe five or six, I sat at the kitchen table, eating an apple and counting the bites. My teacher told us to practice numbers. Mama was scrubbing potatoes at the sink. Her hair was pinned in a greasy knot on top of her head, a loose strand jiggling against her cheek with each motion.

She wore knitted socks and a pair of slippers, a blouse with a pointy collar, and the navy skirt she wore during the week. Her calves were bare, her cardigan stretched and shapeless. I sometimes picked off the woolly pills and saved them for the birds. I would have died of shame if anyone saw her this way. But they didn't. My father was often … angry. And Mama didn't want people at church to find out, so she never invited anyone over.

Cassie slides her back down the porch pillar so she's sitting among the grocery bags. "I see why she became a lawyer. She's got a memory for details."

"Mm. Listen, here's another part:"

On my twelfth birthday I wore my best dress the whole day, white organdy with brightly colored tulips appliquéd onto the bodice. After dinner Papa left for a church meeting, but Mama gave me a box wrapped in beautiful paisley paper and a bow.

I opened it and instantly loved my wooden knitting needles with red balls on the end and my beautiful green Norwegian yarn.

Mama cast on for me and showed me how to knit, and I was off.

By the next afternoon I was well into making a scarf and couldn't wait to show Papa when he came home. But he threw my beautiful work into the fireplace. "And where do you think that will get you? Use your mind, girl!" he roared, and grabbed some heavy volume from the bookcase and threw it on the coffee table.

The flames licked and hissed at my knitting and I felt the heat on my own skin, even though Mama had pulled me away to a safe distance. Lying in bed that night, I vowed to find a career Papa would like. One that would earn me his love and respect. Law, maybe, or medicine. Not teaching or nursing, and definitely *not* being a housewife.

I stop reading and look up.

"Whew," Cassie says. "That's—"

"Yeah. And my Grandma Audrey, who lives in Vegas, left when my mother was fifteen. And then she moved out a year later. I guess they both had enough of him. And Cassie, she was seeing a shrink!"

"Your mother or grandmother?" Cassie says cautiously.

"My mother. Just this spring. It's the whole point of the journal, which her therapist made her write. I mean, I always knew she was screwed up. But I didn't realize *she* knew it."

"It's funny." Cassie hesitates. "When you talk about her, you just call her 'my mother.' Not 'my mom,' or just 'Mom.'"

"'Mother' is a title. 'Mom' is a relationship, that you have to earn," I say without thinking.

Cassie's eyebrows shoot up. "I see. So you don't consider—"

"Not at all. Anyway, so later she got a job in Ann Arbor and worked her way through college. And law school."

"I see," Cassie says again, and I have the feeling she's talking about more than law school. "Well, clearly education is important to her. Which explains a lot, yes?" She starts to gather together the grocery bags strewn around her.

"Important is an understatement. She *idolized* it." I wiggle my bare toes, propped on the end of the glider, and glance up, wary. "And now she's going to be paralyzed."

The plastic bags stop rustling. "Might be," Cassie corrects.

She knew. I guess I'd suspected it.

"The stuff I just read you? That was just a few pages," I say. "Except for those two stories, she sure didn't go into anything deep. So, I'm wondering ..." I concentrate on my dirty toenails.

"Mm?"

"If maybe her dad or someone abused her," I say in a rush.

Cassie gets to her feet abruptly, holding most of the bags. "Whoa, that's a serious—"

"People don't leave home for no reason. And she defends rapists for a living. It's her *specialty*. Don't you think that's weird?"

"Hard to say. Maybe she's got a reason. I guess someone's got to defend those people," Cassie says. "But if something did happen, wouldn't she represent victims?"

"Maybe. I still find it ... odd."

"I see your point," Cassie admits. "In my experience, though, people aren't ... difficult ... unless they've been hurt. Sometimes very deeply. Hey, I'll be right back." She angles her body to open the door and sticks her foot out. She slips through sideways, drops the bags onto the counter inside, and joins me on the glider, redoing her bun with her fingers.

"Yeah, hurt. That's what I'm saying." I set the journal aside. She picks it up and flips through the pages of dense writing, my personal Rosetta Stone I'm desperately trying to decode. Her eyes widen when she sees the blank pages in the second half of the book. She closes the journal.

"So, I think your mom—sorry, mother sounds too cold—needs your support. Read the journal through, and try to understand. Forgive her, whatever it is you have against her, and you'll be free."

My insides twist. "You don't get it, Cassie. It's not about me forgiving her. I need *her* to forgive *me*. W–what if she doesn't wake up?" I cover my face, fighting to control myself.

Cassie sets the journal aside and takes my hands in hers. "Oh, my dear. Ask her anyway. She might hear you—no one can say for sure she doesn't. And if you really feel you've done something wrong, I could help you say a prayer—"

I jerk away and jump to my feet. "You always think religion's the answer." I grab the last two grocery bags and elbow the door open. It swings shut before I can enter.

She catches the door and holds it open. But as I pass, she plucks my sleeve gently.

"Not religion," she says. "That's just a bunch of empty actions. It's like what you said about calling someone mother instead of mom. Christianity is more like … a relationship, with the one who made you and loves you. People think they'll earn their way to heaven by going to church or being a good person. But no human being could ever achieve God's perfection, not even Mother Teresa. Yes, we're all made in the image of God, and it wasn't supposed to be like this. But real faith, Britt, is recognizing our own flawed selfishness and being humble enough to admit we need forgiveness."

I cross the kitchen and drop the grocery bags on the counter. "People who do horrible things don't deserve that," I say.

"No one does," she says. "That's why it's called grace."

"Baloney," I shoot back. "You're so holy, I bet you never did anything worse in your whole life than maybe drop a stitch. Wow, huge sin."

She fixes me with a look and starts to unload groceries. I join her. As I'm pulling out an eggplant, she says, "It's not the degree of a sin that matters. But it's funny what you said, because I did do something … very wrong." She takes a deep breath and lets it out slowly.

"When I was seventeen, I became pregnant. And … ended it."

The eggplant slips through my fingers and bounces on the linoleum floor. I can't take my eyes off her.

"How … far along were you?"

She stoops to retrieve the eggplant, her knee cracking, and sets the purple globe on the counter. "About six weeks." She meets my eyes with difficulty. Hers are a pool of pain. But—

Seriously? "That's not a baby," I say, impatient. "It's just a bunch of cells."

Her jaw juts out slightly. "That's what I told myself. And at the time, I saw no other options. But as time passed, instead of being able to put what I'd done behind me, I felt more and more guilty. I had recurrent dreams—nightmares—in which my baby girl kept calling me."

Ouch. "But those were just—"

"Finally, a few years ago …" She leans against the counter. "I couldn't take it anymore. I had no hope, nothing to fall back on. So I did something really stupid."

I eye her uncertainly. "You don't mean—"

Her bleak expression confirms it. "I made one … attempt. With pills." Her voice drops on the last word.

No. Not Cassie. "What happened?" I finally say.

"Luckily for me, someone found me. Called 9-1-1, and they pumped my stomach. And while I was in the hospital, a woman told me about a Bible study on healing after abortion. It's possible, you know. It's how I met Priscilla, actually. And I learned that Jesus died on the cross for *me.* And I sat and cried, and found peace."

I can't deal. "Some of this food needs refrigeration."

"Okay, enough. But I want you to know, Brittany Warner, that what you're doing with your mom—facing her each day, reading to her—is huge. Really. I'm proud of you."

My throat tightens. "You are? No one's ever … told me that."

"I'm saying it now."

I swallow hard and finger a bag of carrots. "Are these for Joy?"

She smiles, rueful. I pick out the two fattest carrots and fly out the door. It slams behind me, and I'm half-way to the barn on her bike, pedaling between masses of

Queen Anne's lace and purple chicory, when I remember the grocery bags still waiting on the counter.

Cassie won't mind. And for once, I'm thinking that without scorn.

20

I round the corner of the barn to peals of laughter and a scene from some pastoral painting. Luke's truck is backed up to the barn, beneath a beam that extends from the roof like a ship's prow. The tailgate is down, the bed strewn with loose hay and two bales. Jessica and Meghan, standing in the truck bed, shove one bale to the tailgate as I arrive. Meghan grabs a heavy rope dangling from the beam, and Jessica works a large hook attached to the lower end into the twine holding the bale together. She and Will, who's standing by the tailgate, hoist the block of hay as if it's a flag, or maybe a sail. Luke leans out from the hayloft opening above them, pulls the bale in, and flings away the rope.

He leans out again. "Last one's got Britt's name on it!" he calls.

They all turn toward me. "Oh, no you don't," I say. "I'm no hayseed." But both girls jump off the tailgate and Meghan dances about, insistent. So, I set down the carrots and climb into the truck bed. This last bale is massive, heavy and scratchy, and the twine cuts into my fingers as

I drag the unwieldy thing to the tailgate. But I underestimate its momentum and the bale tumbles to the ground, where it seesaws back and forth, threatening to split open. Will stifles a grin and hooks the rope to the bale, and he and Meghan hoist it together to where Luke waits.

Above us, dozens of bales are neatly stacked inside the hayloft opening. These guys have been at this awhile.

"Now me!" Meghan shouts. Will lifts her to the rope. She wraps her arms and legs around it like a little monkey and beams at us.

"Hold tight." Will hoists his squealing sister into the air. A safety inspector would have a fit. Luke leans out of the hayloft, catches the waistband of her shorts, and pulls her to safety.

"Ahoy bonny pirates," she yells, shading her eyes with a hand.

Will and Jessica whoop and applaud. It's a silly fuss … but then I remember myself, at age nine or ten, riding the flying swings at some county fair. My father read a newspaper on a bench below, while I whizzed through space in the outside position of my row. If my swing let go, I'd have hurtled through the air and crushed some fairgoer. Each time around, I peered at the top of his baseball cap.

"Dad," I called. "Hi, Dad!" But he didn't look up. I twisted toward the swings next to me. Empty, and that's how I learned that a thrill, unshared, is really fear.

When the ride ended, I tottered through the exit gate, dizzy. I sank onto the bench, and my father looked up in surprise. "All done?" He folded the paper and checked his watch. "Let's go find Mom. Want a soda?" But it was too little, too late. In the air was where I'd needed him.

Now, high above us, Luke steers Meghan away from the hayloft opening. "Be right down," he calls.

The rest of us wait in awkward silence. "How many bales were there?" I think to ask.

"Just seventy. We made three trips to tide us over to second cutting," Will answers.

"Cutting?"

"Of hay, what else?" says Jessica. "Next month we get the full delivery for winter. But that's easier. A big rig with an electric chute delivers the bales right into the hayloft."

"Oh." I feel ignorant.

Jessica flips her ponytail outside her polo collar. "Well, show's over. Unless you feel like mucking stalls."

Meghan trots from inside the barn, her cheeks pink with excitement. "That's a great idea! You gonna work here, Britt?"

"No!"

"But you could, right? Aren't you by yourself all day when Cassie's gone? Jess, tell her she should."

Appalled, I glance at Jessica. She's startled too, and I'm probably the last person in the world she feels like having around. "What would I do?" I say. "The hay's put away."

Jessica snorts. "There's plenty to choose from. Clean stalls, scrub buckets, shovel plops ..." Now she laughs at my expression. "You don't want to pick up patties? Maybe Will would take you shopping or to a Broadway show."

Suddenly Priscilla's with us, leaning on her cane. "Best idea I've heard all day. If you're serious, Brittany."

"Sure," I say, caught. "I just haven't done it before."

Perfect Jessica and I eye each other for a long moment. "We could use the help," she finally admits. "But you'll need barn boots. There's an extra pair in the tack room."

"My cue to leave. Nice work, guys. Catch you later."
Will flashes a grin and heads toward his car.

Jessica retrieves a manure fork almost my height from inside the barn doorway and thrusts the red plastic tongs at me.

Meghan bursts out laughing. "You're funny, Jess!" To my shock, her skinny arms clutch my waist in a hug. "She's just jerking your chain, Britt. We did the stalls this morning."

My nemesis smirks. "You're right, peanut. It *would* help to show her when they're dirty." She takes the manure fork from me and leans it against the barn. To me she says, "So, six o'clock tomorrow?" She sees my skeptical expression. I've been getting to the barn around seven, and no one's been around.

"How about eight?" I counter.

She shrugs and grins. "Fine. Or nine, or even ten. Any time before noon, that's when the first horses are brought in from grazing."

I tuck a strand of hair behind my ear, pleased to have bested her. "No problem." But there is. *What will I do if someone hands me a lead rope with a horse at the end of it?*

Maybe Cassie will say no.

Cassie's thrilled I've "found something to do." And while I always longed to be a barn brat, it's more work than I bargained for.

Most of the horses have been hayed, grained, and turned out to graze by the time I arrive just before nine. Just as I'd hoped. Jessica hands me the extra pair of barn boots and shows me how to muck out stalls. Pee-soaked bedding and manure weigh a ton, and there are a hundred forty-four square feet in a twelve-by-twelve box stall. And there are fourteen stalls in this barn alone, plus another six in a smaller barn out back. But the shavings are wettest in just a corner or two of each stall, and she warns me twice not to do the last stall on the left, since Joy's still in it. *As if.* Still, once I've done a few stalls and trundled the loaded wheelbarrows outside—a challenge when they're overflowing—I'll be glad to move on to the next chore.

Which reminds me. "Doesn't Joy get room service?"

"Sure—when she's out," Jessica says. "Luke's the only one who handles her. Hey, I've got to go, but maybe you could help Meghan do water buckets. She can't do them alone, even if she thinks she can ... Meghan!" she calls.

Small she may be, but the tyke's a force to be reckoned with. Reaching on tiptoe inside a stall, the tip of her tongue clamped between her lips, Meghan unhooks a bucket from its hanger. She dumps its wet, grassy contents outside. Horses, it seems, are messy drinkers. Then she hoses in a couple of inches of fresh water and scrubs inside the bucket with a toilet brush. I retrieve and wash twelve more buckets under her gimlet eye, skipping Joy—whose gaze bores through me as I remove Saratoga's bucket from the stall across the aisle.

When I'm done, Meghan stands silhouetted against the daylight, less than four feet tall but wielding a burbling hose like she's Napoleon. I snicker, but regret it when she marches toward the first stall, splashing icy water on my feet.

"Oops, sorry. Bring a bucket, Britt," she sings out in her high voice.

Oh. It does make sense to refill the buckets right in the stalls. I secure a bucket on its pin. Meghan hoists the dripping hose and lets it rip. After the first mis-aim, I stand back.

Maybe the sodden sawdust isn't all pee.

At last we move outside, where she shows me how to pick up plops in empty paddocks. Priscilla calls, so Meghan leaves me to work alone at what ought to be a simple task. But I'm a klutz, and the dried balls keep rolling off my manure fork. Finally, I experiment with a cradling motion to keep the plops on the fork and, *Eureka!* It's just like a certain game invented by Native Americans … with ponies. I picture hooting boys scooping dried plops into homemade basket-sticks and hurling them at each other, shrieking ecstatically. I balance a full fork backward over my shoulder and let it fly at a tree outside the fence. *Score.*

Someone behind me gives a long whistle. Will bounces on the balls of his feet, hands in his khaki pockets. His damp hair shows brush marks, and his shirt is freshly ironed. He's off to work. I'd feel an idiotic slob, except for his obvious approval of my aim.

"Thought you hated sports," he says. "You'd be a champ at lacrosse."

I push my hair off my sweaty forehead and lift my nose in the air. "I know of no such game. As it happens, I've invented a pastime—"

He barks a laugh. "Later." He walks away, and my eyes follow him unwillingly. He's got a good bod, even if he is a bit too clean. Unlike me, especially right now. My T-shirt's so damp with sweat it's stuck to my shoulder blades.

"Brittany," someone calls. I head for the barn and a grubby, though dry, Jessica. She didn't work with Meghan.

"Nice job on the stalls," she says, and I nod. Jessica may dislike me, but I can't fault her behavior today.

Meghan leads the absurdly named Tiny into the barn from outside, his hooves clopping on the wooden ramp like cannon shots. Before I can object, she hands me the end of his lead line, and I yelp as the horse noses my hip.

"He just wants a carrot," Jessica says. "Hold the halter just under his chin." She shows me how, and I'm stiff with fright until Meghan returns with a brush and leads Tiny away.

At least Jessica didn't tease me. *Will I ever be free of my fear?*

Priscilla emerges from the barn office and offers me a bottle of water. I swig it greedily. "Not a bad day's work," she says. "There's plenty of tack needs cleaning, but I guess that's enough for your first day." She's so gruff I'm not sure if she's joking. But I haven't committed myself to help out beyond today, anyway.

Luke strides up with that long-legged gait and squeezes my arm, the way he did to Meghan. It feels odd; I'm just not used to being touched the way I have been this summer. But I don't exactly hate it. For a moment, I imagine that Luke is my father. It'd be cool, but that would make Will my foster brother ... *ewww.* I'm glad people can't read each other's minds.

"Thanks for the help, Britt," Luke says. "Between Priscilla's bum hip, Jess being so busy training for her event, and Will working overtime, we're a bit shorthanded."

"It's okay," I mumble. Then I shock myself by adding, "Maybe I could ... come tomorrow. If you want."

His face clears in relief. "Would you? That'd be fantastic, at least 'til things ease up. We'll pay you, of course."

I shrug. "It doesn't matter."

"Of course it does. And listen, the barn can't interfere with visiting your mom, understood? That's top priority. Maybe you could ride in with Cassie or Will when they go to work, and one of us can fetch you home afterward."

"Whatever."

"Fantastic," Luke says again. "And listen … Youth Group meets Friday night. Any chance you'll join us?"

"Um … I'll see." *Oh, man. Give these guys an inch …* I'm ticked at myself too, for getting roped into this, but remember it's only Tuesday. I've got three days to come up with an excuse.

21

Friday night. A beautiful evening, when I could be sitting on Cassie's bench by the lake. Instead, I'm perched on a folding chair at the church, the metal seat cold against my legs below my shorts. Will, Jessica, a dozen teens, and I form a circle. Luke, of course, is the leader. In the center sits Kara, her cloud of black hair neatly, if loosely, fastened in a low knot on her neck. It's flattering, but she's eight months pregnant now and looks like she could go into labor any moment.

"Most of you already know Kara," Luke says. "And some of you have been asking questions. So she's joining us tonight for you to hear what's going on, and then we'll pray."

Kara looks around, her expression as naïve and trusting as if she were handing us scalpels to perform a cesarean section. Actually, everyone seems somber, even some of the rowdier boys. I guess praying's a big deal. Why Luke is enlisting the teens, I don't know. Plenty of adults must already be on the job, like they are for my family.

"I'm not sure where to start," Kara says. "But a couple of years ago I got involved with a guy who was—well, a turd. A man who'd help your granny across the street, then steal her purse. People warned me, again and again …."

Marissa warned me about Benny back home. But I ignored her, and my mother, and the knot in my belly. Benny flung open his bedroom door that last afternoon, exposing me in that raunchy underwear, and my father's eyes bugged out … Not counting having to flush Orangina, it was the beginning of the long, slow catastrophe that almost destroyed my family and landed me here. So, maybe my mother and Marissa were right about Benny. They'd been such snots, though, pointing out that he was a dropout, worked in a gas station, didn't play sports … like those things made him pond scum. But the fact is, I never even got high 'til he and I hung out. And I'd kind of set my mind against college, figuring you could make a decent life without it. My mother would have shot back, "Is Benny's your definition of that?" And, of course, it's not. I just want to figure out for myself whether such a life has to include higher education. I hate being pressured, no matter what statistics say about how much more college grads earn during a lifetime and how many doors a diploma can open. There are all kinds of doors, and there's more to life than money.

I hope.

Kara's still talking, and I tune in again. "… came here as a foster kid, after … well, something happened that made it impossible to live at home."

I straighten with a jolt. That's the understatement of the year. Their house burned to ashes! As she goes on, I pay closer attention.

"Luke and Priscilla were awesome—everyone was—and a few months later, I came to faith in Jesus. I began dating Shawn Newcombe. You all know him, he's a wonderful guy who grew up in the church, but walked away for a while. Plays guitar like a dream. And we'd just about decided—" Kara chokes up. A girl in a plaid shirt and glasses passes her a tissue, and she wipes her cheeks. "We were seeing each other every day and talking about a future together. But then Shawn had to leave for a few weeks—he works on ships—and I was bored and lonely. So, I went to this party by myself. Bad decision. Because the first person I saw there was … you guessed it. And the way he glared, I knew he hadn't forgiven me for our breakup. I should have been on guard. Because that night he, or one of his buds, spiked my drink."

Kara's gaze rests on each of us. The room is completely silent. "Here's the thing. Shawn and I weren't … intimate. We wanted to wait until we were married."

I can't believe she's talking about this at church.

"… and when I talked to him on the phone before the party, he didn't want me to go. I wish I'd listened. Because I have no memory of anything after that, or how I got back to Luke and Priscilla's. And the next morning I realized … I'd had sex."

Yikes. She really said that. Her tone is so mild, her words take a moment to sink in. Her next ones, too.

"Or rather, someone had had sex with me. It would not have been voluntary." A girl gasps.

No. *No.* I peek at Will. He's absolutely still, except for a muscle jumping in the side of his jaw. And his lips are white.

Kara stretches her preggie shirt across her belly and fingers the hem. "It didn't have to happen. My brother would have gone with me, or more likely, talked me out of it, if I'd asked. And honestly I can't even be sure who spiked my drink, and if that was the person who … you know. Either way, I was so ashamed afterward that I didn't tell anyone. Another mistake. But a few weeks later, things got even worse when I realized I was pregnant. I told Priscilla and Luke, of course. I'm still under their roof, even though I've aged out of fostering. But the one who needed to know most was Shawn, because of our plans. And he—well, he freaked out."

Another swipe at her eyes with the tissue. "He actually wasn't sure he believed me. His last girlfriend cheated on him, and he thought maybe I'd had a few drinks and hooked up with … that guy, for old times' sake. As if I would. But our relationship ended. We broke up, and he hasn't been around at all, and … I have no daddy for my baby. Who's a boy, by the way. And innocent. None of this is his fault." Again, she appeals to the circle of teens. "Maybe I *should* give him up for adoption. But that's not what I … want. And people keep telling me anything's possible with God. So … please pray I'll know what to do. Thanks."

She exhales a long breath and peers at Luke, uncertain. "Thank-*you*, Kara, for sharing," he says. "Anyone have questions?" No one does, but a couple of girls fiddle with earrings and their clothes, and suddenly I understand. There'd been gossip—*and no wonder*—and Luke just met it head-on. It was a gutsy move, and I can't help but admire him for it.

"Okay, then let's pray," Luke says. Everyone except me gathers around Kara and places hands on her arms, her back, even on her hair. It's so crowded that some just lay a palm on the person in front of them. Prayer vibes must travel right through people. Luke raises a tiny bottle. "This is anointing oil. It has no special properties—it's just olive oil that's been blessed and represents the Holy Spirit." He upends the open bottle against his fingertip, recaps it, and dabs Kara's forehead briefly. Then he lays his palm on her cloud of black hair and shuts his eyes. Others follow.

Except me. I am so not part of this, though it's hard to tear my eyes from the glistening spot between Kara's eyebrows. It makes her look … almost holy. Lifting my knapsack, I tiptoe toward the door. But I bump into a chair and peek back, to see if anyone noticed. Will meets my gaze above the huddled group. I hurry into the hall, past plates of cookies and rows of water bottles and cans of soda set out on a table.

"Britt," Will whispers. I turn, still backing away. "What's wrong?" he says and comes so near I smell the scent of his soap.

I push him away. "You're Shawn!"

He stumbles, regains his balance. "What? Are you nuts? Kara's my *sister.*"

"So? You're the same. He ditched her when she needed him most, 'cause she was … unclean. You both want someone *pure*, like … your precious Jessica. Luke would need *extra*-virgin oil to anoint her," I snarl, forgetting I'm a virgin myself. I don't feel it, though. I've been tainted by Jeff Cox, who touched me against my will. And by Benny, though he didn't force me to pose in that horrible lingerie. Even the word sounds dirty now.

The classroom door opens and teens pour out, chattering. Will pulls me into an empty room next door and faces me. "Hey, it's me you're talking to. Ex-juvie. Ring a bell?" he says.

He sounds like that stupid cop, and I knock his hand off my arm. "When I kissed you, you pushed me away like I had an STD!"

His face sags in dismay. "That wasn't at all what I was thinking. Look, Britt, I'm no virgin. I've—but Luke helped me see it's not about our pasts. So yeah, I'm kind of … super-cautious. About people's hearts."

I blow a raspberry. "You think my kissing you meant I'm in love with you? Get a life, Will. You're not that hot. I just wanted a little … recreation."

I turn to go, but he catches my sleeve.

"I'm glad you said that," he says. "Because when it comes to kissing and … where it can lead, people can be in very different places. Emotionally, I mean."

"You may as well spit it out. It's obvious you don't like sex."

"Don't put words in my mouth. I've hurt people, Britt. One girl I went with never heard a true word from me. So, for starters, these days I wouldn't even kiss someone outside a relationship. I want to be careful what I start."

I recoil, stung. "Too bad whoever raped Kara didn't feel that way," I retort. "Any sane person would have gotten rid of that … thing in her belly."

His eyes flare wide, but he stays calm. "I just want to be careful," he says again and gazes at me intently. "Can you understand that at all?"

Suddenly I'm uncertain. I mean, every teen mag teaches us to flaunt our bods and make ourselves as sexy as possible. But do teen guys raging with hormones really need extra temptation? My run-ins with Jeff Cox and Benny sure weren't positive, and some girls deal with even worse things. Like, their boyfriends take it for granted they should put out, in any number of ways. And at school we're always being warned about STDs, AIDS, and sex trafficking. TV shows are full of rape, incest, porn, and marriages ruined through affairs. Like the one Chelse's dad had, that her mom thinks Chelse doesn't know about—but of course she does. Not to mention unwanted pregnancies and hard decisions like the one Cassie made. *And regrets.* Finally, I remember my mother at the dinner table, nibbling a tiny rotisserie chicken bone and going on about some case she'd won. Almost always, the guy had undergone some sort of sexual abuse.

Seriously? The big picture, seen all at once, is sort of compelling. And inside, I'm deflating like a punctured balloon. For weeks I haven't been sure whether I've imagined a spark between Will and me. And now that I get why he won't kiss me … somehow, I wish he would.

My eyes smart. "I just—I thought you liked me." I sound like I'm practically begging.

He rubs his forehead. "That's what makes this … ah, forget it."

I rush from the room and collide with Jessica, who's clearly been eavesdropping. "He's all yours," I snap, and beat it out of there as her eyebrows shoot up.

It never would have worked between Will and me anyway. Whoever he ends up with will have to be a saint.

And I'm no saint.

It's almost dark. But there's a steady stream of traffic, and I walk backward toward the road to the farm with my thumb out. A car slows, and I jog toward it. But on the way, I spot the familiar dark SUV in front of Rick's Bowling Bar. I wave the car past and go inside.

Manny's in the back by the bar, his beefy pal on one side and an empty stool on the other. I head toward them.

"Hey." I'm a bit unnerved by my boldness.

He swivels his stool and grins, the frog transformed into a prince again. Without a word he takes my wrist and escorts me out a rear exit to a parking lot. I stumble on the uneven pavement, and have barely regained my balance when he pulls me around to face him, grabbing my other hand, too. He swings my arms from side to side.

"Where've you been? I've missed you, lil' peach," he says.

I wince. Benny called me peach, too. I guess it comes from having coppery hair and a pale complexion. But it's nice *someone* wants me, even if this is all I deserve. Manny pulls me near and I go soft against him, ready to surrender at last to his incredible magnetism and the dizzying scent of patchouli. His lips are beautiful, red and full. He plants his mouth on mine, I kiss him back, and—

"*Ugh.*" I push him away and wipe my mouth. "You taste like an ashtray."

Those amber eyes narrow to slits. "Do I. Lemme guess, Angel Boy smells of peppermint and holy water."

His tone is nasty, and I hoist my knapsack. My blue wallet falls out, fat with my wages from Luke. Manny swoops to retrieve the wallet, but holds it away from me.

"Look, I didn't mean to offend you," I say. "I'm … sorry. But why do you hate Will?" *Maybe I'll grab my money.*

He sneers. "We grew up in the same pigsty. I even saved his life once. Now, I don't exist."

"But what if—"

A violent jerk of his head warns me to stop. "Now for what you really came for." He hefts the wallet as if he's guessing its weight.

"Yes," I whisper, though actually I'm not sure why I've come. I only happened to see his car. But which *is* more important, pills or hugs? And do I want affection from a drug dealer? *I shouldn't have dissed his breath.*

He opens my wallet. "Free ride's over. These babies cost, unless you'd care for some smack? It's cheaper."

"Huh?"

"Heroin, baby girl."

What? "No!" I say. "I'm no junkie, I just—"

"Yeah, right." His mouth twists again while he counts out a few bills. He jerks his head at Z, who's emerged silently from the shrubbery bordering the parking lot and must have seen my reaction to the kiss. I flush. No wonder Manny's insulted. His goons idolize him. Z extends a baggie toward me with about ten more pills. No need to hide them; no one's watching. But his sleeve falls back, revealing purplish needle tracks along his gaunt forearm. Shocked, I raise my eyes to his. They're empty, hopeless.

I've never heard him utter a word.

"What's Z short for?" I ask on impulse. "Is your name Zachary?"

No answer. Manny gives me a grudging look. Somehow, I've gained an advantage.

"Zany?" I say. "Zebra? Zodiac? Oh, wait—Zombie!"

Instantly I'm sorry. Manny barks with laughter, and Z flushes crimson.

"Good guess." The sorcerer drops my wallet into my knapsack. "But it's 'Zero.' Which is how many brain cells his father said he had. At least according to his brother."

"Brother?"

Manny's losing interest. "Yeah. You know him. Our third man."

My gaze shoots to the unfortunate Z. "Buck? Is your *brother?*"

"Half," Manny answers for his pal again, impatient now. "Same dad. And they didn't even know 'til a couple of weeks ago," he adds with relish. He reaches out, almost reluctantly, and cups the back of my neck beneath my hair. His thumb moves against my scalp, caressing it. But then he scowls and mutters something, how I remind him of … I don't catch the rest, but suddenly he pinches my neck. Hard. I yelp and twist away. Manny jerks his head at Z, and the two fade into the night.

Smarting, I slug down a pill with an inch of water from my water bottle and start the trek to Cassie's. If only I had her bike. But I duck into the shadows when Luke's truck, Will's Escort, and a few other cars trundle along the main drag from the church. *They're holy rollers,* I remind myself. Even their exhaust fumes seem smug and sanctified, like a priest's incense.

Well, I'm not holy *or* worried about being a drug addict. The amounts I'm doing are way too small. But I don't fit anywhere. Not with these believers, not with the lowlifes … above all, not in the home I came from.

I'm rootless and without purpose, like a dust speck in the moonlight. Where the earth's concerned, I might as well never have been born.

22

I'm seated in the front row of a courtroom. Kara sniffles on the witness stand. At the judge's bench, robed in black, presides ... my mother. There's no one else in the room.

"Isn't it true," Judge Agatha intones, "that your previous ... lifestyle ... included a premarital affair with this ... gentleman?" Her tone drips sarcasm.

"It was a mistake," Kara pleads. "He wasn't who I thought he was."

The judge raps her gavel, clearly enjoying herself. "Answer the question."

A pause. "Yes." The witness bows her head.

Judge Agatha leans back and clasps her hands across her middle. "Well, silly girl, I don't know why you were surprised. It's not rape when a man avails himself of a privilege freely granted." She leans forward, raps the gavel. "Case dismissed. Prosecution, you may leave the witness stand. Have a tissue, it's on the court."

While Kara sobs, I jump over the low wall between the bench and the gallery and rush to my mother. I tug her sleeve and she turns to me, her expression chilly. Then her lips curve, and she laughs aloud.

"Look who's here. A half-pint judge."

I look down. I'm wearing a robe too. But mine is white, and I lift my chin.

"Mom ... you're a respected judge with a great reputation," I say. "But you're wrong about Kara. She wasn't asking for it like you said, Mom, she was engaged, to someone better—"

"Ridiculous!" my mother snaps. "The young man in question has a promising career ahead of him. He even plays lacrosse." She hurls her gavel at a wall, only somehow it changes to an ax and the blade embeds itself in the plaster. She faces me, her eyes grown huge and her teeth jagged like sabers.

I scream and wake in my bed at Cassie's.

Another nightmare. I sip from the water glass Cassie always leaves by my bed, my thoughts jumbled. Judge Agatha *would* blame Kara for getting pregnant. That's her M.O. But I couldn't have pictured her shredding a rape victim before a jury, much less adding insult to injury by praising an attacker. Yet she wins so many cases that some variation of my nightmare must have been enacted dozens—no, hundreds—of times in her legal career.

Her nerves must be made of steel. How else could she live with herself? I shudder and bury my head in my pillow.

My father calls all the time now, probably feeling guilty about being in New York so long. Despite my suspicions about his intentions, he did say just a few days. And it's already been a week. Maybe he really was roped into some construction project, or maybe he's worried about money now that my mother's not pulling in her usual fees. I talk to him once, but he's so vague when I ask questions that I'm annoyed and decide to give myself the day off from visiting the hospital *and* the barn. Everyone else takes Sunday off, so why shouldn't I?

After church, Cassie and I have deli sandwiches at the farmhouse. A chef, Priscilla is not. But it's a decent lunch, and the first time I've seen Will with both his sisters. He keeps mussing Kara's cloud of black hair, which she pretends annoys her, and Meghan stuffs potato chips inside the neck of his shirt until he growls and chases her as if he's a bear. But then he grabs her and hugs her. They all obviously adore each other. If I had a sister or brother, would we be like this? Or would we have figured every man for himself, like Buck and Z, as we navigated the shoals and reefs in the Warner household? I can't say.

Will meets my eyes a couple of times during lunch, but doesn't say anything just to me. I've barely seen him since the night we argued, and have no idea if he's working overtime as Luke said or hanging out with Jessica. I gave her the go-ahead at the bowling alley, not that I own him or am the grand puppeteer. The longer I live, the less control I seem to have over anything, including myself. Although I'm pleased to have discovered that Manny's pills work just as well as a sleep aid as a daytime escape. My nightmares aren't happening quite so often.

Monday afternoon, I'm slouched on the couch surfing Cassie's limited channels when she hurries in from work. She drops her purse on the coffee table and glances at the TV.

"Did you read to your mom today?" she says.

"Yeah."

"And?"

I yawn, stretch, hit Mute. "It was all about her career."

Her gaze is level and unyielding.

Why hide it? I sigh. "So, I skipped ahead … to where she found out she was pregnant."

"Oh!" Cassie perches on the edge of the couch. On my toes, actually, which I slide away, but she's so excited she doesn't even notice. "You're an only child, right?" she chirps. "So, you must've passed the part where—" She stops when she sees my expression. "What?"

"She wasn't too happy." I don't share my mother's exact words: "I was livid and in despair." I'd slammed the journal shut, my insides churning.

"Oh." A quieter "oh." Cassie chews her bottom lip, her snaggletooth showing. Funny, it doesn't bother me anymore. A crooked tooth is just part of who she is, the way she wears T-shirts and leggings when she's not waitressing, I couldn't picture her any different.

"Well, probably that was just at first," she says. "What woman wouldn't love an adorable baby girl, once she got used to the idea?"

"Not me. I ha—I don't care for babies."

She blinks. "Really? You're young, though. You can't have known many. They're awfully cute, once those newborn wrinkles fill out. Your baby pictures must have been adorable. I bet you were a little petunia."

I don't answer. She's just jollying me, to cover an awkward moment.

"Speaking of which, guess what?" she plunges on. "Mrs. Marino's hired me to cater the family reunion she's always talking about. It's on Labor Day weekend."

"Um … great. Is there a connection?" Though I'm glad to change the subject.

Cassie considers, then reaches into a stack of magazines in a basket on the floor. She pulls out a sheaf of papers I recognize: computer-printed photos of little girls,

Middle Eastern-looking, maybe five or six years of age. On top is the photo that fell off her desk the night I arrived. The one she tried to hide.

I leaf through the images. They're all similar, with huge brown eyes, corkscrew curls, and, okay, achingly vulnerable expressions. But ... "Who are they? Why are they all wearing the same pink dress?"

"Isn't it the saddest thing you ever saw? I guess it's the only nice clothing the orphanage has," Cassie says calmly, as if she's not dropping a bomb. "Some of the girls are refugees, some lost their parents to terrorism or various wars ... I'm thinking of adopting one of them, Britt." She tucks a strand of hair behind her ear, suddenly shy. "I've got a lot of ... love to give, and I can't imagine anything more worthwhile than to be a little one's comfort. To be a—" Cassie clears her throat. "A mommy."

Mommy? When I was four, my mother took me to play on the Alice in Wonderland statue in Central Park in Manhattan. It was large, bronze, and crawling with kids. I clambered from toadstool to toadstool, avoiding the Mad Hatter. His teeth were scary, and so was the creepy White Rabbit. At last I reached Alice's lap, stood to grab somewhere higher for balance, reached out my arm to wave ... but where was Mommy? I slid to the ground, bumping against toadstools and skinning my knee, and took off down the crowded promenade in a panic.

She wasn't anywhere. I wandered through the park, sniffling and trying to imagine living the rest of my life without her. If I never saw her again, how would I live? Who would feed me? Terrified, I forced myself to approach some old men on a bench, clutching their canes between their knees as if they were riding a carousel.

"I c–can't find my mommy," I said, which may have been my first stutter.

They peered at me. "What does she look like, little girl?" one rasped.

"She's beautiful."

The geezers exchanged skeptical glances, and I knew what they were thinking: all little girls think their mother is pretty. "Everyone says so," I insisted, and one guy with a narrow jaw and tweed cap tapped his chin.

"Well, let's see—" he began.

But a big bald guy with dark brown glasses interrupted, "Is that your mommy there, darlin'?" and we all snapped our heads around to look.

She bore down on us like a thundercloud, her briefcase banging against her stockinged knee. At her heels huffed a tall, distinguished old man, his suit jacket flapping.

"Mommy!" I threw myself at her knees.

She stooped. Hissed "Not now" right into my ear, so close I felt her warm breath, and snapped straight into Public Mommy mode. "Why didn't you stay by the Alice statue like I told you? I'm not done!" She grimaced a smile at the men on the bench, and briefly pressed the arm of the gentleman with her. "Judge, you're absolutely right …." As they set off, her free hand flapped hard behind her, motioning me to fall into line like a little duckling following its mama.

Now I pull an afghan off Cassie's sofa and spread it on my lap. "Some people shouldn't have kids," I mutter.

A hurt expression crosses her face. "True," she says humbly. "If I do this, I'll ask for lots of prayer."

"For Pete's sake, Cassie, I didn't mean you. What were you saying?"

Her eyes brighten. "Oh! If I do apply, I'll need to earn more than just what the diner pays." She wrinkles her nose. "It's one of those times a degree would come in handy. I'm so tickled Will's going to college. He wants to study forestry, did he tell you? But if I do a good job on this reunion, Mrs. Marino will tell her friends, and they might hire me, too. I don't mean to brag, but people say I'm a decent cook—"

"You're a wonderful cook," I say absentmindedly, my mind leaping ahead. "Maybe … I mean, you've taught me to chop stuff. I could help, if I'm still here. My dad seems to have vanished."

She clasps her hands. "Would you? Don't worry, he'll be back. But I'd love that, if you've got time between visiting your mom and doing the barn. You're a busy girl these days!"

"Yeah." But something's niggling me. "Cassie, where'd those pictures come from? You don't have internet."

"That's right," she agrees. "But Priscilla and Luke do. And they don't mind—"

"Oh."

Ever-sensitive, she peers at me. "What?"

"Just … I wouldn't ask them. I'm not sure Priscilla likes me."

"Don't worry, it's not you," she assures me. "Priscilla's background was difficult—though you've probably guessed from their place that her family wasn't poor. She's actually from—anyway, she can be a bit gruff, but inside, she's got—"

"A heart of gold," I finish. Cassie's so predictable, never judging anyone. And it's weird if Priscilla and I have something in common. Money is no hedge against dysfunction, that's for sure.

My hostess smiles. "Yes, in fact. She does. But Priscilla's a work in progress, like the rest of us, and she's warmed up a lot from when I first knew her. But I was going to say, I often stop by the library. They have internet and a color printer."

"Oh." I want to kick myself. Why didn't I think of that? I could have been watching YouTube videos all along. "Can I go with you sometime? I've missed—I'd love to check some stuff online."

Cassie tilts her head, her expression puzzled. "Sure. Mostly I stop on my way to or from work, but … we'll work it out."

"That'd be great." *A whole month of Angora Flatline to catch up on.* I cross my fingers, hoping my Aussie guru isn't taking a summer break. She tends to post a couple of videos a week. But if Cassie's going to alter her routine for me … "Is there anything I can do for you, Cassie?" I say. My mother would leap out of her coma in shock if she heard me.

"Thanks, but not unless you can crochet." Cassie gestures toward the incomplete blanket on the coffee table. "Kara's keeping her baby, and the shower's this Saturday. I've got to finish this!"

"She's having a *shower?* But she's not even marr—"

"Babies need things," Cassie says firmly, and stands up. "Time to start dinner. Do you like pork chops? With rice and buttered carrots, and I made a spinach salad."

"Huh? Sure." A million thoughts swirl through my brain, but one looms large: if my mother had a baby shower too, maybe it's in the journal.

I'll find out in the morning.

23

My mother's silvery blonde hair gleams under my last stroke, and I set the brush on the nightstand. "There. You're still beautiful. Which matters to you, I know. And I guess I'll go ahead and say, I've been doing something you wouldn't approve of: cleaning stalls. *Horse* stalls. So now you know, maybe. But now we're going to read this journal, because—never mind."

I settle back into my chair and open the journal. "Okay, you freaked when you realized you were pregnant. Got that, loud and clear. It was kind of hurtful, actually, so I'll skip ahead … here we go." I read aloud: "Finally, following endless go-rounds without making any progress, Steven and I … made a deal."

Her voice takes over in my mind. "He'd raise the baby …"

I almost drop the journal. "… and I wouldn't have to lift a finger. Ever, until it's of age. I would be a hundred percent free to focus on my career."

"What?" I grab my cell and hit the three on Auto-Dial so hard that I might have damaged the button.

"Steven Warner," he answers, but the jackhammering in the background drowns him out. *He did go to work.* My eyes sting unexpectedly.

I raise my voice. "I'm with Mom, reading her journal."

"What? Britt? Talk louder, I can't—"

"Sharonda gave me Mom's journal!" I shout just as a door slams on his end and the hammering stops.

"Ah, shoot." His voice is close in my ear now, and I picture him rubbing the bridge of his nose in the construction trailer. I'd like to claw him right through the phone.

"Okay, what were you saying?"

"She didn't want to raise her own kid."

He makes a noise, and I barge on. "She always said, 'That's not part of the deal, Steven.' But I didn't dream it was—" I swallow hard. "A real deal. I mean, she wanted nothing to do with her own baby?"

Another sigh. "Ah, Britt. It wasn't personal," he says. Same thing Cassie said about Priscilla acting frosty, except that was easier to accept. A *lot* easier, because Priscilla isn't important to me. "Your mom was crazy to make partner in those days—"

"And a baby would be in the way." I glare at my comatose mother. "So you made a bargain. You promised to do every single bit of child care—feeding, changing, burping, and everything involved in raising a kid—for eighteen years? *Seriously?*"

"It was no problem. I didn't mind."

"Why? For some wifey perks? Big house, fancy car, maybe some jewelry?" I practically hear him rub the face of his Rolex. It's one of his prized possessions, and he's always cleaning the crystal. Although normally he's not materialistic, just more of a dreamer. I barrel on. "You know what, Dad? At least Mom was honest about what she wanted. Oh wait, I meant what she *didn't* want. Me."

I punch End on my cell phone and head for the door. But as I round the foot of the bed, I have the odd sense of being watched. I spin around; my mother's eyes are closed. It's creepy. But if she did hear? She spoke her piece in the journal. I should be allowed to reply.

At a water cooler in the corridor, I check to make sure I'm alone and reach for one of Manny's pills. I feel numb, the way I did last year when I sprained my ankle running. It swelled up right away, but between the ice and ibuprofen, it hardly hurt. The pain came later.

As it will today. Taking this pill is the sane thing to do.

For three days, I stay away from the hospital. To see either of my parents would put me over the edge. Instead, I work at the barn, arriving early each day so I can be by myself. One morning, I arrive just as it's getting light, and realize that sunrise here seems to descend on the mountaintops from above. And at night, the sunset disappears the same way, going up. One more topsy-turvy thing about Vermont, but it's kind of cool.

I also spot Luke while he works with Joy—no major change there, unfortunately—and help Cassie experiment with recipes for her catering job. She's determined to use lots of apples, since there are orchards right near here and she's friendly with some of the owners. I suggested she check out the menu at the upscale-looking bistro on the main road. Maybe get some ideas. But she just says Mrs. Marino wants old-fashioned cooking, with an Italian flair. Well, I tried.

I'm still taking Manny's pills to help me sleep. When Cassie drops me at the hospital Friday morning, five weeks to the day since the accident, I only stay a little while and leave the journal in the nightstand drawer. Sharonda's not around, and I wish there were some way to let her know I was here. Somehow, her opinion of me has begun to matter.

Now I trek the familiar mile along Colchester Ave, from the hospital to downtown. But instead of moving on to the pedestrian mall, I cut south on Winooski, left on College … and there's the library. Like an addict released from rehab, I can't wait to indulge in half an hour, maybe even a whole one, of YouTube videos. With headphones, of course. But when I locate the Reference area, a scrawled sign informs me the computers are down.

Aaugghh. "Angora, where are you when I need you?" I wail, pacing past desks. The librarian clears her throat in an obvious hint. "Will these be back online today?" I ask her, gesturing toward the computers.

She purses her lips. "I can't say."

Miserable, I slouch toward the library entrance. I'd so longed for Angora's comforting wisdom. But suddenly, I knock my knuckles against my head. Once, twice. *Hello, dingbat.* What exactly am I expecting from a twenty-two-year-old Aussie, the secret of the universe? No, just a bunch of trivial tips and a cute sign-off. For all I know, Angora's just two steps ahead of me in figuring out life. Maybe the real secret to her cheerfulness is a low dose of Paxil or Zoloft, in which case I'm an idiot for idolizing her.

Talk about the blind leading the blind. I wander to the periodicals rack and flip through a teen mag. It, too, raises false hopes by making impossible promises. Can the editors guarantee that if I buy the raspberry lip gloss they're touting, Will definitely will want to kiss me? *No.* If anything, he'd probably run the other way. Some guys hate kissing lipstick, I've heard, and I'd bet Cassie's vintage knapsack, which I've become fond of, that he's one of them. He's a Nature Boy.

Not to mention, raspberry lip gloss can't do a thing for my guilty conscience.

I'm getting it. Mass media's a racket, a bunch of manipulation. If figuring this out means I'm growing up, it stinks. Better to stay young like Peter Pan, and keep my illusions. With a hollow feeling in my stomach that has nothing to do with actual hunger, I trudge back up Winooski. Soon I'm at Bennett's Apothecary, a block from the pedestrian mall where Cassie and I sipped lattes. Will's at his usual post behind the soda fountain, surprised but seemingly glad to see me.

"What are you doing in town?" he says. When I tell him, he reaches for a tall glass, the kind he uses for milkshakes. "Why don't you just use the South Hero library?"

I stare at him. "How was I supposed to—never mind." Cassie and I tend to shuttle between the island's main drag and the farm, including her cottage. No one told me South Hero had a branch library. But it's too late. I can't undo my light-bulb moment of toppling Angora from her pedestal. So I sit quietly, stewing while Will makes me a Bennett Supreme, that chocolate malted he invented. Within a few minutes, though, my mouth is watering too much to stay angry. Milkshakes must be one of life's most fundamental pleasures. As for Cassie's cooking, I'd try just about anything she made, whether I expected to like it or not. But even food and drink addictions are just short-term solutions for dulling pain. Does *anything* work long-term? Besides religion, obviously, which promises to carry you clear through eternity. *Right*. But a sense of déjà vu comes over me as I watch Will's fingers work the fountain toggles. How far we've traveled since we met; yet in some ways we've come full circle, to be strangers again.

He sets the milkshake in front of me. I sip the creaminess, eyeing him above the rim of the glass. This version's even yummier than the one he made me the day I landed on this doorstep, panting and bloody. I could swear I taste cardamom, but maybe it's my imagination.

"I guess I'm hoping … well, that we can still be friends," he says. "I care about you, Britt."

I snort, mostly for effect. "Friends have things in common. You and I live on separate planets."

He bites his lip, scribbles on an order pad, and slides it across the counter.

A waitress I am not, but even I can figure out that the scrawled letters N/C mean no charge. I peer at the pad again. The tiny letters where the order should go read, "I HEART U." But then I do a double take. There's no "I" or "U," I misread. It's just a heart—and then a cross. Separated by a comma.

Love, God.

These people don't give up.

24

Saturday morning again. I maneuver an overloaded wheelbarrow along the barn aisle. You'd think I'd have learned not to heap it so full, since I'll have to go back and sweep up the sodden, stinky shavings and manure clumps that fall off when I bump the tire over the outer threshold. Straining to keep the thing upright, I push it toward the low wall outside the barn, where dirty bedding gets dumped.

A few yards away in the round pen, Luke snaps the long green lead onto Joy's halter. Today's training is finished, thanks to Priscilla who's standing guard. She unhooks her cane from the top rail and hobbles toward me as I set down the wheelbarrow.

"Appreciate the help, Brittany."

"Thanks." Is she friendlier, or does she just seem different in light of what Cassie said? Either way, for the first time I feel sorry about Priscilla's bum hip.

Suddenly Joy squeals, and there's a series of staccato hoof beats. Priscilla and I spin around. Outside the pen, Joy rears to full height and claps her front hooves together.

Luke pulls her down with the lunge line and grabs her halter. She whinnies loudly, tossing her head and prancing in place, but finally allows him to lead her to the barn. Her hoofbeats resound against the wooden floor of the aisle.

My pulse is racing. "What was that?"

Priscilla shrugs. "Piece of paper? A leaf? The horse is nuts, but Luke's got to see it for himself. 'Scuse me."

She limps away. I empty the wheelbarrow over the low wall, onto a pile of shavings whose top is level with the ground at my feet. It's a balancing act not to dump myself, too. Inside the barn, a stall door rumbles shut. Then Luke appears, mopping his neck with a bandanna.

I pull the wheelbarrow away from the wall. "Is she *any* better, Luke?"

He hesitates. "No. But I believe in second chances, so I won't decide anything in a hurry." His smile is probably meant to reassure me, but fails. "Hey, how's your mom? I give you a lot of credit, visiting her each day. Can't be easy."

"Um … the same." He means her coma, not the sad history revealed in the journal pages. I don't want to talk about either. "So, I hear your career as a horse trainer's about to end," I blurt.

Luke shoots me a funny look. "It is?"

Oops. "I thought—I mean, Will said something about you becoming a pastor?" My face feels hot.

To my surprise he takes my empty wheelbarrow and tips it up against the barn wall, so it won't collect water. Then he says, "Got a few minutes? I've got a chore to do. We can talk while we do it." He heads down a path to below the retaining wall, and I follow. There, almost invisible beneath the mass of dirty shavings, is a large, rusty truck. *No wonder the pile never overflows.* We climb in, and he revs the engine up a trail into the woods. I hang on, teeth knocking, loving the sheer adventure of the ride. Fast-and-bumpy is my favorite speed.

"Will's right," he calls above the engine roar. "I'm taking courses online, studying to be a pastor. Pastor Dave's my mentor."

"Big switch from horse training," I yell back.

He grins and shifts gears as the trail steepens. "Not a total change. But thanks for not saying I'm crazy."

The trail levels out, and a few yards later widens into a clearing. In the center is a mountain, and I do mean mountain, of manure and used shavings. Luke does a K-turn with the truck and backs up.

"Ready?" he says.

"I guess." *We'll be shoveling for hours.*

To my surprise, he points to a lever. I pull it. The bed of the truck rises with a grinding shriek, and masses of dirty shavings tumble onto the pile behind us. Obviously, I don't even know a dump truck when I see one. Still, it's kind of fun to see it work at close range—though I could use a clothespin for my nose as the whole forest now smells sharp and sour. He lowers the truck bed, drives a few yards, cuts the engine. The silence rings in my ears, 'til some brave little bird gives an experimental tweet. Probably checking his hearing.

Luke shifts to face me. "The thing is, I love training horses. The good, the bad, the in-betweens … Their backgrounds and problems can be very different, but underneath, every one of them needs the same thing."

He pauses, waiting.

No reason not to oblige. "What's that?"

"A leader they can trust. It's at the very heart of natural horsemanship, providing what a horse needs most. And recently I've realized … it's the same with people."

Oh, no. "Luke, you gonna sermonize me?" I half-joke.

"Just a story. Okay?"

I nod, wary.

"One day I was having coffee at the diner, and Sergeant Thompson—you've met him, I think—" He checks to be sure I'm listening. I nod. "Anyway, he told me about some kids he'd come across. The Grant family's home had just been destroyed in a fire, and their mom, well, wasn't considered a fit parent."

"*Oh.* You mean Will, and—"

"Yep. Two years ago. Kara was still a minor, and Meghan only six. So Priscilla and I powwowed and did what we needed to, went through the proper channels to become foster parents, so we could take the girls. When they were settled, I visited Will at his 'school,'"—he air quotes—"a juvenile detention center. And Brittany, you wouldn't believe it."

What? They were brain-dead junkies? Buried in tattoos, deaf by heavy metal?

Luke hesitates. Then he pulls a wallet from his back pocket, extracts a photo, and holds it out. I peer at it, and do a double take. It's Will, but not the boy I know. This version is skinny and grim, with a beaded leather headband, shoulder-length dirty hair, and a bunch of earrings climbing his earlobe like ants at a picnic. His enameled mosaic eyes are flat and shadowed.

And haunted. I reach for the picture automatically, unable to look away. He reminds me of … Benny. And … myself. How I feel inside. It's terrifying.

"He looks miserable," I say finally.

"He was lost." Luke holds the wallet open, waiting, but I study the photo again. I hardly believe this is the same person as the fresh-faced, glowing picture of health I know. *What happened to make him like that? Even more important, what brought him to where he is today?*

"I saw a lot of kids there," Luke says quietly. "And got to talk with a fair number of them. One thing stood out above all."

He pauses. I have no idea what he's about to say.

"Not a one of 'em had a decent relationship with his dad. So, Priscilla and I knew we had our work cut out for us."

"To reform the reform school?"

He acknowledges this with a half-smile, then turns serious again. "No. We want Narrowgate to be an alternative to juvie and the opiates killing our young people. One that will help heal their emotional wounds."

I take a last peek at the former Will's lifeless eyes and hand Luke the photo. "So that's why you built—"

"The new bunkhouse, yes. We'll give them a home, teach them about horses … and if we do it right, they'll get a taste of unconditional, fatherly love. As we were able to do with Will. But it won't be easy, and I keep that photo handy for when the going gets tough. To remind myself how important the work is. Especially since … well, I don't know if you're aware, but Priscilla can't have kids. So, this is it for us."

I barely register his last words. *Emotional wounds.* That I can relate to. But … *unconditional, fatherly love.* What would that be like? "I always wanted a horse," I mumble, but Luke doesn't hear.

"… impossible to make it happen this year. Priscilla needs hip surgery. That'll happen in the fall, but next year—hey, I *am* bending your ear." He tilts his head and grins, and I can't help but smile back. Though inside, an ache is rising in me. I push it down.

"It's okay, I guess. If you're gonna be a pastor." For the first time, I feel shy with him. "Though you're not exactly—"

"—there yet. I know, check out my pulpit." He waves at the manure heap and beams, then reaches for the ignition and starts the engine.

Anguish overwhelms me. "Luke!" I blurt out above the roar. "Do you think what happened to my mother was maybe a punishment? For her, or … someone?"

He takes a deep breath and exhales. "I don't believe so, Brittany." A pause, while he gathers his thoughts. "Things like this are always difficult. But it's not for me to point a finger at your mom or anyone else about that accident, no matter how it happened, 'cause no one understands the purpose behind a trial. It's always good, though, even if—well, take the willow by Cassie's cottage, that you got so upset about. Remember?"

I wince at the memory, but manage a brief nod. Exploding at Sandro for chain sawing a tree wasn't my finest moment, and I've had more than my share this summer—but fortunately he doesn't notice my discomfort.

"That pruning we did saved its life. A lot of times, what we go through changes us in ways we don't understand until later. But if we accept it, if we walk in faith in a loving God … well, it's hard. That's why it's called the narrow gate. Few make it through." He gives me a penetrating look. "Britt … we're all aware this has been harder on you than on your mom."

My throat tightens. *He gets it.*

"Speaking of which, if you're going to Kara's shower later—"

"I know, Luke. I need a shower myself."

"Didn't mean that. I meant to say, maybe you … heck, I just hope you'll be nice to Meghan."

His tone is mild, but the rebuke unmistakable. My body tenses. "W–what did she say?"

"Not a word. But she's sensitive … and I'm sure you've noticed, she adores you."

"Yeah, well, I'm not exactly cut out to be a nanny."

"Someone overheard you speaking harshly to her," Luke says gently. "At Cassie's picnic. And I'm not asking you to be her caregiver. Only to dial it back, is all, when you're around her. Meghan's only eight, and she's been through a lot."

My face is so hot, it must be beet red. But in a blink, my shame morphs into resentment. The kid was out of line that day. And today, Luke and I were having an okay time. He was talking to me almost like I was a friend. Why did some busybody have to ruin it?

We bump back down the trail and out of the woods in silence, with me stewing quietly. He parks by the barn and cuts the engine. Hoofbeats thud from the riding ring. Jessica and Captain are practicing jumps again.

Luke climbs out of the truck and rounds the hood to stand before me. I open the passenger door and slide to the ground.

"One thing about you people bugs me," I say.

His eyebrows shoot up. "Only one?" Joking, like my father. I slam the truck door shut and face him.

"You take everything so blinkin' seriously. You know what, Luke? In a hundred years, none of this'll matter."

Those gray eyes darken. "Don't *ever* think your life doesn't matter, Brittany Warner," he says, stern as the father I've never exactly had. "Whoever told you that? It's a lie."

I look down at the gravel by my feet. No way can I tell Luke I invented that so-called lie myself, to help me cope. Suddenly I crave the simple comforts of Angora Flatline. How much easier it is to splash seltzer on a stained comforter than to wrestle with one's entire messed-up existence.

Stepping backward, I meet his gaze briefly. "Thanks for the ride, Luke. I'd better get going if I'm going to make it to that shower."

He tips his cowboy hat in a grave, courtly gesture. His gray eyes radiate sincerity. This guy may be the first real gentleman I've ever known, even if he is a horse trainer. No wonder Will practically worships him.

If I believed in God, I'd go to your church, I almost blurt. Instead, I spin away, my eyes stinging, and sprint down the lane toward Cassie's cottage.

25

Cassie left early to help set up the shower, so Will drives me. He pulls to the curb by the church fellowship hall. Peals of laughter burst through the open door.

"I really, really don't want to be here," I mutter.

"Well, no one's twist—"

"Yeah, right." I climb out of the car and up a short flight of stairs toward the open doorway. My feet seem weighted with bricks.

Meghan runs out, her face split in a grin. "I'm going to learn to change a diaper! And the baby will call me Auntie Meg!"

I scowl. Will's still at the curb, his car windows open. But his attention's fixed on a guy hanging around down the block, too far away for me to recognize. Did Luke tell him how I've been treating his baby sister? She disturbs me, in a way I can't put my finger on.

"Hey, Meghan." I pitch my voice low. "How come you keep being nice to me when I'm, um, not always to you?"

Will's got one dimple, she has two. Even with her scarred cheek, they're—I hate to admit—endearing. Like his.

"I forgive you," she says. "So why shouldn't I?"

"You forgive me," I repeat. "Why?"

She squints and splays her hands in a sort of shrug. "It feels yucky not to."

Two millennia after the crucifixion, a little kid sums up the Christian faith better than anyone I've ever heard. Lives it, too. They all do, actually—Cassie, Will, Luke. They give and give and give with their hearts in their hands, even if Will does sometimes come across like he knows it all. So for once, I have no retort.

Jessica comes outside and offers me a cup of punch. Oohs and aahs burst from inside. Ignoring her outstretched hand, I peer past her and take in the scene.

Kara sits in an easy chair, surrounded by balloons, streamers, and piles of wrapped gifts. To one side, Priscilla as an unlikely lady-in-waiting holds the next present to be opened. On the other, Cassie's recording who gave what on a steno pad. She's also monitoring the five banquet tables crowded with women of all ages, laughing and talking. It's impressive multitasking, but I guess waitressing has sharpened her skills. By the kitchen door, three more tables groan under the weight of enough goodies to host a banquet. Salads, pastas, foil pans brimming with meatballs and chicken wings, a carved watermelon heaped with fruit salad and feta cheese, that I'd watched Cassie construct with painstaking care in her kitchen ... and amidst it all, a humongous sheet cake covered with pink writing. The cake is decorated to resemble a book, so I'm guessing the words are from the Bible. These people probably engrave verses on their shower curtains.

"The cake says 'Babies are a blessing.'" Meghan has followed my glance.

Yep. Not that I agree.

More applause, more laughter as Kara lifts a tiny outfit, beaming. I want to gag. I spin around, push past Jessica and Meghan, and take the half-flight of stairs to the street in two flying leaps. Behind me, Jessica calls my name and Meghan wails as I run alongside Will's car, which is just pulling away. I rap on the window. He brakes with a screech of tires, and I whip open the door and jump in.

"Take me to Cassie's. *Please*," I say.

"Why? What's wrong?"

Here's the thing. At school we learned that a magnifying glass used to focus the sun's rays onto a leaf makes it burst into flame. These days, I am a dry and brittle leaf. In a single moment, the terror, guilt, and rage that's built up within me during the past few weeks contracts to a point under the lens of all the pressure ... and ignites.

I erupt at him. "I'm sick of everyone pretending this is fine. That baby's sire—I won't say father—was a rapist. Its whole life is a m-mistake. But it'll be spoiled rotten, 'cause you people can't tell gold from ... m–mud. Meanwhile—" I break off.

Will squints at me. "Why would it bother you to see a baby be loved? You almost sound ... jealous."

My throat aches, and I look away. "Is it too much to ask for a mother to want you?" I snap. *"Don't answer."*

"Whoa. Okay, got it." He puts on the blinker, checks his side mirror, and pulls into the street. "But I'm not leaving you, so where do you want to go?"

In the end, we get ice cream cones. Butter pecan for me, chocolate for Will. His treat. I don't want to be out in public, even though there's no danger I'd be reduced to tears, so we go back to Cassie's and hunker shoulder to shoulder on the bench on her shoreline. *By* her willow—I can't say under; it's still stubby as a cactus. Though to my surprise, I spot some tiny shoots with bitty green ends.

Will follows my glance. "It'll grow back, like Luke said. Stronger than ever. And right there"—he gestures to the pooling water by the rocks at our feet—"schools of minnows will enjoy the shade."

I snort. "Talk about wishful thinking."

"You'll see." He takes out a knife and whittles at a tiny cross identical to the one hanging from his neck. I attempt to draw with a stick on a rock, but it doesn't leave a mark the way our charred marshmallow skewers did. *Duh.* I toss the stick in the lake. A wave catches it, making it bob and jostle between two rocks, trapped.

Like me.

Just when I've figured we're not going to talk—which suits me fine, it's a beautiful day to just sit by the water—Will says, "So. What was that about your mom?"

Um. "Can't we just forget what I said?"

"Uh, no."

I sigh. "It was in her journal. All she ever wanted was to be a super-successful lawyer, and then later she upped it to being a judge. I have no clue why she even got married or had me. She must have changed her mind somewhere along the line. But it stinks, to choose a career over your own kid."

"Sure does. Or alcohol, like my mom did. Not that she meant to, but it still hurt. When Kara and I were young she was the greatest, always laughing and goofing around." He shrugs. "Then Meghan was born, and my dad left."

That makes me wince. "Yeah. So ... Kara's going to raise that baby herself? At the least, she should do a paternity test—"

"She never reported what happened, remember? That's the last thing she needs. The whole thing's a mess. Better to let sleeping dogs lie."

Ugh. I hate to admit it, but I see his point.

He hesitates. "It's funny, though ... I could have sworn I saw Shawn back there outside the shower. I called to him, but he took off."

"Aren't you mad at him? He didn't believe Kara."

Will shakes his head. "There's plenty of blame to go around."

I breathe deeply. It's quiet here, the ripple of water on pebbles interrupted only by the scrape of Will's knife on wood and a tuneless whistling through his teeth. But my brain won't stop.

"So ... when are you going to tell me about your beef with Manny?" I say finally.

The knife slips. Will makes a small sound and brings a bloody finger to his lips. For a split second I consider apologizing, but this wasn't my fault. I wait.

"Are you sure you want to know this? It's not ... pretty," he says.

"I think I know anyway. Luke said—"

"He wouldn't have told you everything. But maybe it'll help you understand—" He hesitates. Then words tumble out as if he's a bottle of seltzer that's been uncorked.

"When I was a kid, I adored Manny. We lived on

the same street in Burlington. And he was nicer then. His uncle took us fishing with bamboo rods we made ourselves, and Manny even pulled me from the water once when I fell in. But his home life was rotten. His dad was, well, a tyrant. He beat both boys. His brother ended up okay, but Manny … went bad."

"Like how?"

Will shrugs. "Stealing, mostly. At first."

"Alone?"

"Yeah … until he formed a gang. I was the youngest, so they always made me climb in the window to let them in. We hit homes, mostly, in affluent parts of the city and beyond."

His eyes cloud over, giving him a shadowed look. "I was a stooge." He takes the knife again and scrapes a curl of wood off his carving. "We were heading nowhere good, and I quit. But when I was fifteen, I … went back. And by then the jobs were bigger."

"Why?"

"When you're on that track, it's never enough. Especially for Manny. The night our house burned, we ripped off twenty grand worth of electronics."

I'd meant, why did he go back. Some sort of recognition resounds within me. *This is the key to Will, what lies beneath his perfect façade.*

Suddenly the knife and cross drop as he hunches over, elbows on his knees, his hands dangling. They look vulnerable, and I look down to keep myself from taking one in my own. It works; the pebbles at his feet are an audience of stone, oblivious to human pain.

"The truck took off, and we were making off on bikes—motorcycles—when the cops arrived. I was last, and—well, if you play with fire …" Abruptly he straightens and lifts his shirt front, careful not to get blood from his finger on the cloth. The soft flesh below his left ribcage is a roundish, puckered scar six inches wide. As I gape, horrified, he twists and lifts his shirt again, showing me an identical scar at the same place on his back.

Will's got a giant stitch through him. He's tufted front to back like a sofa cushion.

A wave of weakness sweeps through me, the way it always does at the sight of deformity. "What *happened?* Don't tell me, some cop shot you—"

"No. *No.*" He lowers his shirt and speaks to the air in front of him. "I mean yeah, I was shot, and by God's mercy the bullet passed through me. As you see. But it wasn't a cop. That's what you hear these days, but it wasn't."

"Then … a stray bullet. Like a crime show shoot-out."

He eyes me sideways. "Not a stray."

My stomach turns over. "No," I whisper.

His eyes are bleak. "Yeah. But there was no way to prove it, locked away in juvie. Of course, I wasn't exactly innocent. I should never have been there in the first place."

"So, you really were friends," I say slowly.

With a sideways motion, he scoops a handful of pebbles and flings them in the lake. Tiny dents like bullet holes pock the water's surface. "A long time ago. When pigs flew."

"But he *shot* you—"

"When you saw us in the diner, the night of your family's accident? It was the first time I'd seen Manny since I got out a year ago."

Every single thing about that night is etched in my memory forever, including their prickling animosity as they'd glared at each other.

"So now you hate him. And obviously it's mutual."

He shifts uncomfortably. "Yeah. But … there's something else. The night all this went down … was the same night I left Meghan alone with my mother. When she set the house on fire, and my little sister got burned."

My breath catches in my throat. *Of course.*

I look down. "Will." A drop of crimson blood stains the tiny cross between his feet.

His mouth twists as he retrieves the carving and studies it. "Blood on a cross. Says it all, doesn't it." He rubs the blood to a faint stain, then polishes the wood with his shirttail. Slow, exacting.

"What kind of wood is that?" I ask, in an effort to defuse the tension. "It's so pale and smooth."

"Basswood. Or linden. Also called the bee tree, because bees love it. You can hear them humming when the tree blooms. It's funny, on the outside the bark is ridged and crusty, but inside the wood is perfect for carving. Like it's waiting for someone to shape it."

"Wow, you know a lot about trees."

He scratches his neck. "Sort of. I've always dreamed of maybe becoming a park ranger. Vermont's covered in trees, over three billion of them. I love being outdoors, Britt. Couldn't see myself shut up in an office building."

"Like Johnny Appleseed."

He gives a wry smile. "I guess. But now … well, seeing Luke change course, and how he's affected my life, I'm thinking of doing something that would help delinquent kids."

"Like counseling? That would mean studying psychology."

"Yeah. I know it's a stretch. I mean, look where I've been." He tucks his shirttail back in. The cross lies loosely in his palm.

"Huh. Will … you believe that cross means you're forgiven, right?"

"I know it does."

"Well, I think there's someone *you* need to forgive."

He looks up, his beautiful enameled eyes suddenly anguished again. "I can't!" he bursts out. "Before God, Britt, I can't forgive Manny. We're supposed to love our enemies, but … it's hard."

That hadn't even occurred to me. "Yeah, I get that. But I didn't mean Manny."

"Oh. Then …?"

"Yourself, Will. You need to forgive yourself." And I watch, my heart twisting, as understanding dawns on that handsome face.

It takes one to know one. Not that I have any intention of taking my own advice.

Maybe Will and I aren't so different after all.

26

That evening, I sit cross-legged on my bed at Cassie's and hit auto-dial.

"'lo," my father says.

"I need the truth," I say. "What happened to the deal you made with Mom? Something must have. 'Cause you didn't raise me. She did."

"That you, Britt? Yeah, you're right about that—"

"Tell me she took one look at me, fell madly in love, was tempted to quit law ...." I swallow hard past the lump in my throat.

"Aw, Britt. You know your mom. The first week you were born, she was all over me about ... what was it ... oh, yeah. Topping and tailing."

"What?"

"It's babyspeak. How to wash a newborn without a bath. I did it wrong. Actually, I did everything wrong. According to Saint Agatha."

The skin on my arms prickles. He's never spoken about my mother like this. *He's so ... bitter. And why is his speech so slow, so heavy?*

"You gave up."

"More or lesh. I suppose."

I knew it. And was that a slur? "So, your part of the deal was to take care of me. But what was her part? What did she do for you?"

The unmistakable sound of liquid being poured. Ice cubes clink. I hear him gulp.

"It's so awful you've got to drink?" I hope my sarcasm hides my dismay. Is he still buying nips, or moved on to something more substantial? Pints, or even a fifth?

"Jus' make ever'thing worsh if I shay it," he says, definitely slurring now.

He's drunk. I grab my bed pillow and press it against my stomach to contain my urge to scream, cry, yell.

"That's impossible, Dad," I say coldly and hang up. My phone seems to blur, and I toss it onto the comforter. More than a phone call just ended: a relationship, my childhood, my whole view of the world. A lifetime ago, I held my mother's Prada bag out the car window, taunting her while she shrieked. *What was I doing?* In defying her, I'd felt I was fighting to survive, to escape from an all-powerful ogre. But she proved to be unexpectedly brittle … a straw woman, maybe broken now beyond repair.

My mother has been my enemy … but also, I realize now, my safety net. My father should never have allowed total strangers to care for his daughter. Even in a crisis. No matter what my parents' original deal was about me, it wouldn't have stood up in court. He's weak, powerless.

The life I knew is over. Maybe that blinkin' nosy sergeant will ferret out the truth, maybe not. Either way, I'm dangling off a cliff above a rocky coastline, with no rescuer in sight. It's a long drop to the water. The rocks at the bottom are hard and sharp, and the waves are curling upward, calling for blood.

Mine.

Another Sunday slips by. My father doesn't call, and for once Cassie doesn't try to entertain me. She's preoccupied with sorting through recipes for Mrs. Marino's family reunion and keeps questioning aloud whether having focaccia bites *and* assorted crostini is carb overkill, and whether Cajun deviled eggs would fit in at a quasi-Italian gathering. I tell her no, and yes. And assure her that cantaloupe chunks wrapped in prosciutto will be perfect. Cassie's trying her wings, and I want to support her. Not my usual M.O., but hey, the woman deserves a break.

The next afternoon I slip into the shadowy barn, carrying a carrot. Suddenly the peace is shattered by a rapid-fire series of noises: a horse squeals, a woman shrieks, hooves ring against wood. A stall door rumbles shut at the far end, and two silhouettes hurry toward me. It's Luke and a strange woman, rangy and maybe in her late thirties. Her face is distraught but she says, super-controlled, "Think it over, Luke. This situation won't improve. If anything, it will grow worse."

"We'll talk real soon, Susan," he says.

The woman ducks her chin at me and leaves the barn. Outside, a truck roars to life and rattles away.

"What happened?" I dread the answer.

Luke jerks his head toward Joy's stall at the end of the aisle. "Your favorite just reared on Doc Susan. Our vet. Who happens to be pregnant, though you can't tell yet. That little mare is too dangerous to have around, Britt. I'm real sorry."

A black cloud plumes inside me. "You said you'd give her a second chance."

"I have. And then some. But even with all the training, she's just getting worse. Almost every day she does something crazy, and today was … the limit. She endangered two lives back there, not just one. I hate to give up on any horse, but from what I've seen, Joy won't ever be safe for anyone to work with. Least of all, teens, which is our plan, and I won't jeopardize one of them. It'd be one thing if she were afraid of people. That I could handle. But this horse would mow you down right in the paddock if you let her."

"So … you'll sell her? Or give her away. But you'd never, you couldn't—" To my horror, my lips are trembling.

Luke's mouth compresses to a thin line. "I love horses, Britt, and it hurts me to see one gone so wrong. But in all conscience, I couldn't pass this animal on to a living soul. The margin of error in handling her is too narrow. She's an equine … psychopath. And when it comes to people or horses? People are more important. So yeah, I'm afraid the buck stops here."

"But you can't! Isn't there some other … expert—" I'm pleading, desperate, but Luke claps on his cowboy hat and cuts me off.

"Around here, that's me. I'm sorry."

It's the last straw. The tears I've stifled for a decade gush out. I sob, blubber, gulp. My eyes and nose stream tears and snot, my mouth goes square like a little kid's, my throat's a bunch of taut cords. But I don't care how it looks. I bend double, pressing my arms against my aching belly. Luke touches my shoulder tentatively. He means to comfort, but it's intolerable. I twitch, the way my mother always did when I tried to hug her. When I was small, I mean. Luke, being a sensitive adult, removes his hand.

"I'm sorry," he says again.

"So th–there's n-no hope?" I can't stop crying.

He shifts his feet. "I guess as a future pastor I'm bound to say, there's always hope when we pray."

Tears stream down my cheeks. "I can't. I don't know how."

He ducks into the barn office and brings out a fistful of tissues. I blow my nose.

"Just say the words. I've noticed young people's prayers seem to receive special attention," he says.

A pause. "I'll do it, then. But … alone."

He nods, presses my shoulder again, and leaves the barn. I walk down the aisle to Joy's stall. She gives me a look out of the corners of her eye and swiftly presents me with her hindquarters.

I turn back into the aisle and spot a bale of hay a few feet away. It's an odd place to pray, right where Luke chewed me out weeks ago for entering Joy's stall—but he didn't say to do it anywhere in particular. Who'd have dreamed a day would come when Brittany Warner, child of two atheists or agnostics or whatever my parents are, would agree to pray? About anything? Again, I'm embarrassed in front of my own self.

But it's Joy's last hope.

I drop onto the bale and clasp my hands. That doesn't seem enough, so I kneel on the gritty floor and lean my forearms on the bale, bits of hay poking my skin. And for the first time in my life, I ask a being who may not even exist to save the troubled little horse I've come to love. I even end with "Amen," feeling like a fraud but for once taking no chances.

On my way back to Cassie's cottage, it hits me. I've cried, and now prayed, for a horse that's not even mine. But not once have I done either for my own mother. Shame floods through me; my cheeks feel flaming hot. It's another point for the prosecution in the case against Brittany Warner, and I'm guilty as charged. But I'm tired. I can't carry my load any longer. I need help. When I reach Cassie's and she's not there, I stretch out on her couch under an afghan and am asleep within moments.

A beautiful goldfish swims in a round bowl. She has huge, expressive eyes, and orange chiffon fins and tail that sway gently. But the water is dirty. Mud and grit and tiny stones sift through the eddies and rest on the bottom. Barely above them, the fish pales, gasps, lists to one side.

Dying.

An arm reaches into the watery depths and lifts me out of the bowl—of course, I am the fish. I lie in someone's giant palm, my sides heaving, aware of somber multi-color eyes beneath a thatch of wheat-colored hair. The person gently deposits me into a larger bowl, full of crystalline water. I work my fins, water sweeps through my gills—oh, it's heaven to breathe! I right myself and swim around the bowl, exploring my new home.

What an odd dream, I think as I cut a lemon into wedges in Cassie's kitchen. But refreshing, and peaceful. The porch door opens, and Cassie comes in and sets her purse on the counter.

"Do I smell lemon? Are you making something? I figured we'd do burgers," she says. The "we" is because I've actually gotten into the habit of chopping a few veggies while Cassie tries recipes for her catering job. Mostly onions and garlic which, to my astonishment, form the backbone of almost every recipe she's using. And celery. I'd love a YouTube tip on how to stop onions from making me tear up. Labor Day's just two weeks away, and the way things are going, I might actually be here for her catering debut. Even my father would make sure I'm home for the beginning of school right after that, though … assuming he knows the date.

"Yeah, but I'm not making anything. It's just—my mother loves lemons. And the nurse said smells can help wake her." I trim the last lemon quarter.

"Oh, great!" Cassie beams. "For me, it'd be watermelon. Or any melon. I think God outdid himself creating cantaloupe and honeydew. When are you going?"

I sweep the lemon juice and pits into the trash and rinse my hands. Then I grab a baggie for the lemon quarters from one of her perfectly sliding drawers. "I meant to ride in with Will this afternoon, but I fell asleep. I had the weirdest dream, Cassie. But—everything's falling apart. One parent's a vegetable, the other a lush … and now Luke's going to put Joy down."

Her jaw falls open. Suddenly her cell phone rings, startling us both, and she answers it.

"Hey, Luke … oh, no. Oh, dear … yeah. Sure." She hangs up and lumbers toward me, wrapped in the afghan.

"Oh, Britt. I'm so sorry, sweetheart." My stomach tightens. *Cassie doesn't use endearments.* "That little mare, the one you like? She's off her feed. Luke thinks she may be getting colic."

The word is vaguely familiar. "What's that? Is it dangerous?"

"It's a bellyache, and it can be life-threatening, because horses can't vomit. If she can't work through it on her own, he'll have to call the vet."

My mind races. Luke must care a tiny bit about Joy if he wants to save her. Hope flares inside me. "Cassie, you think maybe that's why she was so bad today? If it is, Luke can't put her down!"

"Hm. I'd say Luke would consider the overall picture," Cassie says carefully. "This isn't the first time the horse has misbehaved, is it?"

The empty baggie creases against my fingernail. Once, twice, three times. The plastic was perfect, fresh from the factory. *What is wrong with Joy?*

When at last I look up, Cassie is gazing at me with such sympathy I can't stand it. I stuff the lemon wedges into the baggie and shove it into my knapsack.

"Know what, Cassie? I prayed for Joy. So much for that terrific idea."

She frowns and reaches for my hand. I step away, and her arm drops to her side. I feel a small, vicious satisfaction.

"You can be sure he heard," she says. "You've just got to trust him."

Right. I hoist my knapsack. "Could you drive me to the hospital?"

"Now?" She checks the clock, dismayed. "It's dinnertime."

"My mother's journal is there, and I've got to check something. And visit her. Don't worry, I'll eat something there. And Will's working tonight, I'll catch a ride back with him," I fib.

She sighs and picks up her keys. "All right. I guess. But promise you'll call if you miss him? Even in Vermont, hitchhiking's not safe."

I nod, to end the conversation. But I'm done coloring inside the lines.

27

The lemon wedge in my hand bumps my mother's nostril, leaving a wet smear. But I don't wipe it off, letting the aroma of the juice linger. A monitor beeps, and I glance over. A green line spikes. *Good.*

"You know I'm here, I'm pretty sure," I say softly. "Maybe even why. I'm going to read to you again ... but tonight we're going to backtrack, all the way to the gar-*bage* you spun about your career. Everything's falling apart for me now, the way it was for you, and I want—need—the truth about you and me."

I put away the lemon and wipe my fingers on my cutoffs. Then I settle myself and the journal on the bedside chair, my feet on the low rail, and page backwards.

"Okay, you became ambitious and made it to law school. Already dreaming about the Supreme Court, got that. So, here goes."

I read aloud:

"In September of my second year, I met an engineering student named Steven in the campus bookstore."

Again, my mother's voice takes over inside my head.

Steven who would become my husband, though I had no idea of that then. He'd arrived at the register with one book, I was staggering under a pile of legal tomes. So, he graciously let me go ahead of him—and invited me for coffee.

One thing led to another, and on Friday he took me to dinner. He loved my dress, which was half white, half black, and asked which side I liked best … I said white, but of course have always preferred black since it's best for blondes.

Anyway, Steven was a sympathetic listener, and within a few weeks we often shared a glass or two of wine at the end of a grueling day. But I was too ambitious to allow any romance.

If I'm honest, and what's the point of writing all this if I'm not, I was still smarting from what my college boyfriend Rob said when he broke up with me our senior year. He wanted to marry someone with a great big heart who craved lots of kids, and he felt that wasn't me.

He was right, of course, but—anyway, my second year of law school was hard.

What followed was even worse. The next year, my last, my favorite prof panned an article I'd written for *Law Review* ....

I lower the journal, feeling cheated. "That's all you've got to say about you and Dad?" A machine beeps in reply. I sigh and go on:

In a word, I thought I'd die. I was ready to quit law school and take some minimum-wage job, maybe counting bears at Yellowstone. Though you probably need a degree for that now, too. Anyway, Steven, wanting to cheer me up, persuaded me to go out that night. Our old-fashioned binge made my papa's tomfoolery look like lemonade in the park. We drank vodka, tequila shots, some gin—

"Grandpa Hugo was a lush?" I'm incredulous, though I realize now the journal had hinted at this. But again, there's no answer, so a moment later I read on:

By the end of the evening we were roaring drunk, and my hangover the next day was brutal. Never again, I decided once I recovered. My career, which of course I was not ready to give up, would be derailed. But I decided to show Prof Nichols how wrong he'd been: I'd graduate first in my class!

For the next few months, I stripped anything extraneous from my life, including most of the time I'd been spending with Steven. He wasn't happy, but it worked. And I was on track with straight A's, when I realized I couldn't pinpoint the date of my last period.

In a panic, I did two pregnancy tests and confirmed the horrible truth: I was pregnant.

"You were still in *school?*" I lower the journal to my lap. My mother's face is impassive, even secretive.

They'd gotten married soon after graduation, they always said—but was she pregnant? Even worse—my skin crawls—could I be illegitimate, born before they married? *If the kids at school ever found out ...*

I pick up the journal, my breathing ragged:

> It was the worst possible time. I was livid
> and in despair.

The page rattles in my trembling fingers. This is where I'd stopped reading when I first stumbled on this section. Some self-protective mechanism must have shielded me, because as I mouth the next words, a poison-tipped arrow slides under my ribs and into my heart.

> Having the baby never even occurred
> to me. It would've meant the end of the
> dreams I'd slaved for. I asked around, dis-
> creetly of course, and got a name.

I grip the journal so hard my knuckles turn white. Someone's shoes squeak in the open doorway, and that Jamaican nurse Sharonda brings in a replacement IV bag.

"You're here late." Her nimble fingers unhook the empty pouch from the pole. "Is everything all right?"

When I don't reply, she peers at me. "Are you all right?" she repeats.

I raise the journal, my hand shaking so hard the pages flap. "She wanted to abort me," I whisper.

Dismay distorts Sharonda's beautiful features. "Oh, my dear—"

"*Wait.* Maybe it wasn't me! Maybe I'd have had a brother or sister?" I thumb through the pages wildly, almost ripping them in my haste. The night my father was drunk when I called, did he actually *say* I was the baby she hadn't wanted, conceived while she was still in school, or did I just assume it?

Something buoyant flutters in my chest.

The nurse hangs the new IV bag on the pole and faces me, her expression serious. "Whatever happened, dear, it's in the past. Your mama loves you, I'm sure of that. And she needs you to help her wake, so focus on that. Then you can ask her whatever you like."

She gives me an I-mean-it-look and leaves. I wouldn't want to get on Sharonda's wrong side. I find my place in the journal again.

> Of course, Steven was against it. He even
> told me he loved the name Brittany …

"It *was* me," I whisper. I regard the comatose form in front of me, my mouth lemon-sour. "You didn't want me even when I was already growing inside you. No wonder I felt …" I force myself to lift the journal level with my face, feeling like I'm reading my own death warrant. The letters dance, until finally I can focus.

> … if the baby was a girl.

I finish her sentence and read of the quarrel my parents had, on a path by Lake Superior. It was a doozy, and I picture it as vividly as if I'm with them —which, in a sense, I am. *Was. This happened.* My mother frowns at the small, blue velvet box she's holding. She gives it back to my father, unopened, and walks away. He hurries after her, stork-like. She moves quickly, her words bubbling under her breath like lava.

I made a mistake, but it doesn't mean I can't undo it. The appointment's made. You're a marshmallow, Steven Warner, without a drop of ambition. I won't shackle my life to that.

"Because I don't want s'more?" Even then he's trying to inject humor into a serious situation, but it falls flat. I whirl and glare at him, and his words spill out. "I'm sorry. I've always loved you, Ag, I just didn't dare say it. And now we've got a baby to—"

"There's no 'we,' Steven. And it's not a baby yet."

"Ag! Please, don't say that. I'll do anything, anything at all—"

"Don't call me that."

Her nostrils would have pinched white.

"Look," I tell him. "I was down, you comforted me. We both drank too much."

According to the journal, my mother pauses with perfect timing before delivering the killer punch.

"We were a one-night stand, Steven. End of story."

Every kid probably fantasizes at some point that they're adopted. We daydream of learning we're royalty, or the daughter of a rich gentleman, or heir to some gigantic fortune. It's fairy-tale stuff, and it's everywhere. But I've never run across the opposite: an anti-Cinderella story where someone raised like a princess, more or less, learns she's actually trash. Not temporarily, like *A Little Princess,* but for real. For keeps.

My mother's words are beyond my worst imaginings.

I read the words again: *one-night stand.* A giant fist squeezes my lungs, and I gasp. A few sentences below them, the word "deal" jumps out at me, and suddenly everything's clear. That drunken binge was how I began. Our family's very reason for being, the love I'd always assumed knitted us together, however poorly—is gone, swept away in a moment. It was an illusion. All that really powered us were the empty hopes and dreams of a woman trying to escape her own troubled self. If love makes the world go round, as that old song says, my parents and I are a music box with a broken spring.

More panicky thoughts knife through me, slicing deeper each time. *I'm an accident ... a random collision between two cells, as meaningless as cue balls on a pool table ... I wasn't even meant to be born ... if I were gone, no one would miss me.* My life means nothing. *Nada.*

When I was small, I'd lie in bed and battle the inescapable truth: someday I'll die, and the world will go on forever without me. I'll be annihilated. This is the second half of that punch. This horrible reality snaps over the first part in a perfect fit, like the congruent triangles I never quite understood in math class. I will never recover from this blow, just like the lovely, delicate contour of my mother's left cheek before the accident is gone forever.

Some things can't be fixed.

"One ... night ... s-stand."

Nausea rises in my belly, and I grip the journal until the cover bends. Somehow, I'm on my feet, the journal lying across her legs. Then I'm draped over the toilet in her bathroom, heaving until my ribs ache.

I return to her bedside, wiping my mouth.

My gaze rakes over my mother's body from that once-perfectly-formed face, down her neck and upper body to her flat belly where I once dreamed and kicked and wriggled in a primeval sea of amniotic fluid. Her womb provided my every need, and if anyone had thought to ask about my well-being, I would undoubtedly have given a tiny thumbs-up. But how false that sense of safety was! How complete my ignorance of what lay ahead. My sense of betrayal is boundless. Rage rises within me.

"You … m-monster," I hiss. "You never loved me or Dad. Our whole life was a hoax, it was only about you clawing your way to the t-top." Grabbing the journal, I raise it high above my head, my breath coming hard. I want to smash it onto her belly, punishing the place where I grew and my mother for allowing it. But then … a monitor beeps. I turn my head. See the green line spike. And I cannot do it. But I can't look at her either. I avert my gaze and eye the IV pole. How easy it would be just to knock it over … no, not this time. But …

"I hate you," I whisper. "I w-wish I'd grown any-where except inside you. You … deserve … to die!" I pick up my knapsack, stuff the journal inside, and bolt from the room. Behind me, the monitor beeps an extended confirmation that somehow—on some deep, unconscious level of her pathetic being—my mother understands every word I said.

And why.

28

I streak down the road away from the hospital, adrenaline still spiking through me. A black SUV swerves and screeches to a stop ahead of me, wheels on the curb. The rear window lowers, and Manny peers out above his mirrored aviator shades. They must have been nearby when I texted my SOS moments ago. He opens the door, and I climb over him to the empty seat. Buck's at the wheel, Z riding shotgun and engrossed as always in his smartphone. For the first time, I wonder if he's pathologically shy and uses his phone to avoid talking to people.

Manny studies me in the dim light. The car peels out, and I say, "Go. Anywhere. And hit me with whatever you've got, I want to get obliterated."

A slow smile creases his face. "So, the princess wants to fly. Z, let's help her out." Eyes still on his smartphone, the goon reaches down and passes me a bottle of vodka. I upend it, gulp a mouthful, and wipe my lips with the back of my hand. Instantly my mood improves.

Tonight will be the party to end all parties. I have nothing left to lose.

It doesn't take long to get wasted when you set out to do it. We end up drinking and smoking pot and other stuff at some house near the university, a sad, two-story wooden job missing some porch spindles. A bunch of students live there, and inside, I check out the place with idle curiosity. Maybe college wouldn't have been so bad. Kids can hang their own posters, play their own music, throw their clothes anywhere, and live on Twinkies if they want.

"Where are you from?" I ask a stout, freckled guy, eyeing the can of beer between his splayed knees.

Colorless eyes meet mine. "Stowe."

"What's that like?"

"Skiing, mountains, the von Trapps."

"Really? I love that movie!" And I yodel like Maria in *The Sound of Music.* Louder and louder, and finally I waltz around the room with my knapsack, pretending I'm Liesl and it's her blond suitor, Rolf. Odd glances flash between the students, and I get it. These kids are clueless: they didn't see the movie and have no idea the real Liesl, the beautiful actress who played her, got dementia and died. But I don't care about my audience. Those kid actors who played the singing family stayed in touch like they were really related, even after they grew up, and I bet they still miss their big sister even if it was all fake. And Princess Leia died too, of course I mean the actress Carrie Fisher from *Star Wars*, and mourning her might have brought this crazy country together more than a million politicians ever could.

I pause, panting. For a few brief minutes, I've pushed away the terrible knowledge of my utterly meaningless existence—but now it rushes back like a flood tide. My cell phone squeaks in the knapsack, and I grab it.

"Hello? Britt, is that you?" The tiny, tinny voice belongs to Cassie, who I must have butt-dialed. She always says there are no accidents, but now I tell her she's wrong.

"I'm the *Queen* of Accidents, Cassie." My voice is louder than I intended. "I wasn't even supposed to be born, much less wind up in this godforsaken place."

A guy with eyebrows like sideways commas calls, "So take me with you, I wanna see Times Square." Rowdy laughter.

"No need, dude," Manny says. "We got plenty of stuff right here … Z, introduce our princess here to Molly."

"Brittany! Where are you?" Cassie sounds panicky, desperate.

That's a complicated question, so I force myself to concentrate. "Well, for starters, I'm in the universe. But only by accident—"

"And the solar system. And the Milky Way." Another guy jumps in.

"The Milky Way's part of the solar system," offers a plump brunette cradling a tabby cat in her arms. He gives her an offended look and leaps to the floor.

"That was my point," the guy says. "I'm going in order."

I'm tickled by the discussion, and want Cassie to appreciate our collective brilliance. I press Speaker and hold out the phone to the group.

"You doofuses—or doofi, I'm no English major— are both wrong. The sun and solar system are *part* of the Milky Way. It's a galaxy," says a nerd with glasses who's probably majoring in astrophysics. He strikes a match the same way Benny does, with a flourish, and holds it to a bong like Benny ... but there the resemblance ends. This guy's brilliant.

The first guy tries to focus on him. "Whatever ... so next comes Planet Earth. And North America, the U.S., the state of Vermont, city of Burlington ..." He pauses.

"And a shabby house with missing porch spindles, in the living room, on a brown shag carpet that smells of dog poop," I say into the phone speaker, making everyone roar. "Got it, Cassie? You can send me a postcard, but make sure you write small so the whole address fits." I press the phone against my collarbone and confide to the room, "I love getting mail, but no one ever sends me anything."

"Here you go. Special Delivery." Manny's outstretched palm holds half a dozen pastel pills. I drop the phone.

"Sweet Tarts!"

He laughs without humor. "Not exactly. But here, princess, this one's got your name on it. Just your color."

"Noooooo!" Cassie's tiny voice wails through the phone. But I'm sick of her ruining my fun.

"Bye-eeee." I push the End button and pluck the peach-colored pill from Manny's hand.

We're cruising the city streets again. I'm draped over Manny's lap in the rear seat, blissful. Buck's riding shotgun now and Z is at the wheel, eyeing us in the rearview. Is it my imagination, or is he nervous?

"Need anything else, princess?" Manny's voice is raspy.

"I'm good." I stretch for a moment and wind my arms around his neck. "Y'know, mister, I'm giving you a second chance. Which is more than Luke's doing for … anyway. You're awfully handsome, aren't you." I trail my fingers along Manny's chin. His skin is sandpapery, curiously clammy and pale, even though it's summer. A sun worshipper he's not, plus his jaw is clenched. I slap it gently to loosen him up. I want him to be happy like I am, now, so I crane upward and plant a kiss on his cheek.

"Aren't Mollies terrific," he says through gritted teeth. "The milk of human kindness. Z, it's past eleven, we can't be late for our deal—"

"But, Manny …"

I lean forward, shocked. *Z speaks.* It's the first time ever, in my presence, and his voice is unexpectedly reedy. He looks at Manny through the rearview and cuts his eyes to me. "Not with her," he almost pleads.

He *is* nervous. But why?

Manny laughs. "No worries. She'll be … an asset."

Gratefully, I kiss his stubbly cheek again. *My man will take care of me.*

I'm alone in the SUV, my buzz wearing off. Tired now, I'm content to gaze around. Like the pedestrian mall downtown, the Burlington waterfront is spruced up with benches and tubs of flowers and, at night, fancy lights. No one could say this city lacks civic pride. A massive pier juts into the dark water, but the moonlight cast across it shows it's empty. In fact, the whole parking lot's empty except for the car I'm in and a silver sedan. I check my phone. Eleven-thirty, and six unopened texts from Cassie. A tiny pinprick of guilt stabs me. *She knows by now that I'm not with Will.*

Ahead of me, next to the silver sedan, Manny, Buck, and Z huddle with a trim, fortyish woman in a business suit and running shoes. *That's the dealer?* Manny extracts a wad of cash from a wallet and hands it to her. The flash of blue leather and cash are familiar, and I peer into my knapsack. Empty. As I look up, dazed, the dealer hops into the sedan and speeds away.

Manny strides toward the SUV, smiling, his goons flanking him. But when he sees me, his expression turns … *wow, he looks mean.* A chill passes through me. He opens the car door and says, "Now for you, princess," his voice curt.

He yanks me out so hard I sprawl on the pavement.

"S-stop that, it hurts!" I squint up, bleary.

"Hush your yap. You made a big mistake, you know that?"

"Huh?" I struggle to my knees.

His boot heel forces my thigh down. "Pushing me away … making that crack … no one does that to Manny Sligh."

"What? I didn't—" Dimly, I remember my ashtray comment. But he did taste terrible. I won't apologize for telling the truth.

"Shut up." He snaps his fingers. "Leave us," he orders, and Buck and Z fade away, as if by magic.

Manny grabs my arms and wrestles me to the ground.

Bits of gravel dig into my back. *This isn't happening.* I kick furiously—until he pins my legs, scowling. He fumbles with his belt, the buckle jingling. I'm stone sober, terrified. His zipper makes a *scritch* going down, though his pants mercifully stay on … for now. His head and shoulders form a monstrous silhouette against the moon, blotting out the sky. His weight is crushing, his knees hard and bony against my shins. Then his mouth clamps onto mine. He yanks up my T-shirt, and the night air shocks my bare ribs. Again I smell patchouli, which is supposed to deter mosquitos but Manny's no mosquito, and now I taste hot-sour-breath a mix of ashes-booze-and-something-foul and *how could I ever have found this creep attractive?* I try to punch and kick, but am immobilized.

"Help!" I scream, but my voice won't rise above a rasp.

The wages of sin is death. Where'd that come from?

Maybe I'm about to die; some rape victims do. But my mother defends their attackers. *How can she?* I concentrate on that—until Manny pops the snap of my cutoffs.

His eyes glitter with rage just inches from mine, and my lids squeeze shut. "Please please *please,*" I mumble, not to Manny but to—who? There's no one near to help or blame but myself. I go limp. If I play possum, maybe it will end sooner.

Then. A car roars into the parking lot and screeches to a halt. Running footsteps, full of purpose and heading straight toward us. Then two other sets, one heavy and the other scatty like a cat. There's a thudding, cracking, and I open my eyes as Buck roars with pain and clutches his jaw. A higher-pitched *oomph* and Z cartwheels backward soundlessly, cartoon-like. Manny is lifted off me and spun away like a rag doll. I half-sit up as an enraged Will punches, then tackles him. They scuffle and roll together. Punching, grunting, thwacking.

I snap my cutoffs closed and scuttle sideways, almost sobbing.

Z staggers to his feet and moves toward me. "Help him!" I mouth, and jerk my head at Will. Instead, Z seizes my arm, claps a hand over my mouth to cut off my scream, and drags me behind a bush. He's stronger than he appears. His pale face looms inches from mine.

"Stay here," he squeaks in that freakishly high voice. Then he's gone, his footsteps light and quick.

The punches and grunts continue, and I peer around the bush to see Manny leap to his feet. Will's bent over, clutching his thighs. He wipes his mouth against his sleeve, smearing something dark on his shirt. *Blood.* A gust of wind plasters his hair across his forehead and his white shirt flat against him.

They square off against each other, dark and light. Both panting. "You got a … knack … for showing up where you're not wanted," Manny spits.

"And you've got one for dragging what's not yours … into the gutter."

"She … *was* mine. So were you."

"Never," Will says. "Britt, least of all."

They circle each other like wolverines, and start again. Will rushes Manny and throws a punch. Manny blocks it and hits Will hard in his midriff. My defender drops and rolls away, groaning. Manny rushes in to kick him, but Will grabs his attacker's boot, yanks him off his feet, and leaps onto him. Will delivers blow upon blow, until finally he's got the advantage, but—

"Look out!" I yell. Buck staggers in, swinging his meaty fists. Will tucks his shoulder and rolls to one side like a gymnast. He leaps up, panting, only to confront the towering Buck and incensed Manny. *Two against one.*

A click pierces the silence. Horrified, I recognize the gleam of a switchblade in Manny's hand. It must have been in his shirt pocket. His face blazes with rage and Will, poised on the balls of his feet, turns pale in the moonlight.

Suddenly a siren wails. Two police cruisers speed through the parking lot, their lights whirling. They screech to a stop just yards from the fight, and Sergeant Thompson jumps out and levels his gun at Manny.

"Drop the knife!" he orders.

Three more cops tumble from the cars, guns raised. Will's and Buck's arms shoot up. But Manny grips his knife tighter and throws me a glance—stupidly, I'm in plain view—and my breath almost stops when I realize what he's thinking. *Me a hostage, that silvery blade at my neck.* But thanks to Z, I'm too far away. I scuttle to the bush again.

"Drop the knife," Sergeant Thompson warns again. "Or I'll shoot."

Manny curses. For a moment, time stops. I brace myself for a hail of gunfire. *This is how Will almost died. It's not how I want to die.* But the knife clatters to the ground and Manny raises his hands, his face contorted by hatred. Blood pours from his nose, and for once, the sight doesn't make me faint. While one cop kicks away the knife, another cuffs Manny and pushes him into a squad car. Sergeant Thompson escorts Will and Buck to another. Somehow the cop's stubby fingers on Will's arm look gentle, even protective. *Like a dad.* I move away, my throat tight. The squad cars speed away, lights twirling and sirens wailing.

The removal of noise is deafening. But it isn't quiet, exactly: there's a low roar coming from somewhere. Dazed, I scan the area. A breeze has kicked up, and waves are rolling onto the pebbly shore. *Ah.* My legs and palms sting where the gravel cut my skin. Whimpering, I stagger to my feet and stumble toward the deserted pier. A gust of wind whips my hair as I step onto the damp boards and limp all the way to the end. Dark water swirls around the pier supports. I lean over, hoping to see my reflection by moonlight, but the water's too choppy.

Now the wind is howling, the waves crashing on the rocks. Their motion is mesmerizing. Who knew fresh water could be so violent? My father's words whisper to me from long ago: "And then you'll lie down, and it's just like going to sleep …."

Dying has always terrified me. But tonight, the idea of the earth spinning on forever without me isn't shocking or distressing. I'm already miserable. In a hundred years—or fifty, or ten, or one—it really won't matter that my whole life was a mistake. I stare into the roiling waves, and the answer comes to me: the solution to this problem lies under my nose. As my charming mother has reminded me a million times, I can't swim.

I laugh aloud. It's so perfect, I half-wish someone were here to share the joke. Like Luke, saying my life's important. But he's wrong, and he'd try to stop me, to convince me the events of this horrible night can be reversed. And I'm determined to do this. Slowly … slowly … I lean out from the pier. Feel the emptiness, and the terrible thrill of nothing beneath me …

And I roll into the water with a splash.

29

My fingers brush rough wet pebbles. I shiver, groan. Foggily, I remember bubbles and choking and seaweed and a violent wave somersaulting me over and over. I crack my eyelids open. I'm lying on the shoreline, half in, half out of the icy water. No one is nearby; no one rescued me. The lake tossed me onto its rocky shore like a worthless piece of driftwood.

I have to go on. The knowledge is a stone in my gut.

But someone's calling my name. Someone … dear. A powerful flashlight beam sweeps over me. Then again, blinding me.

"Britt. *Brittany.*" Cassie splashes toward me in knee-deep water, almost crying. Her flashlight beam bounces around me as I pull myself to a sitting position, weak and dizzy. Warm arms span my chilled back and help me to my feet. "Thank heaven you're alive, we've looked everywhere. What was that phone call? But wait, we've got to warm you up …"

We stumble to the car. Cassie helps me into the front seat and disappears. The trunk slams. She reappears, tucks a fuzzy blanket around me, and races to the driver's seat. As she starts the car and blasts the heater, I'm teary with gratitude.

"You should have been my mom, Cassie—"

"Don't."

"But Cass-Cass, I almost di—"

"I said stop! We'll deal with that later. But Will and I have been running all over town like maniacs to find you … Luke and Priscilla are gone, they're in Brattleboro checking out a horse. So, I've just got to tell Will you're safe and take you home." She yanks out her cell phone and punches a number. A tiny, digitized voice invites her to leave a voicemail.

"Will, wherever you are, I've got her," Cassie says, terse. "She's okay, just a bit chilled. No need to call, we'll talk tomorrow. And … thanks."

The minute she hangs up, her phone rings. "Will? Oh, Tommy … yes, she's with me. We're going home." She hangs up and frowns, puzzled. Then she guns the car out of the lot and onto the road back to South Hero.

My head pounds so hard that my brain feels wobbly inside my head. My mouth is full of cotton wads, fuzzy cocoons … and the sour tang of vomit. Someone taps my arm. I moan and open my eyes. It's daylight outside my window.

"Get dressed," Cassie orders. "And into the car."

"There's a bongo in my head," I wail.

"I'll bring aspirin." She leaves.

Groaning, I sit up, swing my feet onto the floor—and yelp. The bottoms of my feet are covered in cuts, whether from pebbles, splinters, or nails I can't tell. Did I wear flip-flops or sneakers when I left Cassie's cottage yesterday?

I have no idea, which is scary. I squeeze my eyes shut in an effort to concentrate. The whole evening floods back in a flash, though parts, like the scene in the student digs, are blurry. What's clear, though, is that for a blob born by accident, I've had several narrow escapes. Too many, almost like someone or something's after me. And Cassie, the one person who's been a hundred percent in my corner the whole summer—Luke no longer counts since he's going to kill Joy—is hornet-mad and offering not an ounce of sympathy.

Why should she?

I open my eyes as Cassie parks by the police station and yanks the emergency brake. She faces me grimly, her hair mussed and her face gray with fatigue.

"He told you, didn't he, about being on probation? What would happen if he got in trouble again?"

Foggily, I realize she means Will. "I thought you cared about me," I mumble.

She picks up her purse. "Heaven help me, I do. But I've been up all night worrying and it's time for some straight talk, Brittany Warner. Because of you, our young friend will be tried as an adult. For assault. He'll have a record, forever. Will broke Manny's nose, did you realize that? Quite badly, from what I understand. Not that the little sh—skunk didn't deserve it."

Next thing, she's out of the car but leaning in again, her keys dangling from her clenched fist. "I told you he was evil. Through and through. But you wouldn't listen, either of you." She straightens so fast she bumps her head on the door frame. *"Ow."* Tears spring to her eyes.

The aspirin isn't helping my pounding headache, and my already-queasy stomach roils from the juice I'd chugged to get it down. I struggle out of the car, and we slam our doors at the same time. And I cringe at the blinding sunlight. Cassie's driveway was shaded, so I hadn't realized. But like a cruel joke, this must be one of the most glorious days to grace Vermont since the beginning of time.

"Either of—who?" I say at last.

Our eyes meet over the car roof.

"You and Kara. It's so stupid, you both had to find out the hard way." She whirls and stalks toward the police station.

"*Kara?* And ... Manny?" I'm stumbling in her wake.

"Bingo." She pushes through the station door and holds it open for me. "Will felt if we told you, you'd be even more ... determined. But you've gone your own way anyway, haven't you."

I sniffle. Who ever dreamed sweet Cassie could be so angry! I ask why we're at the police station, but she just compresses her lips and jerks her purse strap higher on her shoulder.

Right as we reach the main desk, Sergeant Thompson arrives from the back. "Ah," he says. "Visitor and witness, all in one. Keeps it simple. Thank-you, Cassie."

Visitor? Witness? Even worse ... *thank-you?*

A guard escorts us to a good-sized room with four booths in a horizontal row down the middle. Inside each one, a plastic orange chair on the far side faces two others with their backs to us. *One for the prisoner, two for visitors.* Heavy plexiglass separates them. A man in dull green prison garb sits hunched over facing me in the last booth, but the frame blocks my view so I can't see who it is. Cassie nudges me forward and moves away.

"Aren't you coming?" I ask desperately. I never want to see Manny again, and if it's Will—

"No. You need to do this."

I drag myself to a chair and lower myself into it. I count to ten, raise my eyes, and face the prisoner.

Will. His face so bruised and discolored that his left eye is swollen shut. His loosely curled fingers, resting on the counter, just as bad. My entire body prickles with horror, and jumbled memories fly at me like strobes. Will washing my cut foot at the pharmacy. Pointing out Cassiopeia with campfire light flickering on his face. Confessing, haltingly, his role in his little sister's scarring. Making fun of my pretend "manure lacrosse," and explaining why he's careful about romance. Trying to warn me off Manny with bowling pins toppling all around us, and so many more ... right up to last night, when he barreled in to save me from assault. I hear again Cassie's accusing voice, *You know he'll be tried as an adult?* And I know, better than she does, that now he'll lose his scholarship and his dreams of being a ranger or counselor will go down the toilet like my pet fish. But that's later; right now, he must ache all over from that pummeling, his poor flesh inflamed and his face a purplish wreck. By his hairline, there's dried blood like my mother's after—

And I nearly retch as a second wave of memories assaults me, of that last fateful day at home, where I posed in that horrible silky lingerie for Benny and saw my father's shock, then provoked my mother later about the testing prep materials, and actually, really, dangled her expensive Prada bag out the car window.

It's all my fault. Every single terrible thing that's happened since I came to Vermont. Mine. The enormity of my sin hits me and I want to flee like I always do, but this time there's nowhere to go. I'm actually in a jail, with an armed cop standing behind me and my rescuer before me, a mess.

"Oh, no. Oh, Will." I can hardly get the words out. "I'm so sorry, Will, so very sorry. You look awful, why'd you come after me … no, why did you ever do *anything* for me? I'm the worst scum—" My voice cracks.

"It's okay," he says into a metal tube fixed in the plexiglass. "Don't cry, Britt. *Please.* Last night I felt rotten, that I'd screwed up again. But guess what? Now, I never felt so good." He starts to smile, but winces and touches his swollen lip. "Except for this."

"*Huh?*" I'm gulping and hiccuping now, trying to control myself because falling apart in a jail is the last thing I want to do. I am not crying! But something hot and wet plops on my arm. Then twice more. Tears. So I must be. I swipe my eyes with the heel of my hand, fierce now. "How can—how can you possibly feel *good?* Your life is … is … ruined, don't you know that? You'll be here for who knows how long, and—"

"I did it, Britt. Maybe overdid it, I didn't mean to break Manny's nose. But I *protected* you."

I stare at him blankly, sniffling.

"Remember I said I joined the gang again when I was fifteen?" he goes on. "That was for my sister. Kara was head over heels for that dirtbag, glued to his side day and night, and I was petrified for her. I had to keep an eye on her, just in case. My plan worked for a few months, 'til the night everything … went down and I ended up in juvie."

The night you got shot.

"After that Kara was with Luke and Priscilla and had nothing to do with Manny," Will says. "And when I came back a year ago, she'd met Shawn and I relaxed a bit. Huge mistake. I never dreamed she'd go to that stupid par—never mind." He glances toward the door, where Cassie stands rigidly with the guard.

"But what I've done is so much worse, Will." I swallow hard. He still doesn't know. And what I'm about to say will end forever any chance of gaining—no, keeping, he's given me nothing but grace all along—this extraordinary guy's approval. Because he's pure gold, I understand now that it's too late. Even the wrongs he's committed, he did for someone else. And last night he threw himself into danger, sacrificing his own safety—and freedom. All his hopes for the future.

For me.

It's a new feeling, knowing someone valued me that much. But I can't enjoy it. Poison spews from my lips like vomit.

"Will, I … I c-caused my mother's coma."

There's a pause as long as a lifetime.

"Not on purpose," he says softly.

I gape at him. "How did you—"

"I don't know everything. But Cassie heard you talking in your sleep."

My eyes stream more tears. "I've made such a mess of things. I was so angry, she made me flush my Siamese fighting fish down the toilet, but I never, ever meant to—"

"Yeah. We humans do that, screw up."

There's a tissue box on the counter before me—someone knew I'd need it—and I grab a few and dab my face. For a non-crier, I'm making up for lost time. "And it's too late to fix anything," I bawl into the soft whiteness.

"No. It's never too late, as long as we're alive. Are you ready to make it right?"

"But it's done. I … can't."

"Not by yourself," he agrees. "But remember what Pastor Dave said, first time you came to church? God will forgive anyone. No matter who we are or what we've done."

I go still. Will tents his fingertips against the plexiglass, a clear invitation. I long to spread mine to match his and go from here, forgetting the past. The barrier between us will dissolve and we'll fly through the sound-deadening ceiling tiles above us into some mythical blue Neverland, holding hands, like Peter Pan and Wendy. But—

"Except me," I say slowly. "I just found out I wasn't planned. Or wanted. My whole life was a mistake. Built on sand, wasn't that in one of Pastor Dave's sermons?"

Will lowers his hand. "Never. Not even a sparrow can fall without God's permission, remember Pastor Dave said that? No baby could be born outside of his will. It's impossible. God planned you and knew you, Britt, even before he made the universe. He's been with you all along, and loves you more than you can imagine."

If only it were true. "You really believe that?" I whisper.

He nods. "Just look at my life, if you want proof. Even here, Britt, I'm not alone. God is taking care of me. He'll do that for you, too. But you need to ask, and be forgiven."

They've told me this all summer long. Over and over, plus every Sunday from the pulpit. But today, in this prison I've made myself, I'm finally hearing it.

"Then how—"

"Just say you're sorry—"

"I *am*. But that can't be enough. He wouldn't—"

"It is," Will says simply. And suddenly there's nowhere to go but forward. I squeeze my eyes shut.

"Um, hello, God? If you're there … it's me. Brittany. You know how awful I've been—" And for the second time in my life I pour myself out to an invisible being. But this time …

Sometimes words aren't adequate. I'll just say that something—Some*one*—has heard me. And is responding. I might say a quiet peace surrounds me … that I feel I'm being hugged … that I'm warm all over … or even that the air is pierced with an impossibly sweet aroma like nothing I could imagine, that makes me want to cry. But it's each of these, and something more. Like a melody just beyond my hearing, or a great, lionlike heart beating next to mine, pouring love and comfort into me. What a glorious relief! I sit absolutely still. And bask in it.

I'm forgiven.

Forgiven.

Peace.

And love.

I … believe.

I believe.

I open my eyes. "Will … I felt him. Like a hug. And such peace … oh, Will, he's real!"

With a lopsided smile, he places two fingertips on his lips, kisses them, and touches the plexiglass again. Slowly, tentatively, I follow his example. It's like a finger-kiss between toddlers, and for a moment I'm a little kid again.

Awareness jolts me, a sense of urgency like I've never felt before. "Will, I need—"

"I know. Go to her."

In one fluid motion, I whirl and run from the room, as I've done so many times this summer. But this time I'm not running away. I'm running toward.

And Cassie's right behind me, her car keys jingling.

I burst into my mother's hospital room and rush to the bed, perching on the edge of my usual chair. "Mom, I've got something to tell you. Something amazing!"

She's pink and serene today, doll-like. I lean over her, no longer fazed by the machines and beeps and IV pole. I could almost convince myself she does hear me, that any moment she'll open her eyes, say my name, or squeeze my hand.

But I have to make sure. "I've been here almost every day these past few weeks," I say clearly. "Reading to you. Maybe you've heard some of it. But now, if you can—please, please focus harder than you ever have on anything. Harder than … if you were hearing your first case at the Supreme Court."

I moisten my lips. "What I did that day in the car was terrible. I've … prayed for God to forgive me. It worked, he did. But I need your forgiveness too, so badly. Please, think about it?"

On an impulse, I take her hand and squeeze it. "I have to go now, Cassie's waiting, but—whoa, you're hot!" I feel her forehead. It's burning. I snatch up the call button and jam it over and over.

"Yes?" says a sing-songy nurse voice.

"We need help!"

"Someone will be right in." The woman's calmness eases my panic a bit. *Everyone gets fevers, it's probably nothing to worry about.*

A minute later, my favorite Jamaican nurse hurries in.

"Sharonda, she's sick!" I say.

She scans the monitors. "Yes. Her temp spiked last night. Dr. Patel had us draw blood."

"*Blood?*"

"For tests."

"But what's wrong?"

The nurse straightens a blanket that doesn't need it. "Her white count is elevated. It appears to be an infection. We may change to a more specific antibiotic when the results come back."

I twirl a strand of hair. "Is it dangerous?"

A pause. "Possibly. Being in bed for an extended period weakens the immune system. In addition … there is a crackle in one of Mrs. Warner's lungs," she says in the formal phrasing I've grown used to.

She moves past me to leave. I clutch her sleeve, but release it when she looks down at my fingers. "A crackle, what's that?" I say.

"It means there is fluid. Where there should be air."

"Which means …" I'm dreading the answer.

She hesitates. "Your mother may have pneumonia."

My strength drains out through my feet. I sink onto the bedside chair. "Does my fath—"

"Of course, he is on his way. There was a delay at his work. We had already called him, because your mama … well, she is waking. There are no overt signs yet, but … you see?" She points to one of the monitors.

Mom's brainwaves are spiking. Her head moves, restless. Hope and dread fill me in equal proportions.

"Help us," I whisper.

30

My mother does have pneumonia. And the next couple of days are a blur. I'm with her almost constantly, napping on a couch in a nearby lounge when I can no longer keep my eyes open. The rest of the time, I straighten Mom's sheets. Sponge her brow. Massage her hands and feet and talk to her. But mostly, I sit and wait while endless rounds of doctors and nurses come and go and huddle together, whispering. Dr. Patel, a nice-looking Indian in his fifties who I've met before, repeatedly listens to her lungs and pulls stethoscope bulbs from his ears with a grave expression. The belt-like halo thing that encircled her head and chest is gone. At some point my father arrives, his eyes bloodshot and his skin gray. I throw my arms around him and hold him close for a few moments. His palm rests lightly on my back.

I bolt down candy bars from the vending machine, Skittles and Milky Ways and Peanut M&Ms. My stomach turns acidic with sugar and worry, until I'm forced to hit the cafeteria for an omelet or bowl of soup. Cream of broccoli, minestrone, vegetable beef … I spoon nourishment into my mouth mechanically, barely noticing flavors. Cassie meets me in the cafeteria a couple of times, bringing fresh clothes and iced caramel lattes from Starbucks. What a difference small kindnesses make. She also brings a tiny book of Psalms and a giant card signed by Luke and Priscilla and the church teens, including Jessica. Everyone says they're praying, which for once I'm grateful to know. I'm praying, too.

My father and I take turns sleeping on the too-short couch in the lounge. Sometimes I curl into the easy chair next to him. Like Meghan's favorite horse Tiny, the chair's misnamed; there's nothing easy about sleeping in it. So, I read a line or two of a Psalm, again and again. Who knew there were so many verses about God being a refuge in our troubles? This sure qualifies. Once I wake from a couple of hours' nap in the lounge and arrive at Mom's room just as a nurse emerges with a canvas carrier full of blood vials. We exchange grim smiles, skirting each other. Later, another nurse brings yet another IV bag. Sometimes I'm asked to leave the room while they tend the catheter snaking from beneath the sheet over my mother.

On the second evening, I do return to Cassie's cottage for a shower and a few hours of real sleep. In the morning I dash to the barn, aware I haven't heard a word about Joy's colic. I haven't asked, either, afraid of what Cassie might say. As I bolt down the aisle, I hear Luke's voice coming from Joy's stall, then a woman's.

It's worse than I could have imagined. Joy stands between two IV poles, her head lowered and her forelock disheveled. Her eyes are dull. Luke scratches her behind her ears, facing her rear end, where … well, the vet is clearly performing an extremely intimate exam. Her shoulders are pressed against Joy's hindquarters as she feels around inside … and lets out a loud *Whoa!* She withdraws her arm, strips off her long glove, and says, eyes shining, "Well, Luke, there's always another bend in the road. She's a very sick little mare … but if she makes it through, she's got a cyst on her ovary the size of a baseball. It's got to be pouring hormones into her 24-7. Take it out, and those behavior problems will be over."

I let out an involuntary sound, and Luke pivots and sees me. "I see you heard. Talk about timing," he says. Then, courteous as always, "How is your mom?"

I tell him the basics and let myself into the stall. No danger now; Joy is beyond caring about anything. I finger-comb her peroxide-orange forelock into a little braid like mine and lay my cheek against her hot face as I've longed to do from the first time I saw her.

"How long until you know?" I ask, and Luke looks to the vet.

"It'll be clear which way she's going by tonight," she answers bluntly.

I hug Joy and make Luke promise to keep me posted.

Back at the hospital, I resume my vigil for a third day. At some point I pick up my recent nemesis, my mother's journal, and read about the slow unwinding of what I've come to consider a devil's bargain: the deal my parents made about raising me. Their marriage was forged in desperation, panic, and logic. Never love. One of the saddest things I've ever read is how my mother gritted her teeth and finished law school while pregnant with a baby she didn't want, and engaged to a man she didn't love. I can't imagine why she followed through with it all.

My father must have been very persuasive, which is also difficult to picture.

Yet there were poignant moments, too. Neither of their families knew the truth. Grampy Warner gave an emotional toast at the wedding reception, welcoming "our newest flower" and "the bouquet to come" … meaning grandchildren. If he and Grammy were disappointed that I'm an only child, they never showed it.

Though the journal doesn't say it outright, I suspect my other grandfather was in rehab that day. But even Grandma Audrey was gracious. My maternal grandmother, a snob through and through, shook hands with every member of her son-in-law's extended family—even his cousin Bettina's two-year-old son Georgie, who according to the journal whispered questions throughout the ceremony. My mother was ready to throttle him.

Our extended family are strangers to me. Maybe they're in and out of each other's lives, gathering at reunions and speculating about their unsociable, high-flying Warner kin. My parents went their own way, just what Cassie accused me of. But my mother included this account of her wedding in her journal, so maybe she harbored hopes of more closeness than actually developed. Did she regret distancing herself from her kin? Or was she just relieved when Grandma Audrey treated her future in-laws with civility? Maybe her mother's support that day was the high point of *their* relationship. If so, how sad that my grandmother didn't know I was there too, in utero.

There's little hint of what drove my mother for so long. Near-poverty, yes, and deep wounds made by her father, my grandfather Hugo, who—reading between the lines—was alcoholic *and* abusive. But lots of people go through hard stuff without making a habit of defending creepy criminals. A mystery lurks here but I realize, watching yet another nurse check my mother's temperature, that I'll probably never solve it. Even if she recovers fully, it's not her way to tell.

Late on the third night, I pass the Emergency Room on my way to the vending machines and stop short. Priscilla is pushing Kara, who is clearly in labor, in a wheelchair. Priscilla steps away to speak to a nurse, and Kara's eyes meet mine. Our gazes lock, and in those few seconds we somehow exchange a volley of silent messages. We are both in crisis. She's about to have a baby, and has lost her mother; mine is upstairs, fighting for her life. Neither of us knows what lies ahead. We've both been attacked physically, her far worse than me. And humbled before God and man. Yet, amazingly … her face is serene. Despite everything, she has come to terms with her situation, and will cherish this baby as much as if he were conceived in love. Even if she raises him alone.

And amidst all this, the compassion in her eyes says she understands what I am going through, too. We all make mistakes, but as Will says, there's grace.

Finally her lips curve in a smile, and she nods. Encouraged, I move forward to speak with her, but fumble on what to say. Good luck? May your labor be quick and your baby healthy? All this is new to me.

"You know you're not alone," I finally bring out, hoping she understands that I don't mean Priscilla being there, but God protecting her.

Her eyes dart sideways, and her smile broadens. "I know, thanks. But I'm not as alone as you think," she says, and tilts her chin toward the doorway. I turn to see a young man race in and stop before her. I dimly recognize Shawn, the guitar player at Cassie's picnic.

They exchange a long look, his tender and searching, before Kara stiffens with pain. He gives her shoulder a gentle rub and moves to take the wheelchair handles as Priscilla returns with a nurse.

I stretch out my arms in a giant, double-thumbs-up *Yes* as they disappear down a hallway. *Way to go, Kara!* I've just seen a miracle, and now am hoping for another.

Brisk footsteps jolt me awake in the easy chair by the window. It's daylight again, and dread grips me as I realize that Sharonda is fitting an oxygen mask over my mother's face. It looks much more serious than those little plastic nose plugs. How gleeful my father had sounded, weeks ago, when he announced that she was breathing on her own.

"Is she worse?" I whisper, so low the nurse may not hear me.

But Sharonda does. "It will give her a higher percentage of oxygen," she says, which isn't an answer.

I'm sinking into despair—nothing has changed since the dreaded pneumonia diagnosis—when my cell phone beeps. It's six a.m. Who would text me now? Luke, it turns out, and I realize I've completely forgotten about Joy's colic. But the text just says, "Check voicemail."

"Hey there, Brittany," says Luke's recorded message. "Hope I'm not waking you, but I couldn't wait to share the wonderful news. Your prayer was answered—Joy's going to be okay. Especially after we get that cyst out. Keep us posted on your mom, you hear?"

I listen to the message a second time and even a third, clutching the phone like a lifeline. Finally, it sinks in and for a moment, even my mother's rasping breathing takes second place to my relief. I leap to my feet and hurry to the waiting lounge. My father's still snogged out on the couch, so I grab my wallet and the journal from my mother's room and head for the cafeteria.

It's morning, and I'm hungry.

I wipe egg off my fingers—another messy breakfast sandwich, but they're so yummy and full of protein—and sip coffee. Green Mountain again, which is sold everywhere here. I open Mom's journal to where I left off. So much has happened since the horrible night when I learned about my origins and went on that bender. Now that seems less … dire. I've felt warmed, even oddly reassured, ever since my encounter with … okay, with God. Who wanted me, even if my mother didn't. Now I need for her to know he loves her too.

Before I read, I notice a pimpled teen with exhausted eyes, another refugee from an all-nighter upstairs. What's *his* story, I wonder as he sets down a tray and lowers himself into a plastic chair as if he's a million years old. Then he looks around blankly, and I realize he needs salt and pepper. I leap up and bring him mine. The kid looks up, mumbles something I take to be thanks, doses his eggs, then spoons them in automatically. He's probably sleeping in a chair, too.

I turn back to the journal. Of course, I don't read aloud here, but my mother's voice fills my head, as always.

Now for the grain of sand in my little oyster life, the grit that did not become a pearl. The missing link to everything, the sine qua non missing from this account. I've got to deal with it now, if I'm ever going to be free.

What? I read on:

I hoped I'd buried it forever, but I keep having the same dream. I'm swinging almost to the treetops at the school playground, when a girl runs past with Bobby Layton at her heels.

I recognize my twin sister, but they disappear into the woods. A nervous giggle, then a cry from behind the trees … and I wake in anguish. Its meaning is clear, and I can no longer bear this. Maybe writing it out will exorcise it. So …

My last year of law school, I'd studied late at the libe for an exam. As I passed the building where our classes were held, I saw a single window lit up on an upper floor. My professor's office. I turned in, meaning to ask about a summer internship. Big mistake. Outside Room 202, my highly revered prof's name etched on a brass nameplate, I raised my hand to knock—and heard a moan from within. Then the words, clearly female: "No … no, stop!"

Horrified, I backed away. I knew that voice, she was in my class. A slutty dresser, with morals to match ... the kind who'd trade her body for a better grade. Except in this instance, she obviously hadn't. Or it back-fired; whatever was going on was more than she'd bargained for. And I didn't want to dirty my hands.

Of course I didn't admit this to myself then. I just scuttled out of that building, checked to be sure I wasn't observed, then eased myself out of the shadows and strolled down the quad as if I hadn't just left the scene of a crime.

That night, I donned my favorite black-and-fuchsia polka-dotted nightshirt and brushed my hair until it hurt in our dimly lit bathroom, staring at myself in my cheap mirror. My hollow eyes matched the pit in my stomach as I justified my actions. *It's the age of free sex,* I told myself. *If she's screwing the prof, it's by her own choice. Who knows, maybe she moonlights as an "escort." Be smart, Agatha. That prof could ruin your career before it's even started.* But my stomach heaved and I vomited diet soda and saltines, the only food I'd eaten that day. Then I lay awake until the next morning, when I pulled myself together to take the exam.

It was our last final. I never saw the prof or that student again. But now and then I'd look her up, to see where she might be practicing law, and ... crickets. I should've checked the obits.

I slam the journal shut, my breakfast sandwich sour in my belly, and toss the paper wrappings into the trash. That poor girl! How many years did it take to get over her trauma? Did she ever? Back in Mom's room I distract myself by raising the blinds, to check how far the dawning sunlight has crept down the mountaintops. Not very; it's early yet. I settle myself in my usual chair, my mind racing. Remembering the feeling of gravel digging into my back as Manny stood over me on the waterfront, unbuckling his belt—

Enough. "I'd like to chew you out," I say to my mother. "Like you always do to me. I can't believe this. You should have stopped that horrible man, or at least come clean afterward!"

Maybe … she did? "Okay, you've got two seconds to prove me wrong." I open the journal again.

> "I felt ashamed," I read aloud. "Evil. With no way to make it right." My fury drains away. *That's exactly how I felt. After the accident.* "I never told a soul," I read on, to myself now.
>
> One night, before what I later dubbed the *Law Review* binge, I almost unburdened myself to Steven. I mean, he'd shared with me his deep dark secret, even if it was pathetically tame.
>
> Who gets that traumatized from being locked in a closet? It was a kids' prank, though his cousins were older. But he was trapped in that tiny space a few hours and swears it made him—I forget the word he used. Powerless, or passive.

He couldn't move, so he retreated to such a deep place inside himself that he just lost his will. Like, permanently. Which does explain a lot. Pushing marriage when I got pregnant was obviously the one exception of his life, and that took all he had.

Despite the terrible start, though, I guess it's worked out. He's a decent husband. And Brittany's a sweet child, though her teens are a bit bumpy. But we'll survive.

The worst part? Straddling this powder keg for so long.

Oh, Mom. The journal continues:

One day, in my first job after passing the bar exam, I defended a man accused of rape. It wasn't fun, but I won the case by blaming the victim. My new boss, impressed, gave me a similar case … then another … and promised I'd make partner if I kept up the good work.

Blaming the victim became my go-to defense. Every win upheld the justice of my logic. The system affirmed that I was right. And somewhere along the way, I let myself believe that young law student was responsible for her own rape.

My strategy worked. But truth always wants out. Two decades later, I'm quaking with shame in a shrink's office. The cost of keeping this secret, walking a wrong road, has been higher than I could have imagined.

Whoa. I get to my feet, heavy with sorrow. My mother used her whole career to justify what she did, or rather, didn't do, on a single tragic evening. I'm staggered by the emotional price of her denial. Her life—and mine—might have been so different if she'd helped that woman, or told *anyone* the truth afterward. Even a priest, though now it's clear why she avoided church. She had no peace.

Criminals do deserve a fair trial. But defending them in order to justify her own guilt warped my mother into a near-monster.

I shut the journal and set it on the nightstand. "I've—got to go, Mom. Be back in a while." My father's probably still asleep in the waiting lounge, so I just tiptoe away from her bed and curl up in the easy chair by the window. It's far enough away. And I shut my eyes.

Like she did.

31

It's full daylight now, but according to Mom's wall clock it's still only nine-thirty. I haven't slept long. But I wake with a song in my mind: "Hush, little baby, don't say a word, Mama's gonna buy you a mockingbird. And if that mockingbird don't sing, Mama's gonna buy you a diamond ring." I hum the song right to the ending: "... and if that horse and cart fall down, you'll still be the sweetest little baby in town."

I twist sideways in the chair, my legs over the armrest. *What the heck?* How do I know this song? My eyelids drift shut. An early memory floods my mind, and I jolt upright. I'm nestled against a stuffed bunny in my crib, wearing a pink-checked little romper, and above me, someone is stroking my hair and singing. *Hush, little baby, don't say a word.* I roll onto my back and fling out chubby baby arms, gaze up into smiling cornflower blue eyes ...

"Mommy," I whisper, my eyes moist. And again, *"Mommy."* Whatever she's done, this woman loved me the best she could. Being human, she's capable of appalling evil. Well, so am I. Concealing it is a sin we share, as my lies this summer prove. But she wanted to set things right. The journal confirms that, too.

Who am I to judge my mother? A new love for her pours through me, and I savor her words:

Brittany is a sweet child.

I jam my feet into my flip-flops and cross to the bedside. Perching on my usual chair, I lean forward and take her hands in mine.

Her skin feels so soft.

But even with the added oxygen, she is laboring to breathe.

"Don't die, Mommy," I beg. *"Please don't die!"*

The third-floor lounge isn't especially chilly. But I'm shivering as I wait by the couch where my father snores under one of Cassie's afghans. He shifts onto his back, his forearm across his face. "Dad?" I whisper. He jerks his arm away and eyes me blearily.

"How is she?"

"Not good. Listen, Dad. I've read her journal, and—did you know about what happened at that frat?"

He rubs his face. "Yes. Your mother … regretted it."

I brood a moment. "Dad, I love her."

He nods, unsurprised. "I know."

"But I—I need to tell you something … terrible. About the accident."

The afghan slides to the floor as he pulls himself to a sitting position. "There's no need."

"What?" I cannot move. Surely, he can't mean—

Elbows on his knees, he leans forward and rubs his face. "Some noises at the job site sparked a flashback. And bits and pieces have been coming to me ever since … even our meal at the diner, where we met Cassie."

I bite my lip.

He meets my stricken gaze. "And yeah, the argument afterward. What can I say, Britt? Mom was riding you pretty hard. We both know she can be a tough cookie. And you—well, you did what you did. No point in dwelling on it, we just have to go on."

I stoop to retrieve the blanket. It's more than I deserve. And one less worry on my shoulders, about what he remembers.

Now his face grows stern. "But Cassie filled me in on what's been going on here. It's appalling, Britt, and has to stop. All these shenani—"

"It already has," I cut him off. "I'm even giving Chelsea and Marissa another chance, back home." *Maybe even Benny. If any of them will have me, once they understand who I am now. If not, there's got to be someone back home who believes.*

"Dad, I've changed," I say.

His brows draw together. "So … you got religion." His tone makes clear his opinion.

"Um, it's more like a relationship …" My insides are in knots.

"Whatever. I'm not there, Britt. At all. But I can see you're different, something's—well, Mom will be proud of you when … I mean if …" He covers his eyes. I move next to him and take his hand. It seems I'm the adult now, and he the child.

We hunker together, heads bent. One of us prays.

It's still the same day, though it seems a month since this morning. Four in the afternoon. Dr. Patel and two other physicians confer by Mom's bedside. She moans, and the two doctors we don't know nod to us and leave.

Our doctor comes to the window, where my father's slumped in the easy chair. I'm perched on the arm, and we await the verdict together.

"Her white count is very high," Dr. Patel says. "Her fever has spiked, and she is beginning to wake. I regret to say that her latest scan confirms lung damage beyond what she could recover from. I recommend we sedate her more fully."

Dad stares at a bit of medical plastic on the floor. "What about putting her back on the ventilator?"

The doctor shakes his head. "To assist breathing artificially would only prolong the inevitable. Please understand, there is no hope of recovery. Our primary objective now must be to ensure Mrs. Warner's comfort."

"We don't want her to suffer," my father murmurs.

No hope? I pluck his sleeve. "Does he mean—" I whisper.

"Her lungs are filling with fluid," the doctor says. "Her ability to take in oxygen will only worsen, until … again, I'm very sorry. The situation cannot be reversed." He looks at my father with compassion and adds, "If there is no other family to call … with your permission, we will go ahead and deepen the sedation."

No. I'm jumping to my feet to scream my protest, when there's a noise from the bed. We all whirl and gape as Mom's eyelids flutter. *Yes!* I race to the bed, take her hand.

"This doesn't change anything," Dr. Patel warns behind me.

"Mom." I bend over her. "Mom, can you hear me?" To the doctor I say, "I know. But I've got to tell her something. *Now.* And I'd rather do it alone."

"Of course." He leaves the room, and Dad follows. Sharonda retreats to a corner by the door. I could ask her to leave, but decide against it. We might need her.

"Mom, I read your journal about … that young law student."

A monitor beeps. A line spikes.

"And I get how you felt for … letting it happen. I've hated myself too, all summer. But I started to tell you earlier, something's changed."

I feel her forehead. If possible, it's even hotter than before. Her labored raspings are louder too.

"Your journal says you wanted to make things right. And there's so much I wish we—but barring a miracle, time's running out. I want to give you hope."

And I tell my mother, simply and gently, about the One who loved her enough to die on a cross for her.

"Do you understand, Mom? Can you squeeze my hand?" I say.

And wait, my breath suspended. Her hand lies passive in mine.

Tears flow down my cheeks. "Can you—blink?"

An eyelid flickers. I gasp and lean closer. My mother's eyes open fully, for the first time in two months, with a softness I only recognize from my single hazy, infant memory. They glisten with tears. Then … she blinks. Just once. As relief and joy course through me, she forces in a gulp of air, her mouth contorted with effort, and it hits me like a punch. To prolong this would indeed be cruel.

But I've just found her. Now I have to let her go? *It's not fair. I can't.*

A nudge, the slightest intimation of words floats through my mind: *You must. Tell her.*

I lean in, as if someone's pushing me. "Mom," I whisper. "It's okay. Whatever you … need to do … is okay."

Her eyes blink slowly once more, then flicker and drift shut. The ragged breathing eases. Then, with a small sigh, it stops. My eyes move to the heart monitor. The line is flat.

"Thank-you," I whisper, and rest my palm on her burning forehead. My eyes feel desert-hot and dry too, and my insides are dissolving.

But an arm reaches past me, and I peer into Sharonda's somber face. I'd forgotten about her.

"I have to. Your father hasn't signed a DNR." She pushes a button on the wall by the bed.

"Code Blue! Code Blue!" an intercom blares, and I realize she meant a Do Not Resuscitate order. Three nurses run in, their eyes veering to the flat line, and take instant action. One seizes my mother's wrist to check her pulse, eyeing the clock on the wall. Another jiggles the IV; the third starts doing CPR. Dr. Patel pushes in a wheeled cart with a machine labeled "Defibrillator" in red block letters, my father on his heels.

"What was that? What's happening?" Dad cries.

But Dr. Patel and a nurse block his path, so he moves back, fists clamped in his armpits and bouncing on his toes.

"Clear the room!" the doctor barks. As he hurriedly attaches electrodes to my mother's chest, I slip into the hall and straight into Cassie's arms. My father stumbles out behind me, and she releases me so the three of us huddle together.

"I can't lose her," he sobs.

"Dad. She's gone."

He moans, more quietly.

Cassie shifts from one foot to the other. "Mr. Warner, I mean Steven … may I pray with you?"

Dad pulls himself together and, to my surprise, gives a shaky nod. She wraps an arm across his shoulders and another around mine, unself-conscious in her role of minister. I bow my head as she quietly asks God to give us peace and comfort.

My father steps away when she finishes. Dr. Patel emerges from Mom's room, somber, and stops short when he sees me. "Your face. It is … bright," he says slowly. Then abruptly, to Dad and me, "I'm so sorry for your loss." He hurries away.

I press my hands to my cheeks, but feel nothing unusual. I can't explain what he sees, any more than I could teach Latin declensions to a kindergartener. But I'm numb now anyway; the grief will hit me later.

Sharonda walks past and squeezes my upper arm. I instantly forgive her. She was just doing her job.

"May I speak with you?" the doctor asks my father. They move away. Cassie looks at me, questioning.

I exhale. "It's okay," I say. "I think … *she's* okay."

Joy, surprise, and relief mingle on her face. "That's wonderful."

"Cassie, how did you know when to come? You arrived at just the right moment."

She gives a faint smile. "I've actually been over in Maternity the past few hours."

"Oh!"

"Yes. Kara delivered a baby boy this morning. Lucas Shawn Newcombe. Six pounds, seven ounces. Mommy and son are fine. In fact"—she beams—"they're lovely."

For some reason this, not losing Mom, is what starts my waterworks. For the third time in less than a week.

32

I take a shower the moment I'm back at Cassie's, scrubbing myself 'til my skin is raw. It feels so good to be clean. I'm exhausted, though, so for a few more minutes I let hot water stream over me and my mind go empty. Then I rub my hair dry and work on the tangles. But voices reach me from the kitchen, and my hand halts mid-stroke. Cassie and ... Will? I toss the brush on the bureau and scramble into a T-shirt and cutoffs.

I rush into the kitchen and he turns toward me, his shiners an even deeper purple than they were when he was in jail.

"What are you doing here?" I cry. I want to throw myself into his arms and press myself against his chest and hear his heart beat. But I'm afraid of hurting him. He's still so bruised.

"Britt. I'm so sorry about your mom," he says. "I wish I'd been there with you." He reaches out and squeezes my shoulder, then rubs it gently.

Instantly, my eyes fill. "It's okay. Cassie was, she prayed for us. And, Will—I talked with my mom. She

… for just a little bit there she was awake, and understood. And I'm pretty sure she's … okay. She blinked at me, to let me know."

Will's eyes go soft. "Wow," he says.

I nod. "But … what are you doing here? How'd you get out? I thought you'd be in jail for ages."

"Well. You won't believe this. Guess who called the cops to the waterfront?"

I turn to Cassie, who's grinning like a Cheshire cat. "I assumed—I mean, you were searching for me, so—" I break off. If she'd made the call, the cops would have known I was there and searched enough to bring me in, too. But before she can explain, her phone rings and she picks it up and leaves the room, motioning us to continue.

"Remember how Z ran away?" Will says. "He made an anonymous call. Then he thought about it some more and turned himself in at the station. Told them everything, including that you were there. I'd tried to explain that, but wasn't too coherent." He laughs, a carefree laugh full of joy and relief. "Sarge Thompson thought I'd stood you up for a date."

I'm still puzzling it out. "So, the Sarge called Cassie to see if she'd found me. I can't believe Z did that! Does this mean—"

"Yep. They've dropped my charges. And I'll try to help Z … visit him, whatever."

He'll give Z a Bible, like he gave me … and friendship. But Will's still talking, and I force myself to pay attention.

"… and this is for you." He pulls a creased paper from his pocket and presents it to me. It's a crayon drawing of a girl who's obviously me, the pink hair being the main clue, and—my throat tightens—a woman in a hospital bed. The bed's tilted to a near-vertical position, and the girl and woman are hugging sideways, cheeks pressed together like in a selfie. A halo crowns the woman's blonde hair. A childish scrawl across the bottom of the page reads: "For Brittany. I cried for you. Love Meghan."

I trace the last two words with my fingertip, my throat tight.

"And she sent those." He indicates the barn boots I've been wearing, on the floor by the back door. They're sparkling clean, and look brand-new.

"She says someone washed them for you, but didn't say who … and gave a funny little shrug. I think she hopes you'll come back to Vermont."

"Huh. She's an amazing kid, Will. I don't know, she's like some little … prophet. She's taught me so much about love. You … you all have."

His expression changes to one of surprise, even wonder. He steps toward me.

"Britt—"

"Check this out!" Cassie re-enters, proudly displaying a text pic of Kara's new baby. We all crowd around and admire him, and even though he's red and wrinkled I've got to admit there's something appealing about him. But I'm acutely aware of Will, of the skin of his arm pressed so close to mine. What would he have said if Cassie hadn't interrupted us? Somewhere I've heard that in the midst of life we are in death; is it possible the other way around is true, too?

After a moment, he gently takes Meghan's art from me and hangs it on Cassie's fridge.

In the few days following Mom's passing, I feel as if I'm made of glass that could shatter at any moment. And yet,

I'm aware of an odd sense of peace. I walk carefully, talk little, and live in the moment, pushing away any thoughts of leaving Vermont. Meanwhile, the church showers my dad and me with kindness. Flowers, endless food, visits … he's stunned, and keeps remarking on the generosity of what to him are perfect strangers. But finally, he reminds me we have arrangements to make back home. Our last evening in Vermont, after dinner, Dad drives me halfway up the island for some homemade ice cream at a place we've heard about. It's a gorgeous, balmy summer evening.

"What flavor?" my father says as we inspect an enticing list of possibilities posted by the service window.

"Butter pecan," I say. "All my life."

His brows draw together in a frown. He clears his throat. Finally, he says, "I've let you down. Haven't I."

My eyes smart. "Kinda."

He wraps an arm across my shoulders and pulls me close. "I'm sorry," he whispers.

"It's okay," I mumble. To my astonishment, suddenly it is.

Back in the car, he cruises across South Hero and pulls into a park by the shore. The lake is glassy and still, so we seem to be inside a silver-blue sphere. Dad gets out of the car and strolls to the shoreline, where he pokes about and picks up a rock. He hurls it across the water like a discus, and I stare in amazement as the thing makes one … two … three … four … *five* skips. He picks his way toward me, pleased, dusting his palms together.

I grab a rock too, and … it's a blast.

Skipping rocks isn't a sport, it's a marvel of physics. Pick the flattest stone around, heft it into position, and let it fly over the lake. Depending on aim, arm, the angle of entry, the wind, and the waves, a rock either slices the surface and plunges in—not what you want—or bounces across the gleaming water like a kid let out of school for the summer.

Almost two months ago, I scorned those girls who batted a balloon back and forth at Cassie's picnic. But today, a gritty slab of granite skimming above glassy water equals sheer, pure pleasure. Go figure.

He tosses another rock, then I do. It's good to be with Dad. But the strains and sorrow of the past weeks are etched on his face. I realize he doesn't have the hope I'm clinging to, that Mom's in a better place. My nightmares have stopped, but he can't sleep. Maybe he's still buying nip bottles, or worse. Once we're home, I think, I'll guard him like a warden and get him help if he needs it. I already flushed the rest of Manny's stash down Cassie's toilet. That's over.

Now, holding a large dripping rock in my hands, I screw up my courage to address the final fear that's tormented me all summer. The one dug deep into my mind, that won't let go. I take a deep breath.

"Dad."

He hefts a flat, triangular rock. "Mm?"

"I still have to talk to that cop."

His rock skims across the water and disappears into a last ray of sunlight, angled low across the water. My father turns, and again my world changes in an instant.

"No need," he says. "Your mom was driving. What happened was her responsibility. End of story."

What? "Are you sure? You talked to him?"

"I'm sure. And yes, I did."

My lungs seem to fill with helium. Even holding my rock, I could float through these treetops. *Thank-you. Again.*

"Dad. Would it be okay if I pick some verses for Mom's funeral?"

His smile is pained. "That would be perfect. Your mom used to read poetry, years ago."

A pang. *I didn't know.* But—"Um, I meant Scripture."

"Oh. Well, you know I'm not—"

I fix him with a look, and he stops talking. "Uh, how about some of each?" he finally says.

That works. I sling my rock and manage two skips. He picks up another. Three this time. So my dad and I play for the first time in my memory, taking turns until our feet are drenched, our throwing arms sore and elbows aching, and our minds blissfully blank because right now there's no need to think of anything else. Except slapping the occasional mosquito.

Finally we drive back to Cassie's, and Dad parks by her cottage porch. It's almost dusk now, and the whole sky, over the lake and between the mountains, is striped in brilliant orange, pink, and purple. A reverse sunset. Meghan slouches on the glider, wearing denim shorts and a pale green T-shirt with tadpoles on it. Something in me softens even more at the sight of her.

"Who's this?" Dad says.

"My boss," I joke. I rush up the porch steps and give Meghan a huge hug.

"Meghan, meet my dad. And isn't it your bedtime?"

"Yeah, I'm waiting for Cassie to bring me back. Hi, Mr. Dad." Then she drops the casual pose. "Britt, guess what? Shawn's back, and he and Kara are getting married! And I'm Auntie Meg now." Her grin splits her face.

My father smiles and climbs the steps to the porch. "Cassie?" he calls, and she appears in the doorway.

"I had a feeling," I say to Meghan. "Hang on." I dash past them all, duck inside, and bring out a wrapped gift with a gold bow. "Would you give this to Kara? Tell her congratulations?"

The kid takes the box, smirking. "Bet I can guess what this is."

"Really? How?"

"Well, I went in the gift shop at the hospital and found what I'd pick for her."

"Oh. What's that?"

She screeches, "The blue stuffed pony that plays 'Hush Little Baby!'"

She's right. Though only I appreciate the irony. I ruffle her dark hair. "You're one smart cookie, you know that? You'll knock 'em dead at debate someday." *Where'd that come from? Maybe there's more of Mom in me than I thought.*

"Huh?"

"Never mind. You've got your whole life ahead of you. Go in peace."

Beaming, she squeezes my waist, the highest part of me she can reach. Her silky dark hair brushes my arm, and I catch her sleeve when she turns to go inside. "Hey, Meghan?" I say.

"Yeah?"

"Wish Perf—I mean, Jessica—luck from me at her big event. Okay? When Joy had colic, she stayed with her all night."

The half-pint checks her watch. "Sure. But she and Pastor Dave left this morning with Captain in the horse trailer. So, I'll have to text her on Priscilla's phone. Jess is so excited her dad's the one taking her that she's not even nervous."

"I don't get it."

Meghan fixes me with a severe look. "It's not easy being a PK, you know."

"PK?"

"Pastor's Kid. A lot of people take his time when he could be with his family." She sounds as earnest as a rookie newscaster reporting on her first nor'easter, and I try not to laugh. "And … well, her mom left for a while, but she came back. People should cut Jess some slack."

My amusement disappears. Suddenly I'm near tears, which I hide by bending to kiss the top of her head. It blows me away—and shames me—that this wise little girl sees through Jessica's gleaming façade, which I missed completely. What made me think owning Captain meant her life was perfect?

If Mom had met Meghan.

If I'd understood Mom.

I'm starting to hurt.

Cassie's guest bedroom seems empty without my belongings, which are packed—neatly, for once—in the duffel at my feet. So is her moose nightshirt, which I've worn every single night since I decided to stay in Vermont to wake Mom. Sometimes I put it on straight from the dryer. The window is latched shut for the first time this summer, and the Bible Will gave me is stowed in my new knapsack. Which is, actually, the same one I've been using all summer, and have gotten sort of attached to. Cassie presented me with a blank journal, "to keep track of what's going on in that head of yours." I held it above the open knapsack, teasing, and she laughed and hugged me.

"All right, it's yours. Think of me when you use it."

As if I wouldn't. Whatever she suspects about stuff I've done this summer, Cassie's no fool. Even if she never did go to college.

Luke is sweeping the aisle outside Joy's stall when Dad and I go to the barn. My father cranes his neck to examine the rafters, and I follow. A dozen small birds with forked tails swoop and soar in a whole other world high above us. I'd never noticed them before, because I didn't look up.

"We're here to say goodbye, Luke," I say. *I hate to leave.*

He sets the broom aside and nods to my father. His eyes crinkle at me. "Take a good gander at this little lady, 'cause after the surgery she'll be a different horse. That colic was a godsend, Britt. I was never so happy to be wrong. I usually do a vet check before buying a horse—but Joy's so young, I never thought of hormones … anyway, Priscilla's glad, too. She says burying horses is a pain."

I crack up—that's so Priscilla, always dour—and toss a carrot into the stall. There's no cuter sound, in my opinion, than a horse munching on a treat. It gives me shivers, I'm so happy. I whisper sweet nothings, wishing I could bring Joy home with me. *After* her surgery.

"This construction is mortise and tenon with pegs," Dad says to Luke. "I always wanted a post-and-beam barn."

He did?

"Mm?" Luke says.

"Besides engineering, I studied historic preservation.

But my wife—anyway. I do commercial construction."

"That's good work."

"Yes … Agatha thought so." His voice trembles.

I turn. Luke is balanced on the balls of his feet, giving Dad his full attention the way he does with anyone he's talking to. My father is gaunt and exhausted, his skin pale under the tan he's gotten in the past few days.

He runs a finger along the edge of a stall door and clears his throat. "All the guys at her law school were drooling over her by the end of the first week. But she picked me … it's hard." He covers his eyes, and for the first time I understand that despite their tense, fragmented history, my father truly loved my mother.

"I'm here if you ever want to talk. About anything," Luke says. "Hey, I've got something in the office you might like."

They walk away. Joy raises her head, still munching. Only a few feet separate us, plus the wooden half-wall and upper metal grille of the stall. I imagine opening the door and hugging her neck, the way Meghan does to Tiny. When his head is down, of course.

Joy snorts and backs away.

Someday. I blow her a kiss and head up the aisle to join my father and Luke. Dad's got a book tucked under his arm. I tilt my head to read the spine: *Historic Barn Plans.*

My eyes meet Luke's.

He'll make an awesome pastor.

We emerge from the cool interior of the barn into the sunlight. Priscilla limps over from the farmhouse, mopping her face with a bandanna. Cassie and Will pull up in Cassie's car. My father and I are finally leaving, and I don't want to blubber yet again.

"Thank-you for lending us your daughter. We've come to love her," Luke says.

"The debt is entirely mine," Dad replies. "You've been … exemplary." He shakes Cassie's hand. "Cassie, you've done yeoman's duty in an extremely difficult situation."

She brightens. "It was no trouble."

Ha. Liar.

Dad gestures at Will's bruises. "William. What you saved my daughter from is unthinkable. If there were any way to repay you … any of you …"

"Actually, there is." Priscilla turns to me. "We hope you'll come again next summer, Britt. Maybe you can learn to ride this year at home. Joy will be in training, and if things go right—by next June, the place'll be crawling with teens. What were we thinking?" She strikes her head in mock dismay, the first glimmer of humor I've seen in her. "You'd be a huge help."

Exhilaration whooshes through me. "Dad?" I say.

"Hm." He scratches his earlobe. "No reason why not, I guess. It might even count as community service for your, uh, college application. The resume."

Yes, yes, yes! I groan, for form's sake, but in my mind, I'm doing cartwheels.

Cassie says, shy, "I'd love for you to stay with me again, Britt, if you don't mind … sharing. I've decided to apply to adopt."

I put my palms to my cheeks in mock horror. "Don't tell me you still want a girl!"

She twirls a finger at her temple, acknowledging she's nuts.

I hug her hard. "You'll knock 'em dead at the

reunion."

"Not by food poisoning, I hope," she says and grins.

Next I hug Priscilla, who excuses herself and leaves, muttering about something she has to do. I suspect she's a softie after all, and hates goodbyes.

Now it's Luke's turn. I don't think a hug can feel *wise*, but his comforts me as his hat brim grazes my hair. "Never forget. You're not alone," he says softly as he releases me.

I nod, touched. "Take care of Joy," I say.

I turn to Will. Time grinds to a halt, and we seem frozen in place.

"Britt—" He hesitates and says to my father, "Mr. Warner, could we have a minute?"

Dad nods, surprised, and Will takes my elbow. "We'll just be a sec," he says.

We slip around the corner of the barn and face each other. Will swallows hard, his Adam's apple jerking between the lapels of his checked shirt. It's a work day.

"It's weird," he says slowly. "We've been through so much this summer … but it feels like I've just found you. And now you're leaving …"

"Yeah." I feel shy.

He reaches out and smooths my hair. "I've always loved the color," he whispers. "It's like autumn leaves. They'll remind me of you this fall."

Emboldened, I step forward. His arms close around me in a long hug. I'm pressed against his chest, my head tucked under his chin, and it feels so right. His freshly ironed shirt smells faintly of fabric softener, and his heartbeat thumps warm and steady. I stifle tears and swallow hard past the lump in my throat, which makes my ears squeak. I wish I could stay in his arms forever.

"Ssh." He releases me and pulls something from his pocket. A leather cord, attached to the bit of wood he's been carving. A cross like his, sanded 'til it glows, the bloodstain a mere memory. And now, half-gilded like the original. As he eases the necklace over my head, his fingers brush my neck and a thrill races through my body. He settles the cross in the hollow of my throat and lifts my chin briefly. Our eyes meet.

"So, next summer …?" I say tentatively.

"I think … anything's possible," he says, his eyes bright.

I smile. He leans in again and kisses my forehead. Then he takes my hand and we rejoin the others.

We roll down the lane from the barn, me hanging out the window and Dad beeping the horn. In the barn doorway, Luke, Cassie, and Will wave. Luke's expression beneath the brim of his cowboy hat is wise and gentle, like some pioneer in a vintage photo. Cassie, smiling bravely and wearing her usual T-shirt and leggings, blows me a kiss and mimes a hug with her arms. I suspect she'll burst into tears the moment we leave. In front of Will, Meghan holds a manure fork in one hand and waves with the other. I wave harder. She hoists the fork like a warrior's lance, nearly braining her brother. He ducks in alarm, and all three of them bend double in hysterics. I wave one last time and turn my attention to the road, my throat aching with the effort not to cry.

These friends, these amazing people, saved my life this summer. Not to mention my soul.

We drive between the white fences, past the lush

pastures and horses grazing peacefully. At the turnoff to Cassie's, I finger Will's cross that rests in the hollow of my throat and peer toward the sparkling lake, where the fragile, shorn willow keeps guard on the rocky shore. A light breeze lifts its slim shoots, and I catch a shimmer of pale green.

Then it happens. My mind's eye fills with a vision I could not have imagined. The scene is the same, but now the willow is fully restored and magnificent. Its long, soft fronds sway in the breeze, arching over the cool water and providing shade for whatever minnows lurk below. Just as Will said.

Something indescribable plumes within me. It's been forever since—no, I've never felt such peace, a long, calm, oceanic swell that sweeps through every cell of my body.

We pass beneath the rough, high-arched NARROWGATE FARM sign. All of a sudden, it's too real. I'm leaving, and won't see my new friends for ages. *I'll be back*, I promise them silently. We turn onto the main road. After a bit it curves, and the mountains wheel around us as we enter the causeway leading off the island, toward home. My father gazes straight ahead, his mouth set beneath the visor of his baseball cap. His hands grip the wheel in a perfect Driver Ed ten-and-two, and I'm filled with love for him. No one is born without a biological father, and I've had my share of disappointments. But mine stood in the gap for me when it mattered most.

An involuntary smile spreads across my face. "Dad?"

"Mm."

"I can't stop thinking."

His mouth tightens, his eyes still on the road.

"Me either, Britt. You know, about Mom, it'll take a while to—"

He glances at me. And then again, and wonder replaces his frown as he recognizes the inexplicable, exhilarating joy that's bubbling from somewhere deep within me.

"I know," I say. "We'll grieve. All the stages. But I'm thinking about life. Being alive. I'm sad *and* happy, all mixed together … and, Dad? Doesn't it almost feel like Mom's with us?"

My dad adjusts his faded pink baseball cap. "Now that you mention it … yes."

"And there's the future to look forward to. That's something."

"Uh. Yes. But … I've never seen you like this."

I look over at him, so intensely that his skin must prickle. "I've never felt like this."

Another quick glance. "Why don't you tell me."

So as the car rumbles onto the causeway off the island, I take a deep breath. And tell my dad about my summer.

We talk the whole way home.

AFTERWORD

Almost two decades ago, a family member described waiting tables on a family who had come north for a "Vermont Christmas." The next day, she heard they'd had a terrible car accident, with ultimately only one survivor—and realized she'd probably been the last to see them alive. She was shaken, and I was horrified. Later, I learned that two southern cousins of mine actually knew this family, and how their community grieved, which made it even more personal. Then I heard of a second fatal accident in Colorado, in which only a teenage girl survived out of a whole family—and I had known the mom. Again, grief and horror. But also, a sense of deep significance. As a Christian, I asked myself, could there be hope amidst such tragedy? And somehow the idea of Cassie was born, and subconsciously added to a writing exercise I'd done about a teenage girl with a reddish braid.

In fiction, imagination and memory and real event combine in a synergy that's difficult to explain. Cassie is not my family member, Brittany is definitely not me, nor are Agatha and Steven my parents—but my people were not churchgoers, and as a small child I did suffer greatly from being told there's nothing after death. Their explanation, that someday the world would go on forever without me, was too awful to bear. I wrestled with it nightly, and grieved it for many years until, at almost thirty, I came to understand God's perfect plan and promises, and received hope and comfort through faith.

And Joy is a real horse! I owned her for two challenging years, during which she really did rear on a pregnant vet. Sometimes you can't make this stuff up. You can read her story on my website. We also had a magnificent willow …

But more real and significant than anything in this novel are the eternal truths that God is Sovereign, and that in an ultimate act of love He sent His Son Jesus to die on a cross, as a living sacrifice for the sins of His wayward children who come to believe. I've long dreamed of sharing these with others through writing. The result is this book.

Today, with death and danger seemingly everywhere, these truths are more important than ever. My prayer is that this story brings hope to any reader who needs it. God is real, and He loves you. And if you're searching …

It's no accident. Please, pay attention.

In His love,

Lori

www.narrowgatemedia.com

AN INVITATION

If this story has touched your heart, and you sense God calling you to a deeper relationship with Him, here is a next step. Pray this simple prayer:

> *"Father, I admit that I fall short in following your commandments. Up to this point, I have been lord over my life and you have not. I am a sinner.*
>
> *I believe that you sent your Son, Jesus, to pay the penalty for my sin through his death on the cross. I trust in his sacrifice as full payment for my self-determined will.*
>
> *Jesus, I ask you to be Lord in my life."*

Congratulations! If you have prayed these words from a sincere heart, it will change your life on earth and give you eternity with Him in heaven. But don't try to go it alone. Check out your local church, and find other Christians to connect with.

QUESTIONS AND TOPICS FOR DISCUSSION

1. At five, Brittany Warner has everything materially she needs, but is a scared little girl denied the comfort of believing in some sort of heavenly afterlife. Do you remember what you were told about death as a small child? How did it affect you, positively or negatively?
2. A decade later, Brittany is emotionally starved and estranged from her non-nurturing mother and ineffectual father. Have you or someone you know ever been in a similar situation? What was your response?
3. Early on, the waitress Cassie says the Narrowgate clan are like family to her. What does family mean to you?
4. Why does Brittany find Manny so attractive? Have you ever found yourself drawn to someone you know to be so lost and broken that they are dangerous? How did you respond?
5. When faced with trouble, Brittany's lifelong response is to flee. That's not an option in Vermont, so she

turns to substance abuse. Discuss more helpful coping strategies for stress.

6. Several people offer Brittany comfort and wisdom in Vermont: the pastor-in-training Luke, her new friend and potential love interest Will, and the warmhearted waitress Cassie. How is their love different from that of Manny and his pals?

7. Seventeen-year-old Will befriends Brittany after the accident and is very attentive to her needs, even to the point of self-sacrifice. What are his motivations? Has anyone ever helped you that way? Name a time you helped someone like that. How did it make you feel?

8. At the beginning of the novel, Brittany detests babies and small children, a reflection of her own lack of nurturing. Trace how events in the novel cause her to change her feelings about babies and small children, and herself. How does it feel to nurture someone and be nurtured?

9. Discuss the impact of Agatha's journal on Brittany. Why was it so devastating to learn she'd been lied to about her parents' relationship? Did Agatha benefit by concealing her secret? Which did the most good or harm—keeping mum, or telling the truth? Can you think of a time in your own life when telling the truth, even belatedly, allowed a process of healing to begin?

10. How does Brittany find hope? Despite her terrible loss, she is comforted by a sense of peace from God and others' prayers. Have you felt this peace? If so, is there anyone with whom you'd like to share it? If you haven't experienced this, do you think peace and hope are possible for you? How?

ACKNOWLEDGMENTS

When a story's been this long in the works, many thanks are due. Foremost is my brilliant longtime mentor, friend, and comrade in the trenches, David B. King, who has encouraged me eloquently and vigorously all along the way. Thanks, too, to my critique groups over the years: Susan Dominguez and Bethany Clemons and the rest of our "Local Yokels," the inimitable Bob Hale and his coterie, and the zany Poets & Writers INK of Cape Vincent, New York, who remind me periodically that writing can be fun. And my earliest encourager, the late Susan Litowitz. I also owe various professional debts to Catherine Andrade, Carmen Barber, Hope Bolinger, Erin Burke, Teresa Crumpton, Geoff Culkin, Cher Gatto, Deb Haggerty, Tessa Emily Hall, Masha Hamilton, Harold "Rink" Jacobi, Nicole Quigley, Karen Sargent, Linda Seger, Liz Soule, Cindy Sproles, Katherine Towler, Cyle Young, Nick Zelinger, and Jody Zorgdrager. And to Movieguide and WeScreenplay for appreciating my screenplay version, and the Fletcher Allen hospital in Burlington, Vermont, for a tour and information. For loving encouragement and feedback, thanks to my parents and various family members—you know who you are! Likewise, to all my dear friends who cheered me on, some of whom read various versions; you too know who you are, and (I hope) how much I appreciate you. And thanks to my new southern friends, screenwriting pals, newsletter subscribers, anyone I may have forgotten, and future readers.

Special, heartfelt appreciation to my penultimate cheerleader, my husband Gary, who does me the great honor of tearing up when he reads my writing. With faithful love and a million small kindnesses, you're my rock on earth, without whom this project would never have happened. I love you dearly. Thanks, and abundant love, to my three precious grown children, their wonderful spouses, and our six darling grands, for bringing me joy beyond anything I could have imagined.

I thank my heavenly Father for each one of you, and for His love and blessings beyond measure.

ABOUT THE AUTHOR

 Lori Closter is a wife, mom, grammy, and lifelong writer who is fulfilling her dream of giving people hope and faith through stories. A native New Yorker, she holds degrees from Cornell (BA) and Temple Universities (MA). She served as writer/researcher and assistant producer on various projects, including an educational film series produced for National Geographic. At almost 30, she became a Christian, married, and moved to Massachusetts, where she homeschooled her three children, kept assorted badly behaved animals, and began to write fiction. During the summers she and her husband hosted family, friends, and weekly rentals in the Thousand Islands, where panoramic views and fabulous sunsets over the mighty St. Lawrence and Lake Ontario from her favorite waterfront deck brought rest and inspiration.

Today, Lori and her retired pastor husband live in coastal North Carolina and are focused on sharing her work and their spiritual journey with a world that needs hope. Her short stories have been published in several places and recognized in contests, and her unpublished collection *Riding the Elephant* was an Eludia Award semi-finalist. Her screenplay of *Topping the Willow* has been multiply recognized including Kairos Prize finalist, won Best Script at the 2025 Purpose Film Fest, and is in development as a faith-based feature, *Breaking Joy*. To find out more, visit www.narrowgatemedia.com.

Connect with Lori:

Lori Closter

@lori_closter

linkedin.com/in/lori-c-007b6255/

9 7989 8649 9802